UNITED STA

KEN JACK

ISBN-13: 978-1466444980
ISBN-10: 1466444983

CHAPTER 1

Cold evening air rushed in on the Prime Minister, followed by two men on ropes, black clad, skin daubed with black, swinging in the study window as it flew abruptly up.

One moved swiftly behind him at his desk before he had time to react and gagged him with a gloved hand.

The other pulled back his arms, bound his wrists with a plastic tie in one quick motion, and jabbed a needle into the back of his hand.

'Go!' he rasped, and they walked then dragged the Prime Minister quickly backwards to the window, as he slumped in their grasp.

The first passed a lifting strop under his pinioned arms, and the other clipped on a steel cable dangling just outside the window. A gag was drawn tight on his mouth and a hood pulled over his head.

'Up and away!' one hissed into the microphone on his headset, as they sat the Prime Minister on the ledge and pushed his head down to clear the raised sash.

Seconds later he disappeared sharply skywards.

Moments after, the abductors were gone too, the windows were closed as before, and the 'do not disturb' sign hung on the study door.

Two hours later the Prime Minister's private secretary in the office below yawned, looked at his watch, and decided the President must be delayed indefinitely. Sleepily, He made his way up to the study and tapped lightly on the door.

The Prime Minister had stayed in Downing Street after the phone call from Brussels, instead of going to Chequers as planned – the Union President would be in London within the hour and wanted to see him urgently.

'We've certainly created an effect!' he'd said to Neville Edwards, when he phoned him to ask him to take his place hosting the Cabinet dinner that evening.

Then came the message the President's flight was delayed. He could be two hours late. Would the Prime Minister please wait as it was of such importance.

So he'd settled down in his study to tackle another of the endless red boxes.

Now, getting no reply, the private secretary assumed his boss had dozed off as he sometimes did. So he headed for bed, leaving instructions to call him if there was any word of the President's arrival.

Nobody called him, and next morning, being Saturday, he treated himself to a brief lie-in. He wondered idly if the Prime Minister would still wish to go to Chequers.

Then he heard the sound of firecrackers coming from St. James's Park. He tried to think when the Chinese New Year began.

As he listened, puzzling, he realised there was a lot more aircraft noise than usual – and then that it was small arms fire he'd heard.

Jumping out of bed, he made for the window – then the alarms went off in Downing Street.

The Prime Minister came round as the hood and gag were taken off.

A door flanked by two civilian guards swam into focus.

Half right from the bed he lay on, a man sitting at a small table poured tea from a decorated china pot.

'Just in time for a cuppa,' he said matter-of-factly.

The Prime Minister sat up slowly, looking dizzily at the proffered cup.

'What is this?' he said.

'Lapsang Souchong,' said the man at the table.

'Treasonous bastards,' gasped the Prime Minister. 'What is this about?'

'Come, Prime Minister,' said the man, sneeringly, 'you only stand for one thing – what would it be about? The United States of Europe – one and indivisible! That's what it's about.

'You threaten the whole structure by your attempt to secede.

'But I'm sorry, It's too late for that. We're not having it,' he drawled laconically.

The Prime Minister's mind fought to focus, and then cleared. 'And you think abducting me will change minds?'

The man at the table now dropped the mask of urbanity, thrust his face close to the Prime Minister's, and snarled, 'You have poisoned the country's mind!'

'This puny gesture won't alter it!' the Prime Minister retorted, showing a bravado he didn't feel.

'No puny gesture, Prime Minister – the fixed determination of the President and Council. You will see!

'You will not be harmed, and we will speak again. For now – enough!'

He motioned to the guards, and they, pinioning the Prime Minister's arms once again, jabbed his hand a second time, and a second time consciousness slipped away.

The teapot had a large pink rose on its side, perfect in form, each curled petal bursting out from the centre, pushing plumply against its neighbour in the rich fullness of summer.

It seemed perfectly harmonious, and yet perfectly incongruous, in that it had its existence only there, there on the teapot.

No thought. No feeling. Just the teapot. And the rose.

Other objects in the room swam into view.

The table, old, oak, rather Civil Service looking, upon which the teapot stood. The chair, oak, swivel, wooden slatted back, brass-bound legs, metal castors – this time empty. Behind on the pale green wall, a picture of flowers in a vase.

The Prime Minister sat up. No one else was in the room. He rose and moved unsteadily to the table.

Leaning on it with one hand, he felt the teapot. Cold. He thought it was the same day, but couldn't tell. He wasn't hungry or thirsty. His bladder was – at least, not full.

He looked round for a camera, but saw none.

There was a Judas-hole in the door.

'Kind of them to give me such privacy,' he thought. 'In deference to my position, no doubt.'

He turned to the bed – metal-framed, mattress cover, pillow, two blankets – very barrack-room.

On the floor beside it – he hadn't seen it – a radio.

'More privileges,' he thought sarcastically. 'But why leave me a radio…rather strange.'

He bent to switch it on. Tentatively he tried the knob, slowly turning it between finger and thumb till it reached the 'click'.

'Oh God! A bomb!' he gasped, spinning round with his back to the set and flinging his arms around his head, as it did click.

'...Viking, Forties, Cromarty, south west four, showers, good. Forth, Tyne, Dogger....'

He felt foolish.

But then, it would've been an easy way to get rid of him.

Crowding on this was the thought that his abduction hadn't caused much of a ripple if the shipping forecast was going out as normal.

'Who's in on this?' was his next thought. 'It must include Cabinet members.'

There were strong views in the Cabinet, certainly. Divergent views.

But this? No one had even resigned yet.

'...the news headlines. Delegates at the Developing World Debt Forum being held in Washington have so far failed to reach agreement, but the British delegation says there is still time to do so.

'Three boys whose small boat was found drifting in the Bristol Channel were found safe and well in a cave they had been exploring when their boat drifted away on a rising tide.'

'So much for me!' he said out loud. 'Not even mentioned!'

'The Prime Minister has had to cancel a number of engagements as he is "temporarily indisposed", Downing Street has announced, but the emergency meeting of the Cabinet at Chequers this weekend to discuss the crisis over the Secession Bill will go ahead as planned.

'The row over commuter train services into the Capital....'

Chequers...Chequers made him think of Lynda. Though it hurt to think of her, it hurt more not to think of her. Lynda Stalker, Minister for Women - a post which had become de rigueur in the Cabinet, and women could not be better represented, in his view.

He had looked forward to this weekend at Chequers, fraught though it would be, as it would give them some more relaxation together, some time to get back on an even keel after her last little indiscretion, which had hurt him so much.

It seemed incredible now that he'd only left her a short time before he was snatched.

He could still feel the brush of her cheek against his, smell the perfume, hear the rippling fun-filled laugh. He knew she loved him – but she could not be content with love alone, as he must be.

Desire rose in him – a desperate panic yearning fuelled by the insistent thought that he might never see her again.

What price then his principles and prudence? To love her as he did, and never to have made love to her, was torture now.

How he'd restrained himself until now he hardly knew, for when they were together, he burned with passion.

But his sense of mission overrode all other considerations with him. If he fell by the wayside, victim of a supposed scandal, who would pick up the torch and bear it aloft with his fervour?

He felt duty dictated he must avoid at all costs giving the tabloids any excuse to distort the relationship and cry 'scandal' – which of course they would at the drop of a hat..

For her part, she might have any man she wished, and had had many, but had chosen him – apart from her wanton indiscretions.

Why him, he was at a loss to understand. Yes, he was Prime Minister now, and now had power and patronage, but this had begun before all that – before anyone could divine his destiny.

Most men didn't see past her stunning looks, and the low-buttoned blouse she invariably wore.

She flaunted her sexuality, it was true, and on occasion couldn't restrain her passion, and cast fidelity to the wind. But there was more, much more, to her than that.

'...and after a check-up the three boys were reunited with their families.'

'It is understood the Prime Minister is resting quietly at Chequers this weekend, to be on hand for consultations at the crisis meeting to discuss the Secession Bill.

'However, he will not be taking part, and Deputy Prime Minister Neville Edwards will chair the meeting, which is expected to be stormy.'

'Edwards!' gasped the Prime Minister. 'Of course – it was Edwards! Bloody Judas! The Trojan Horse!'

He stood up quickly and banged the table. The teapot jumped.

Then he fell back with a groan as a searing pain shot through his head and it began to throb violently.

He lay gasping, stunned again by this flash of pain. Somewhere, far away, the newsreader continued with the details....

'The Prime Minister is thought to have suffered a recurrence of the digestive trouble for which he underwent tests last autumn. His public engagements over the next few days have been cancelled, or are to be undertaken by Mr. Edwards.'

This filtered into his consciousness as he lay motionless, his gaze fixed on the ceiling, partly numbed by the pain when he had jumped up, partly unwilling to move in the hope that the pain would leave him alone.

But through the blur of pain he saw it now – Edwards bargaining for his place, not openly, but with a thousand hints, a thousand nuances. Him and the rest of the federalists.

Party unity necessitated his promotion to the Cabinet. Cabinet unity had necessitated his promotion to Deputy Prime Minister.

One could admire many – most, even – of the federalists. Principled men with committed views, long and deeply held.

One could not admire Edwards – unprincipled, self-serving, tacking to and fro with every wind shift. But he'd always been effective in insinuating himself into key positions.

He believed in nothing except himself – not even the democracy he affected to preserve.

His argument would be that we had signed the Single European Act, Maastricht et al, Lisbon, and – with the Treaty of Berlin – had committed ourselves at last to the United States of Europe.

These and myriad other measures, he would hold, had been ratified by the elected representatives of the people, who after due deliberation yielded up sovereignty to Brussels for the greater good of the country.

Now, he will argue, the status quo must be defended. The people decided in favour of the Union. The people's will must be upheld.

'God, I could write his speech myself – I can see it all,' the Prime Minister thought. But again the waves of pain lapped over him, and consciousness ebbed away.

CHAPTER 2

Neville Edwards stood back to the fireplace, legs astride, hands clasped at his back, a synthetic smile hovering around his mouth, but with a tense expectancy immobilising his other features.

'Good morning, ladies and gentlemen. Trust you slept well after our excellent dinner last evening.

'The Prime Minister will not be putting in an appearance, and I will be in the Chair.'

Surprise and consternation were evident, but Neville Edwards brushed it aside with a schoolmaster-ish, 'Sit down, then, everybody, and let's get on.'

With hurried ends to conversations around the room, and much shuffling of chairs and papers, the Cabinet took their seats around the table in the conference room at Chequers.

'There is only one question before us now,' began Edwards without preamble.

'As we all know, it's now certain that the Secession Bill will secure a majority in the Lords as it did in the Commons.

'Those of us opposed to the secession of the United Kingdom from the Union cannot accept the situation as it is developing, and neither can the European Council....'

A gasp from the other end of the table, and the Home Secretary half rose in his place – ' The Prime Minister is a member of the Council, and he proposed the policy!'

'...as I was about to say, Charles, the Council, with the exception of one voice crying in the wilderness, cannot accept it.'

'Well, they'll bloody-well have to this time next week.'

'Charles, please allow me to continue.

'The arguments have been well-rehearsed in Cabinet, in the House, in the media. There's no need to articulate them again here. We're all familiar with them.

'But the nub of them is this – the United States of Europe is now de jure one and indivisible, and has been so, de facto, for some years.

'Since the Treaty of Berlin it has been politically one and indivisible also.

'Untold damage would be caused to the Union and to this country by secession.

'It would result in the unravelling of the whole warp and weft of the economic fabric of Britain, and substantial weakening of the economy of the Union as a whole.

'It is as unthinkable as the secession of Scotland, or Wales, or Northern Ireland, from the United Kingdom.'

'Neville, in case you hadn't noticed, Scotland's halfway there, and Wales and Northern Ireland haven't been too happy with Westminster rule for years.'

Across the table, the Defence Secretary, thrust forward his burly frame – ' Neville, we're not here to listen to you and Charles digging over yet again the ground you've been digging over for months past. It's been through Cabinet. It's all but through Parliament. You've lost, and that's that.'

'I have to say to you, my friends, that it cannot be left there.

'There is no constitutional provision for secession from the Union…'

'Which is why we've just passed a unilateral declaration of independence,' boomed the Defence Secretary.

'…therefore the Bill is an unconstitutional measure….'

'In terms of the Constitution of the Union, but not in UK terms,' put in the Chancellor.

'And the UK is a member state, therefore this action is unconstitutional,' Neville Edwards rejoined. Then he continued.

'I have to tell you that at the Special Summit of the European Council, it was decided that should Parliament vote for secession, the Council must intervene to prevent it.'

'I beg your pardon!' gasped the Attorney-General, rising to his feet as turmoil spread round the table. 'I beg your pardon!'

Now several were on their feet, gesticulating, angrily remonstrating.

Then as they stormed their protests, one by one their gaze fell on some of their number who sat unmoved, no show of surprise, and silence fell.

But again the crescendo of voices rose as they flung bewildered, angry, incredulous questions, at those impassive colleagues.

A sudden shudder shook the Minister for Women. 'What's really happened to the Prime Minister? Where is he?' she demanded.

'Yes,' thought Edwards, ' you'll be missing your little friend for some time to come.'

Then he continued, 'Friends, by authority of the European Council, I am, as of now, assuming the powers of Prime Minister....'

'Not my friend! This is treason! Over my dead body you will assume the powers of Prime Minister!' said the Home Secretary with quiet determination, then rose, and strode to the door.

He pulled on the two brass handles. The doors swung open.

Three soldiers in combat dress stood facing the door, a foot from it, sub-machine guns at the port across their chests.

'What is this, Neville?' said the Home Secretary, suppressed rage suffusing his face. 'Where is the Prime Minister? You'll never pull this off. This belongs in the seventeenth century. You will go down in history as another Guy Fawkes. Little children will burn your effigy this day in all time coming!'

Around the room incredulity struggled with anger, and now fear, as to which was the dominant emotion.

'I am assuming the powers of Prime Minister....'

'What about the King? What about Parliament?' shouted another minister.

'We will take powers under the Civil Contingencies Act and prorogue Parliament here and in Scotland, and the Welsh and Northern Ireland Assemblies.

'The Prime Minister is safe – the former Prime Minister. He will not be harmed. This is not, Charles, the seventeenth century.'

Lynda Stalker was on her feet. 'Safe? Safe? Where is he?'

'You don't need to know that. He is not being harmed. He is simply being replaced.

'As you see, some colleagues are in agreement with this action. I invite any others of you who wish to remain in the Government to join us.

'No harm will come to you if you do not, but it will be necessary to detain you.'

'You bastard! You Judas! You snake-in-the-grass!' burst out around the room.

'Any of you who wish to join us now may stay,' said Edwards, now suddenly cold and machine-like. 'Otherwise you have twenty-four hours to advise me of your intentions. Captain!'

Soldiers - Dutch, French, Polish - filed into the room at a signal from one of the three at the door.

They silently took up positions around the walls of the room.

'Gentlemen – and ladies!' said the young Dutch captain urbanely, as he gestured towards the door. 'This way, please.'

CHAPTER 3

The boy clutched the bag of pigeon food and gazed upwards.

Pigeons scrambled round his feet and over his shoes. Another flock wheeled in over the lake in St. James's Park.

The boy's attention was riveted in the sky, but his gaze was focussed far beyond the wheeling birds.

'Look at all them planes!' he gasped to his friend, who was madly waving his arms to keep the pigeons off.

'Cor!' said the friend, and let out a long low whistle, as he looked skyward where the other pointed.

'It's like the – wha'd they call it? – the blitz!'

'Must be the King's birthday or summat!'

'No, that was last month – I know 'cos I went up the Palace with my Mum and my Auntie. Must be an airshow.'

'Yeah, look, it's an airshow – there's parachutes jumpin' out!'

'Blimey! There's a lot of 'em!'

'They're comin' down 'ere!'

'But there's no spectators – an' it's only just after breakfast! Can't be an airshow.'

Booted, helmeted, camouflaged figures started to hit the ground around the boys, roll over, then pull in their parachutes.

Rapidly they unclipped harnesses and ran in different directions – but as though knowing exactly where they were going.

The boy went up to one near him.

'Mister – is it an air show?'

'No – not an air show! Go to house! Go your home!'

''E's foreign, 'e is,' said the other boy as the soldier moved off in a low crouching run. 'Did you see 'is gun?'

Then they heard firecrackers. A lot of firecrackers.

'It's not firecrackers. They're shootin'. It's a army exercise.'

A policeman ran past, shouting into his radio.

A soldier came from behind some shrubs, tripped him with a booted foot, and smashed the radio with his rifle butt.

Then pinioning the policeman's arms behind his back with his own handcuffs, he marched him off to the pavilion in the centre of the Park.

'They're really tough, ain't they?' said the first boy. 'See 'im trip up that copper?'

They could hear sirens all around them now.

Lines of soldiers advanced through the Park, moving in small, tight, tactical formations – some towards the Palace, some towards Whitehall, but most making for Birdcage Walk.

As the firing continued, the boys could see figures running fast, crouching low along the wall of Wellington Barracks.

The boys followed them round the end of the lake.

They could see more soldiers fanning down through Green Park.

Another wave of planes passed overhead. No more parachutes. Must be going somewhere else.

Some of the soldiers now had trucks with guns behind them.

'I think we should go 'ome like 'e said,' said the second boy.

'No, let's watch. It's excitin',' said the first.

'What's the time anyway?'

'I dunno. I'll ask 'im,' the first boy said, pointing.

He walked up behind a soldier crouching by a tree, sub-machine gun trained across Birdcage Walk.

The boy tapped him lightly on the shoulder. 'Mister, what's...'

The soldier spun round in reflex action, finger instinctively closing on the trigger, sending off a burst of automatic.

The boys lay across each other on the path by the boathouse, the paper bag still clutched tightly in the first boy's hand.

A pigeon bobbed round, investigating, but soon went away, put off by the bright red stain on the bag, and the dark pool spreading on the path beside it....

Fifty miles to the south-east , another drop secured the UK landfall of the Channel Tunnel.

Within hours the shuttles were disembarking tanks, guns, trucks, stores. Then hundreds of troops, then thousands, pushing out a bridgehead deep into the Kent countryside.

At Heathrow and Stansted and Gatwick still more paratroops secured key points, and then unscheduled flights began to arrive – plane, after plane, after plane.

More tanks, more guns, more trucks, more troops.

Warships flying the Union ensign appeared off Spithead, and in Plymouth Sound, and the Dart Estuary, guns trained shoreward.

And to seaward, aircraft carriers and supply vessels.

At military airfields across the country, the unexpected incoming aircraft, requesting diversionary landing facilities, had identified themselves with correct Union codes.

The visitors appeared with no fanfare, screamed through at low level, and climbed steeply into the blue, leaving heavily-cratered runways in their wake.

The crowds of bewildered Londoners which had gathered spontaneously in Trafalgar Square milled round, almost heedless of the troops all about, and the armed figures high up in Admiralty Arch, Canada House, the National Gallery, and the buildings at the mouth of the Strand.

It looked like New Year's Eve, but sounded quite different. No singing, no music, no champagne corks, no screams and splashing from the fountains. Instead a loud grim hubbub of voices.

Even without hearing the words being spoken, a clear emotional tone overlay the whole Square. Shock, fear, incredulity, indignation, and anger, were all part of it. But mostly indignation and anger.

Snatches of conversation drifted up.

'If Nelson's watchin' this lot, 'e must be turnin' in 'is grave!'

'Well, they've bitten off more than they can chew.'

'It's a thousand years since the last Conquest. We'll just stuff this lot right up the Chunnel an' stick a flamin' great cork in it. Then 'istory won't even notice 'em.'

'Edwards'll end up hanging upside down from a lamppost.'

'They ain't got the King – 'E was too quick for 'em.'

'The Prime Minister was right to pull us out when he did. We might not have the troops in, but we'd be under the heel of Brussels just the same.'

'If this is how they act, it just shows he was dead right about them.'

The troops around the square stood silent, sullen but watchful.

Things might have been well enough had the huge throng been left to give vent to its feelings.

Who first decided to disperse them was not clear. Perhaps it was thought it could be achieved with loudhailers and riot shields. But one thing borrowed another.

No Londoner wasn't goin' to be dragged off of Nelson's Column by no Frenchman, nor no I-tie neither.

A few helmets were knocked off in getting this message across. A few punches were thrown, and skirmishing broke out.

Finally someone pulled a trigger, and very finally, a Londoner came down from Nelson's Column and didn't get up again.

A long quiet pause followed, then a cry of rage rose in crescendo from the collective throat of the throng.

Probably the troops did show restraint, because at least three were kicked to death before general firing began.

Several more died then, victims of the massed violence confronting them.

But the violence and the crowd ebbed away as the firing continued.

Down Whitehall, and along the Strand, and up Charing Cross Road, and into the Mall, the human tide flowed out from the Square. And as it ebbed, it left along its receding margin a terrible toll of creatures from its midst, dead and dying, like marine detritus strewn on the sand, disgorged by the retreating sea.

CHAPTER 4

The Prime Minister struggled up, up, up through the waves of unconsciousness, back from the oblivion which had enveloped him with the prick of the hypodermic. As he did so, his mind began to range back over the last few months, and then over the years, hazily reflecting on how it all began.

He remembered the heady atmosphere of election night, not yet four weeks ago, how he watched with Party stalwarts as the TV Election Special filled the big screen at Party headquarters.

The gasps and excitement as the swing-ometer moved inexorably into the red white and blue sector, the presenter pacing in front of it, gesticulating, darting this way and that, eyes popping, as he interpreted the movements, or announced another blue or red seat turned red white and blue.

This was the Election Special that the whole country watched – and indeed much of Europe and the world.

Viewing figures peaked at seventeen million, and as few children were included in the count for the late-night slot, every second adult must have tuned in. Projecting that through the night, with viewers coming and going, it was calculated that eighty per cent of the population watched it at some time.

Not surprising, perhaps, as ninety-one per cent of the electorate had cast their vote, in an unprecedented and historic turnout.

Queues had formed outside traditional polling stations from early morning, it was like the Christmas rush over again at Royal Mail with postal votes on demand, and online voting really took off in this election after its troubled start in the previous one.

Nothing had galvanised the people and brought out the vote on this scale, ever.

Europe yes or no – not just the limited issues of the referendums which had gone before. For the first time in decades they were being given their true voice.

They had been led by the nose by know-best politicians for the last time – never again!

'...And so, how many of these red seats here, and how many of those blue seats there, would have to turn red white and blue to enable them to form the next government? said the presenter, dashing eagerly from left to right of the studio.

'...Well, let's see, here it comes...the computer's bringing it up on the screen now...and here we are.

'So you see, we only need a swing of five per cent, and already, with only a third of the results in, we are seeing a swing of nine per cent.

'Let's see how many seats would turn red white and blue if this swing continued through the night.

'And...look...it's a landslide...which is in line with our exit poll findings.

'But let me emphasise, the night is still young. The exit poll figures can only tell us what we think the result will be, but the swing we're seeing now bears it out.

'If this is accurate, Britain will be out of Europe! Out of Europe! David, over to you!'

The anchor-man ran bony fingers through silver grey hair.

'Thank you, and if I can turn to our panel of distinguished guests in the studio – Dick Clark, for the Union Party, surely this is a wipe-out for you and the pro-Europeans, isn't it?'

'David, as has just been said, the night's young. Polls have been wrong before...'

'Not when they predict a complete landslide, though. You're going to be swept away, aren't you?'

'...as I was saying, yes, it looks as though we may be in for a disappointing evening, but so far most of the results are from the south-east, and we are confident our vote will hold up better in other areas'

But brave words and brave faces were not enough. And as the night went on, the words faltered and the faces fell, as three of the four studio guests had to acknowledge that their parties had suffered a terrible drubbing. The fourth guest wore a grin from ear to ear, which nothing could shift.

And in the red white and blue bedecked Party headquarters, the champagne bottles were being lined up and the glasses polished.

The night was not much older before the corks were popped, the glasses filled, and toasts rang round the room.

Lynda Stalker, always close at the Prime Minister's side in these gatherings, urged him to join the celebration. But in spite of all the indicators he gently refused her urgings, and those of many others, smilingly shaking his head and saying, 'There's many a slip....'

Round Europe the gloom was tangible. All knew what to expect from Britain now, knew also that this could be just the first crack in the dyke, for the British weren't alone in their reservations about the Union.

Round the world, brokers in dealing rooms scrabbled to translate the news into currency movements and share prices, and the great trading indexes shot up and down like yo-yos.

And at last, there at the centre of the dancing throng under the red white and blue garlands was the Prime Minister. Only now did he relax and allow himself to accept congratulations.

But as all the while his majority mounted, accompanied in the Election Special studio by dervish-like gyrations in front of the swing-ometer, his smile widened into a broad grin, which remained fixed there until breakfast-time, when he and Lynda left together for a quiet hour, before he had to ready himself for the visit to the Palace.

'This is it, then,' she said, as they sat in the private sitting room in Downing Street, moving close to him as soon as the steward had left after serving coffee.

He pulled at his tie, undid the top button of his shirt, and lay back against her on the settee. He felt the rhythm of her breathing under his head, and caught the fragrance of the discreet perfume she always wore.

Sometimes, passing other women wearing the same perfume, he resented the fact they were not Lynda, resented their use of it. He so loved her that he felt everything of hers should be hers alone.

'Yes, this is it,' he murmured. Then his eyes closed, his head lolled against her breast, and sleep rushed in upon him.

CHAPTER 5

More than twenty years before, he had come to the House of Commons amid the economic euphoria of the mid-80s.

He had seen it all – the Iron Lady's reluctance over Europe, the attack on her by her one-time Chancellor, characterised though it was as 'like being savaged by a dead sheep', the Decline and Fall.

And then the demi-European, less reluctant, but still practising safe sex as he got into bed with his European partners, the Maastricht opt-out condom his protection against Acquired Sovereignty Deficiency Syndrome.

But the Government's hands were still tied by the commitments of Maastricht and the insidious tendrils of the Exchange Rate Mechanism, unable to follow its own lights to lead the country out of the recession which had enveloped it in the early 90s, and so came Black Wednesday.

Maastricht was already 'A Treaty Too Far,' and with Amsterdam, Nice, Lisbon, and the Euro, Westminster was fast heading for a role as a rubber stamp.

Then it was he had raised his voice and cried, 'Enough!' – the first of the coming men to be loud in the cry against further political integration, though the old guard thundered and fulminated in the Other Place.

Romantics, and ideologues, and not a few xenophobes, fell in behind him, the Great Britain-ites singing Land of Hope and Glory and Rule Britannia!

The Government ignored them as cranks and crackpots – and in truth many were – and ground relentlessly on down the road to the Berlin Summit and the Treaty of Union.

As that historic summit began he delivered the speech which was the watershed for the Party.

Even its leaders had added their signatures to the Treaty, determined to translate their vision of Europe into reality, discounting the growing opposition, so that that opposition consolidated and became ever more vocal.

'So we are to be the United States of Europe,' he began. ' And no doubt those other United States are the model which some in Europe wish to emulate.

'But unlike the Good Ol' U.S. of A., these United States are no conjunction of coinciding interests, of like-minded peoples from one common ancestry, settled but a few years in the land, seeking to be masters of the land they work, casting off the tyranny of the Old Country across the sea.

'This is an edifice artificial from the start, a veritable Babel of different tongues and peoples – discrete nations with thousand-year histories, whose common history is of divergent interest, rivalry, and war.

'Though many warning voices have been heard, yet this new super-state is to embark on its grinding course of yoking together, creaking and groaning, all the disparate elements of a heterogeneous assortment of peoples, cultures, and customs.

'Strange the irony that it should have begun to take its final form just as the monolithic blocs of Eastern Europe disintegrated.

'Strange that many of those who led the way in closer cooperation with Europe were the first to sound the alarm when this cooperation threatened to become political conjunction.

'And now the Euro rules – but as a tyrant to its peoples. Lost is all the romance and sentiment of the Pound or the Franc, the Deutschemark or the Lire, as evocations of home and country – but worse than that, lost is the control of our own economic future.

'As anonymous and all-powerful as the Euro is the Central Bank which spawned it – a Central Bank elected by no one, and answerable to no one.

'National treasuries are its pawns, the economy of a continent its chessboard – on which it plays both sides. Move and counter-move are games played with itself.

'Thus hardly into this new millennium, when the Balkans have torn themselves apart, when Russia strives to contain its diverse nationalities, when the other one-time states of the USSR fall foul of ethnic conflict within, and the Middle East continues to disintegrate in the face of religious and political division, and the grip of terrorism, we are intent on tightening the bonds of Europe.

'These United States are to yoke together Greek and Dane, Portuguese fisherman and French farmer, industrialists in Milan and the Ruhr, the high sierras of Andalusia and the Dutch polders, North Sea oil and Sicilian subsistence farming, the City of

London and the Paris Bourse, the Church of Rome and of Constantinople, Canterbury and Calvinism, Jew, Moslem, and Hindu, and all the unbelievers in every language, and the believers in every dialect, ancient monarchies and late dictator states.

'All are to bow the knee to Brussels, pull down their tricolours and their imperial eagles, and become a single star on a monochrome background, nameless, indistinguishable from its neighbour.

'Nations of seventy million and of two, Romance language and Nordic, Celtic and Slavic, Frisian and Catalan, Udine and Buchan.

'Regions already marginalised economically, politically, socially, in their own country, are now in danger of disappearing off the edge of the known world – the world, that is, known to Brussels.

'All this diversity, all this disparity, all the dichotomies, all the anomalies, all in-gathered, thrust together, held together, opposite poles attract, like poles repel – is this to be the model for the new Millennium?

'Is this to be – the United States of Europe?'

Lying on his bed in the bare room - now become a cell, no teapot, no radio, no picture - a prisoner now, he thought of that speech, and thought how, as Brussels continued to turn the screw in the first year or two of the newborn Union, tightening the grip of the centre, support for him had swelled.

Not now just with the die-hards and the lunatic fringe as before – but with MPs concerned for their own self-interest as they saw Westminster's powers being drained away, and more significantly, with the pragmatists, the level-headed, sensible centre.

All recognised that with so many new accessions, the much greater sway of majority voting threatened the significance of Britain's voice in Europe as never before.

The first High Representative may have been a Brit – but a Brit who quite properly felt it her duty to leave her nationality behind when she took up the post, though not all her successors had been as scrupulous.

The eurosceptics, and the anti-federalists, and those by any other name committed to national sovereignty, fell in behind the rising man.

Meanwhile the flood of legislation threatening to swamp Westminster, also enlisted the support of many originally enthusiastic about Europe.

And as he was swept on and up, the Party began to turn its back on those who still clung to Europe.

Even the business interest, taking fright at the flood of directives from Brussels, and the ever-decreasing scope for economic manoeuvring, swung behind him.

Before the United States of Europe had reached its third birthday, the balance of opinion in the UK had fallen clearly on his side of the argument, and the Union was judged a mistake.

He was the clear favourite when, as a result, the inevitable leadership challenge materialised that summer, and he was the clear winner in the contest.

And then, just two short months ago, he found himself kissing hands, and going home to No. 10.

Determined to make his stand within a secure perimeter, to make his sorties into the high councils of Europe with no anxious backward glances at the support lines in his rear, he went to the country, calling a general election on the issue of Europe alone, adopting red white and blue as the new Party colours, to reflect the support flowing in from across the traditional divides.

The first to give the people their voice, to concede the supremacy of democratic choice, the first to be willing to inform and empower the people, and accept their decision, the people gave him his reward.

Now not just the Party, but the nation, backed him.

All the previous elections since he had come to the House had failed to put the issue to the voters. The politicians knew best, but the people knew different, and the politicians knew that they knew different, and would not take the chance.

And later, as party opinion divided, tacit agreement kept Europe off the agenda – the divided main parties keen not to expose the rifts within them.

No longer. His Party had fallen in behind him, and only a rump of the official Opposition supported Europe – although this rump was headed by the Leader of the Opposition, and could not be ignored. So the Opposition steered a middle course. But they knew the mood of the people, too, and could not have opposed it outright, without being overtaken by a swift Nemesis.

Many men of conscience crossed the Floor, as did many who were merely self-serving.

Only the Union Party stood its ground. It could do no other, its raison d'etre since its foundation by Dick Clark, a prominent Euro-enthusiast in the House of Commons, being a federal Europe. And now it was spearheaded by Euro MPs of different colours. In their anxiety for the preservation of their ideal, they had stepped over party boundaries to join forces on the great issue looming for Britain, and become the only unequivocal voice in opposition.

Then the Prime Minister had stood on the dais at the largest election rally ever seen since the dawn of the television age – taking the message direct to the people.

And that keynote speech had beamed out on the eve of poll on all channels, into every living room in the land.

'Not the French in the Middle Ages, nor the Spanish Armada, nor Napoleon at the height of his imperial might, nor in modern times the Kaiser, nor Hitler's storm troops, nor the wolf packs in the Western Approaches, nor yet the Luftwaffe or the V2s, have won over us by force of arms.

'But now, these endless streams of Brussels diktats, and its creeping economic hegemony, and the judgments from its courts, so often running counter to our age-old legal traditions, conspire to subjugate us more surely than would have the Imperial Guard, or the SS.

Let us have partnership, yes, but of dominion – let us have none!'

And they cheered him to the echo that night, and the next sent him back to Downing Street with the largest majority for more than 60 years.

CHAPTER 6

And in this time, too, a young politician had risen in the east. From the back benches of Germany's smallest provincial Landtag, this Matthias Weurmann had made his voice heard in Bonn, in Berlin, and in Brussels, too, and then made his power and influence rule.

He had stood at the Brandenburg Gate that night in 1990, as the fireworks burst overhead, and the shouting, laughing, crowds surged to and fro, hugging, weeping, waving flags, drinking champagne.

That night all Germany seemed to throw off the last shackle that bound it to its past, the last desperate legacy of those bitter years over half a century before – a divided nation.

And he thought of that other night a few weeks before, when he had walked through the Berlin streets, a cold chisel in one coat pocket and a mason's hammer in the other. Thought how he had come, with countless others, to that hated symbol of division, and defeat, and foreign oppression, to the Wall. How he had chiselled and hammered block from block with a fierceness of purpose and a fixed passionate stare as the masonry crumbled under his blows.

He had tried to destroy this Wall with thought, and word, and pen, and seemed never to have marked it at all.

Now, at the Brandenburg Gate, the memory of that physical assault was glorious.

He had carried home not bricks or blocks or wire, as many did, but the handful of dust remaining from a block dislodged from the Wall, pulverised under his hammer in a final frenzy.

He had kept it in an ornamental glass jar in the middle of his desk ever since.

And as the starbursts and rockets lit his upturned face at the Brandenburg Gate, so a light of understanding had dawned from within, and shone from his eyes, and took him over with a religious intensity.

This coming together of the Germanys, this healing of a nation by demolishing the political barriers dividing it, must be the pattern not just for Germany – but for its neighbours, for East and West, and for the World.

All in that instant, the idea grew in him, and possessed him, and imbued him with Messianic fervour, and his watchword became "Unity!"

It was his voice which fanned the flagging spirit of the Brandenburg Gate, as that first fine idealism faded away under the economic strain of immigration from the East – jobs for the workers, houses for the workers, and in the East disillusion at the failure of Unification to empty into their outstretched hands the cornucopia of all the good things of the West, and gave rise to the unholy face of neo-nazism.

But he was a European, and a German only incidentally, and many of his countrymen with him.

'What is Germany?' he would say. 'There never was a Germany until Bismarck, and that is only the blink of an eye in the vista of European history.

'We must go to the opposite extreme from Hitler. He sought to build his Reich by including all Germans, and excluding all non-Germans. That is to create enmity and division amongst peoples, and between nations.

'We must go the other way. We must create a great European family, perhaps, in time, a world family.'

And this ideal – shared by many – had carried him from the Landtag to the Bundestag, and from the Bundestag to Brussels.

There, he preached his Gospel in the Parliament, then in the Commission, then in the Council of Ministers.

There he had gathered disciples and they had carried forward together the programme of ever-closer union.

They had seen the Central Bank become supreme, the Euro established as a common currency and then the only currency, majority voting the way of all decision-making, the permanent president in the Council of Ministers.

His was the vision which lit the way, his the voice that cajoled, exhorted, enthused, the European federalists to live their dream.

But his, too, was the voice which for many turned uncertainty to anxiety, and mild doubt to reasoned and entrenched opposition, yes, and to xenophobic ranting and marching in these islands off the mainland which never had known whether they were of Europe or not.

For all that he was charismatic, and handsome, and popular, that he won hearts and minds as well; for all that he carried nations with him, and not only his own; for all that he personified the aspirations of all the long years of Europe since the Treaty of Rome, yet he was a German, and the long-dead of his country's past haunted him still in the long memory of his country's foe.

To hear a German voice shrill in passion and exhortation – even in passion against that hated predecessor – struck in many of his listeners discord, not the harmony Matthias Weurmann longed for.

And nowhere more than in the Kingdom across the German Sea.

CHAPTER 7

But in Germany the delegates to the Berlin Summit were proudly conscious that history was being made in these days, and that they were making it.

This was the Summit which would set the final seal on Europe as a federal union.

Now after more than half a century the great endeavour would be brought to completion, the dream realised.

And the greatest dreamer of that dream, whose vision and fervour for that goal had elevated him in power and influence above all the rest, so that he was now the embodiment of Europe, of the aspirations of two generations of Europeans – was to get his great reward.

And though the first attempt at a Constitution had fallen victim to popular doubts in more than one referendum across Europe, finally this Summit would institute a permanent elected President – a President not just as chairman of the Council as before, but a President now with full executive powers.

And in the manoeuvrings to get the process back on track after the 'anti' vote in the referendums, even greater powers were arrogated to the Presidency – if a battle was to be fought, it might as well be fought for the whole nine yards.

And of course there was but one serious candidate.

So Matthias Weurmann, architect of the federal Union in its final form, would have the great privilege of piloting it through its first ten years.

All other credible contenders had bowed out, acknowledging his formidable lead, and wishing to avoid humiliation as candidates.

Only a few fringe contestants remained to challenge him, knowing it was no challenge at all, but taking advantage of the electoral platform to advance their views.

The European Council of heads of state or government would be under his authority, and a re-styled Council of Ministers would be, in effect, the President's Cabinet, with one minister responsible for each portfolio, and enjoying Europe-wide powers.

But the final agreement had yet to be hammered out, and the delegates to the Summit had known the hard task they had in hand.

Maastricht, Amsterdam, Nice et al, and the wrangling over the Euro and Lisbon, were walks in the park, compared to the knock-down, drag-out, this quickly became, as members wrestled for maximum national advantage before the end of the old order.

This was the great test, too, for the enlarged Union, for the newest accession countries of Eastern Europe had their voting rights too, and were manifestly planning to use them.

So long used to the harness of regulation and direction in the command economies they had laboured under in the past, they had found the conflicts and competitive pressures of the free market too heady a cocktail.

They did not wish to turn the clock back to the quotas and five year plans of the communist era. They did in truth revel in the freedoms of the new economics, and had spread their wings, and expanded – but yet they yearned for some structure, some framework, within which they could harmonise with neighbouring economies, and escape the tossing on the stormy seas of their early ventures into the economy of the free world.

The bloc mentality still had its grip – and they wanted to come in from the cold, so they had knocked at the door, and eventually entered in.

But since their entry – and before – the great fear of the anti-federalists had been the spectre of new members, speaking with one voice, and bringing chaos to the fickle but fragile group dynamics of the early twelve.

And at the first time of asking it was clear their fears were justified.

The traditional grouping had been increasingly riven with dissension as the new members' interests clashed or coincided with their own.

Agreement had been hard to achieve, consensus impossible.

Deadlock was the result, and the consequences of deadlock threatened stagnation – of the political process, of the economy, of Union-wide social issues.

Under such intensive pressures the only way forward had been through majority voting – long advocated by the power-axes of the original Community, long resisted by the sceptics and anti-federalists of the later adherents. After all, the latecomers had joined not from commitment to a political ideal, but in response to economic imperatives, as the Six flourished and prospered.

So in joy, in grief, or with resigned pragmatism, each member state had cast into the melting pot its last vestige of national sovereignty – the veto, hoping that the new form forged from the remains of the old would break the deadlock, and restore the vitality.

And it had. And the Treaty of Berlin signed that day, giving birth to the United States of Europe, testified to that. Europe had cast off the inertia in which it had languished since the death of consensus.

It moved forward again, ponderously enough at first, but gathering momentum, and finally its progress as a federal union seemed inexorable – but at what cost to many individual members was hardly foreseen.

Redistribution of resources between net contributors and net beneficiaries fuelled internal tensions, and rekindled old national jealousies.

Regardless of the checks and balances and national weightings so carefully built into the voting in the new United States, the Federal Government sooner or later steam-rollered over some legitimate national concerns, economic interests, or the cultural sacred cows of each and every member, as voting majorities imposed decisions.

Some called it 'democracy', though it was not the people but the states which voted, and decision-making could hardly be farther removed from those who would have to live with the consequences.

But now the transition was complete – from acknowledgment of mutual interdependence and economic cooperation as neighbours, to political and economic integration with all that implied for the subjugation of national interest and national sovereignty.

Thus was the dream of many realised – a dream nurtured at first in secret places of the mind and then in secret rooms, with other secret men. A secret they kept lest a premature acknowledgment of that ultimate end should frighten faint hearts, or set the ghosts of nationalism and xenophobia stalking abroad in Europe again.

Yet what bitterness that dream, realised, created in others. Willing peoples, gullible, hanging on the honeyed words of their leaders, tempted on into ever-closer ties, believing all the while the blandishments of 'harmonisation', and 'cooperation' – and never seeing the snares of 'integration', and ' federalisation', until too late, when the trap was sprung.

And all too soon, the solution became the problem, and the yoke of the Federal Government began to rub and chafe.

CHAPTER 8

From the first time Matthias Weurmann and the Prime Minister had seen each other, rising young men both, there had grown up a bond of mutual respect between them.

Now, these many years later, they sat reflected in the polished mahogany on opposite sides of a conference table in a Belgian chateau.

They nodded, with wry faces, across the table.

Each knew what the other stood for, knew that it was that which had elevated them to the great offices they now held.

Each had come to respect the other's intellect, integrity, power of debate, political shrewdness, and capacity for action.

Each acknowledged that the other's stand for the juxtaposed views they cherished was as principled as his own.

And each quite simply liked the other.

They shook hands that day in Liege – but hands across a political divide which was, in truth, an unbridgeable chasm.

For this was the meeting at which the Prime Minister – a landslide majority behind him - was to state his case unequivocally.

His position was clear, his popular mandate unarguable, and his course inexorable, unless at this eleventh hour some concession could be wrung from Weurmann and the Federal Government – or at the very least some form of words, which might hold out hope of a changed status, a reversion to some sort of associate relationship or other.

But really those around the table knew they were just going through the motions, and none expected any substantive change on either side.

And so it was.

Weurmann said to his aide later that day, 'This Prime Minister will do as he says he will do, or he will perish in the attempt.

'But still I like him - I wish he thought with us, but I fear we are on a collision course.'

Then after a pause he said, 'I like this lady minister, too,' For Lynda Stalker had accompanied the Prime Minister to this conference.

The aide, knowing his chief as he did, felt compelled to respond to what might ordinarily pass as a casual reference.

But he had seen Weurmann's gaze fall again and again on the low-buttoned blouse of the Minister for Women, and the flash of long-buried passion in his eye.

Weurmann had loved and lost many years before and been badly wounded in the fray. In the years since, he had devoted himself single-mindedly to his European dream, and sublimated all passion into the pursuit of that.

But Lynda Stalker bore an uncanny resemblance to his lost lover, and stirred a deep well-spring of desire within him even at this first encounter.

She, always sensible of the sensual attraction she commanded, and the desires she aroused in men, became acutely aware of a deeper intensity in Weurmann's regard, a quality beyond the ordinary lust she encountered in men in general, and to which she had become inured.

And she became aware of a flickering response in herself, beyond the flirtatiousness which she often affected in appropriate circles, and sometimes could not control in inappropriate ones.

She tried in vain to keep this out of her eyes, and kept them downcast on the notes in front of her. But every once in a while she was compelled to look up, and always when she did so, found his eye meeting hers.

The watchful aide saw the fire that flashed between them – and the Prime Minister saw it, too.

'You know that she and the Prime Minister are...involved?' the aide asked later.

'I have heard a rumour – but also that they are not lovers.'

'No', said the aide. 'He uses the utmost discretion – very wisely.'

'We cannot always be wise,' said Weurmann in a faraway voice.

A few doors away in his suite at the chateau the Prime Minister discussed Weurmann with the Foreign Secretary.

'Even though I like him, he's so thoroughly imbued with this vision of his of Europe as one nation, that he's not "a man I can do business with",' the Prime Minister said.

'Of course, that's what we expected. When Maggie said that about Gorbachev, he was taking off the blinkers, loosening the reins, of a closed society – looking outwards....' said the Foreign Secretary.

'...Whereas Weurmann is putting the blinkers on, tightening the harness, reining in the team,' the Prime Minister concluded.

'Exactly,' said the Foreign Secretary. 'He may be doing it for the right reasons – he wants the Union to move forward together, harnessing the strength of each....'

'But he thinks one harness will fit all,' said the Prime Minister, 'get all to pull in harmony. Instead, the tighter he pulls it, the more it chafes.'

'Well,' the Foreign Secretary put in, 'we're not alone in feeling it chafe, though perhaps we're the only ones who've got to the point of casting it off.'

'I'm even more decided now,' said the Prime Minister. 'I thought I might turn his course by argument, with some support from other members. But his determination flows from a deep conviction. I don't think we'll change it.

'But I've left him in no doubt about where we stand, and I think we're going to have to adopt the radical approach.'

Then the two men parted to dress for the formal dinner.

As he fumbled with his black tie, the Prime Minister recalled painfully the affinity which had developed almost instantly between Lynda and the President, even before any words were spoken.

In the hour before dinner, Weurmann quietly arranged for a minor change in the seating plan, and when they took their places for the meal Lynda Stalker found herself sitting on Weurmann's right, with the Prime Minister on her right.

Throughout the meal they exchanged only social conversation, and a few passing references to the formal session, but she was aware of an electric tension between them.

Only once did they touch. As he bent forward to speak across her to the Prime Minister, his knee accidentally pressed against hers. But that momentary touch sent a frisson of desire through her whole body, and she turned to him with a yearning gaze.

He stopped in mid-sentence as his eye met hers, then quickly recovered himself, sat more upright, withdrawing his knee, and continued with what he was saying.

It was barely a surprise to her when in her room later, she answered a knock at the door to find a footman bearing a discreet little note on a silver salver, inviting her to join the President in his suite 'to touch on some discussion points before tomorrow's session.'

It was no surprise to her at all when she accepted the invitation, but not before she had spent some time in front of the mirror, and effected a quick change from the formal gown she had worn to dinner, into a black cocktail dress in wild silk, with a deep vee cut in the front and panelled in sheer chiffon.

He was charismatic, handsome, distinguished-looking, powerful, and still had relative youth on his side, but it was not to these qualities she responded. None of these, nor even the combination of them, would have been enough for her. It was to the hidden spring of love in him, which, buried deep as it was, she had still discerned.

To that, and to her own intense need for sex as the consummation of love. For though she truly loved the Prime Minister, she did not have the messianic sense of purpose which in him could sustain their celibate relationship.

The President and she spoke but little, and touched on no discussion points, but they did touch the point of passion in each other, and let it flood forth, clinging to each other, pressing kisses upon each other's lips, neck, breast – holding, caressing, trying to cleave ever closer together.

Then the black dress slipped to the floor, and the two fell upon a rug before the open fire, and drained themselves of all desire.

Next morning the Prime Minister knew without being told.

When they met at breakfast and exchanged chaste kisses, he immediately perceived the soft radiance in her that meant one thing.

It had happened before with other men. He didn't blame her. He understood. But he never flinched from his determination to put the duty he conceived was his before all else – personal happiness included.

But this was different. There was no doubt who it had been. He'd seen the fire in their eyes. And he felt compelled to speak.

'Lynda, this man, honourable though he is, is my political enemy,' he said, 'and he dishonours himself – and us – by this.'

She had known he would know. He always knew – they were so close. She did not dissemble.

'I didn't go with him as a politician,' she said. ' You know how it is with me. You know it will happen every so often.'

'Yes, I know,' he said. 'But him?'

'Yes, him – I had to.'

CHAPTER 9

The week following the weekend conference in the chateau months before had been one of feverish activity for the Prime Minister.

Returning on the Monday, by the evening he had convened a special Cabinet Committee, which deliberated long into the night, and after a few hours of sleep reconvened for a working breakfast.

In the days that followed, there was much to-ing and fro-ing of ministers. Parliamentary business managers, and whips.

The Prime Minister himself burned the midnight oil night after night, and cancelled his weekend engagements.

The next week's meeting of the full Cabinet opened in sombre anticipation.

A number of matters were dealt with in short order, which at any other time would have produced lively interchange.

Now, however, there was a detachment, and impatience to be done with these more or less routine items.

Some inkling of the Cabinet Committee's deliberations had percolated through the Cabinet at large, and all knew the course to which events, and the Prime Minister's thoughts, were tending. All expected that their formal expression in Cabinet would provoke impassioned debate, the like of which had not been seen in the Cabinet Room for many years.

Each of them round the table knew that history was in the making that day, that what was to come would be more written about, and talked about, and argued over for twenty years to come – perhaps for fifty – than any subject in living memory.

It had no parallel in British history, or Party history – unless it was the Irish Question, or the withdrawal from India, or the Wind of Change, and there the role had been different.

As the Prime Minister turned to it, every eye was upon him.

'We've long sought to convey to our partners in the Union our view of the need for reform, to take us towards a more flexible partnership structure, and to move away from the increasingly inflexible forms and relationships which some members advocate.

'It's my view, and the view of the Cabinet Committee which has been considering this – prompted by the tenor of the recent

Conference in Liege – that as the most powerful voices in the Union remain intransigent, we must proceed to active consideration of secession.'

No murmur was heard from the listening Cabinet. All had expected this.

The Prime Minister enumerated the key reasons for embarking on this course, to the increasingly sombre group of ministers, who might have written the text of his address themselves, so often had these points been the subject of discussion in and out of Cabinet.

But to hear them enunciated one by one in the wake of the first formal expression of this resolution – a resolution which, though it had been anticipated, was still startling – was to view the irrefutable logic, in the existing political context.

As the Prime Minister summed it up – 'We have an unimpeachable mandate from the electorate to resist the further encroachment of Brussels and the Union, the further erosion of the powers of our own national institutions, and the dilution of our own culture and tradition.'

The eyes now turned from the Prime Minister to his Deputy, to Neville Edwards, arch-federalist, anticipating a stormy reaction.

Federalists for the most part – honourable federalists – had resigned the Party whip long since, recognising that on the Government side they were an ever-dwindling minority, and would be much more at home with Dick Clark and his Union Party.

But they had been a sufficiently strong and vocal minority for Neville Edwards – as the most vocal, if not the strongest – to find himself borne upwards, as a sop to maintain their goodwill, while that was still possible.

But as his support drifted away to the Union Party or to other groupings within their own party, as thinking on Europe changed with the march of events, speculation was rife as to how long the Prime Minister would endure his presence at the Cabinet table.

But for now, he was still the principal mouthpiece of the other faction with which the Prime Minister had to contend.

Thus, the eyes of the Cabinet were upon him.

The atmosphere was tense, the expectation keen, the anticipation electric, that now was to be the showdown – the repudiation, finally, by the Prime Minister of any further need to rely on the support of him and his cohorts, and on Edwards' part, the eruption of all the rancour, jealousy, and personal bitterness towards his chief, which the Deputy Prime Minister harboured.

It might even bring Edwards' resignation this very morning, his stated principles certain to be compromised by any other course, with all the public and press furore which would ensue.

The Prime Minister, too, though almost imperceptibly, braced himself for the onslaught.

No one spoke a word. Hardly a breath was drawn.

The gauntlet had been thrown down. It lay squarely in front of Edwards, in almost tangible form.

Edwards straightened in his chair, leaned forward slightly, ran his gaze around the twenty expectant faces confronting him, and finally rested it on his notes, without looking towards the Prime Minister.

He cleared his throat.

'I would like my dissent from the decision to consider secession to be noted,' he said.

It took some moments before the Prime Minister and the rest of the Cabinet quite realised that nothing more was going to follow.

As it became obvious, glances were exchanged around the room which seemed to say, 'What's Edwards up to? What's his game?'

At three-thirty p.m. the next day the Prime Minister entered the Chamber of the House of Commons, bowed to the Speaker, and took his place on the front bench. A great throaty murmur rose around the House, and as quickly died to silence.

Members squeezed together on the benches, sat on the steps, stood at the Bar of the House, pressed around the Speaker's Chair.

Incredibly, with the entrance of the Prime Minister, every single member was present – the House in its entirety. None could remember having seen it so full.

The galleries, too, were packed – lobby correspondents, peers, members' wives and families, public, union officials and politicians, all craning, and peering, and straining, to catch every new actor making his entrance on the stage, every word of every speech, every alarum and excursion on the Treasury bench.

The Speaker dealt with the remaining business items with even more than usual dispatch, and turned at last toward the Government bench.

'The Prime Minister,' he called in his sharp, businesslike tone, and the great murmur rose again.

Then the Prime Minister was gripping the side of the Dispatch Box in his familiar attitude, but with none of the twinkle in the eye or the ironic smile about the lips, which the House was wont to see.

A serious, even grim, manner fixed his usually mobile features in an expression of purpose and determination.

And, unusually, he had before him no notes, not a scrap of paper, nor even an Order Paper.

'Mr. Speaker,' he began, 'I rise to speak to perhaps the most momentous motion this House has been asked to consider in half a century.

'The House will forgive me if I speak at unusual length, but the motion, if carried, will represent the close of a long chapter in the modern history of this country, and the opening of another chapter in which its future course will be very different....'

In the hour which followed, he delivered to the crowded benches a pellucid chronicle of the previous fifty years of relations with Europe.

Britain's initial indifference, followed by doubt and the formation of the European Free Trade Area with the non-'Common Market' countries, the agonising over possible entry, problems with the former Dominions' favoured trade status.

The eventual entry, the contentious issues, Common Agricultural Policy and butter mountains, contribution levels and regional aid, social chapter and single currency, veto and qualified majority voting, fast-track and slow-track, convergent economies and divergent economies, European Court and Central Bank, directives, and labels, and Euro-speak.

Thence to sovereignty and subsidiarity, European Parliament and Westminster, European Council and British Cabinet.

Now on to the shift in mood, the change in sentiment, as the politicians outstripped the people in pursuit of their own

European ideal, And the people, unwilling to be led along blindly any longer, making themselves heard, making their strength felt, making their votes count, whether in referendums or, as now, in national elections.

Business and industry, too, so long champions of Europe, beginning to falter in their support as they bowed under the burden of increasing regulation, harmonisation, labour policy, and the never-ending streams of bureaucratic forms and directives.

And finally, as the Community grew, consensus becoming unwieldy, qualified majority voting resulting in ever more frequent reverses for Britain, Parliamentary authority being eroded, economic flexibility being circumscribed, effective political control moving to Brussels, culture and character, heritage and tradition being submerged – and then the Treaty of Berlin and the United States of Europe.

'And so now, in these first decades of this new millennium, we have to ask ourselves, "Do we want to go into the new age as citizens of the Union, or as Britons once again?"

'We have to ask, "Do we wish to become submerged ever-deeper in the European sea, or rise as before 'from out the azure main', independent, free, and British?"

'We have to ask, "Into whose hands do we wish to commit our future – to the Council, the Commission, the Central Bank? Or to King, and Parliament, and Country?

'And we have to answer – "Into our hands, not others" !

'We have to answer – "Arise, not submerge" !

'We have to answer – "Into the new age, as Britons once again"!

'Mr. Speaker, I beg to move.'

In vain Mr. Speaker cried 'Order! Order!', as the house erupted in cheering and shouting, and waving of Order Papers.

The public galleries erupted, too, and ushers escorted more than one from the Chamber for no more serious offence than unbridled enthusiasm.

The press gallery emptied almost magically, the instant the Prime Minister sat down.

The House knew the arguments the Opposition would array against the motion, had heard them before, did not feel the need to hear them again, and could read them up in Hansard if really necessary.

So the packed House flooded into lobby, and tearoom, and bar, and dining room, and out on to the Terrace in the gathering dusk – breathless with speculation, buzzing with their own comments on the Prime Minister's speech, and muttering over the contributions with which they hoped to follow on, if they could catch the Speaker's eye.

In the next forty-eight hours the Bill was read a second and a third time, and though it had raised murmurs in the Lords, it was set to complete all its stages there too, and receive the Royal Assent, at the beginning of the following week.

CHAPTER 10

President Weurmann drummed his fingers on the arm of the carved oak chair, and let out a long whistling sigh, then dejectedly addressed the members hurriedly assembled for an extraordinary session of the Council.

'I did not think it would actually come to this,' he said, 'until, perhaps, my recent meeting with the Prime Minister – then I realised what we were up against.'

And inwardly he wondered whether he had given him a fresh and personal motive to drive his political antagonism, with the night in the chateau still fresh in his mind.

'He is undoubtedly a deeply-principled man. For some time I wondered if he had become merely an opportunist, but not so.

'The question is, what is our response to be?'

This Summit had been called at such short notice that, even as he spoke, one or two heads of government with their foreign ministers were still tiptoe-ing in, mouthing silent apologies.

'I would like to have your views,' he continued after a pause to let the new arrivals settle in.

'Let them go, and good riddance,' said the Dutch premier. 'They've been a thorn in our side. All the time since before Maastricht – 'we don't want to do this, we don't want to do that, down with Spanish fishermen, we want more funds, we want to pay less money, protect the British "banger", we keep our border controls, we will never give up our rebate...on, and on, and on. Everything takes two times as long if Britain is involved. They don't want to be in the Union? I say "good riddance"!'

A smile rippled round the room despite the seriousness of the occasion. Always amusing, even with the driest or most serious subject, the tall, lean, Dutchman had certainly neatly encapsulated how most of them saw the British.

'We cannot realistically do that, though we might like to,' said Weurmann. 'To establish such a precedent at this stage of the Union's development is to risk everything.'

'What options do we have?' said the Hungarian premier.

Weurmann nodded to an aide, who began to pass out papers. 'We have outlined several options in the briefing paper now being passed round.'

'Well, you have just ruled number one out,' said the Italian Prime Minister. 'Why do you even put it down?'

'It is put down because it is, of course, one option – to let them go. But as I have said, it is a risky precedent to set.'

'But should we try to hold anyone in who does not want to be in?' asked the Dutchman.

'That of course is for discussion,' said Weurmann.

'Option 2 is to continue negotiations and seek to persuade them to stay. However, I am not hopeful that we would make much progress with that. Having been very much involved in the discussions to date, I feel that we have passed that stage, but again, it can be discussed.

'Option 3 is to offer some kind of associate status.'

'I would not favour that,' said the Finnish premier. 'Why make exceptions?'

'I agree,' said the bespectacled Danish minister. 'Either they are aboard or they are not. No in-between.'

'Nevertheless it is an option,' said Weurmann.

'Option 4 is to use legal sanctions'

'How would that work? Presumably they will now not accept the jurisdiction of federal courts,' observed another. 'That has been one of the contentious issues all along – they have never liked interference with their traditional "British justice".'

'I think that is correct, and this one does not begin the race,' replied Weurmann.

'Option 5 – economic sanctions.'

'I believe that is how we must go,' the Austrian premier put in, nodding his head vigorously. 'Everyone feels it if his pocket is empty. Also this is why we want Britain to remain in – her economy is so closely linked with all of us. She damages us all if she will leave now.'

'But it damages us to make sanctions, too,' said another.

'This is true,' said the Austrian, ' but which damages us more? Sanctions are damage for the short term. The British secession is damage for the long term.'

The president continued, 'Finally', he said looking gravely round the table, 'Option 6 – military sanctions.'

There were gasps, sighs, exchanged glances, and a long pause.

'Britain will not give in because she is threatened,' said the German Chancellor, breaking the silence.

'What sort of military sanctions?' asked someone else.

Weurmann said, 'General Le Blanc is outside and will brief us on this if required.'

'A blockade?'

'There are several possibilities here. I think we have to ask the General.'

'This would be an even more dangerous precedent than letting them secede,' said the Dutchman. 'And what would the cost be – in men as well as money? The people will not stand it – not just to keep an unwilling partner in.'

'The cost is secondary to the principle,' said Weurmann. 'But we only contemplate a limited police action.'

'How could we justify force?' rejoined the Austrian premier. 'How could that be right?'

'That, too, is for further discussion,' replied the President. 'But these are the options. Now we must consider them and make our decision.

'I think there is general agreement that option one, option two, and option four can be dismissed.'

There was some shuffling of papers, and murmurs of assent, but the Dutchman again pressed his point, more seriously now. 'Mr. President, I would like full discussion on option one – letting them go their way,' he said.

'All right, in that case we discuss four possibilities.'

Discussion ranged around the table, groups forming and re-forming in favour of one or other option.

Coffee came and went.

The debate became heated at times, and stagnated at others.

General Le Blanc gave a presentation outlining several scenarios and the feasibility of military options.

The only consensus to emerge after some three hours, was that somehow Britain must be kept in the fold.

They broke for lunch and then resumed, with no substantive progress made.

'Are there any other possibilities anyone wishes to suggest?' Weurmann asked after lunch.

Heads were shaken.

'We could call on them to resign as a government,' said one, ' on the basis that their actions are unconstitutional, and call fresh elections.'

'But the electorate has already given them a huge majority,' said the President. 'Fresh elections might or might not go our way. We intend to act whether they do or not. We should not run the risk, or we might weaken our case.'

Silence ensued.

Then Jiricek, the Czech foreign minister said tentatively, 'Not all British are against the Union. What if those who are not – those who are pro – ask for our assistance?'

All eyes turned to him, questioning.

'Well, we Czechs know all about that from 1968, and the Hungarians, too.'

The Hungarian minister nodded, 'Yes – in 1956,' he said.

'The Russians did not like Dubcek bringing in liberal reforms,' the Czech continued, 'and they engineered a request for help from Czech hard-liners.'

'Gentlemen,' said Weurmann, looking round the table with rising interest, I think this is a proposal which merits serious consideration.'

The discussion rolled on, but with a new and sharper focus.

Coffee came and went again, but by dinner-time they had concluded what their course must be.

Resuming later, they were able to get down to the principles of how to implement the action they had decided on, and the timetable for it.

By midnight, having passed the ball to Le Blanc, they retired to sleep, or sat in little knots to drink schnapps or cognac, and smoke, the decision made.

Shortly after, in the privacy of his room, Weurmann telephoned Lynda Stalker. He wanted her out before the balloon went up.

Though they had only had that one night, he was unable to get her out of his mind, and phoned her frequently.

He'd never known love-making as he had experienced it with her.

He'd transcended the base desire to pretend she was his old lover, and she had provided him with a glimpse of transcendent sexual fulfilment.

Now he wanted her for himself as he'd never known want of a woman.

'I would like you to come to Brussels,' he told her, naming the dates.

'Why?'

'You know why.'

'Why these dates?'

He had to lie.'To fit my diary.'

'Matthias,' she said gently, 'I'll never forget our time together – but I thought it would be a one-off.'

'No!' he cried emphatically. 'Never! How could you think so?'

'But in any case,' she continued, 'I can't make these dates.'

He swore to himself as he put the phone down a few minutes later. How to avoid her becoming embroiled? She was unlikely to be swayed easily from her support for the Prime Minister.

He did not know how, but he must contrive something.

CHAPTER 11

Weurmann's staff had quietly canvassed sympathetic opinion in the UK in the wake of the ministerial summit.

'If we can find a strong, credible leader, we can tap the support of the Euro-enthusiasts,' the President said to his political advisers after the conference.

'Jiricek is right. It will put a completely different construction on whatever action we take if we are invited to give assistance.

'We will be seen to be – and we will be – supporting the significant section of the British establishment which believes the Government should honour its commitments – not just those who are pro-Union.

'Find me the man, and let's stop the rot now.'

The trawl of Union supporters had begun almost immediately.

A Council committee oversaw this process and drew up a short list.

Approaching potential candidates was not without its dangers, as one or two of the political staff found out. Discreet and casually offhand as they were in their contacts they yet aroused the suspicions of some – and the hopes of others.

Senior political figures began to realise something was brewing as they chatted in their clubs and the lobbies at Westminster, and related the tenor of their surprise late night phone calls from Brussels.

Clear pointers quickly emerged nonetheless, and realistically there were but three credible contenders – only two of whom were to be approached in the first instance.

One was the founder and leader of the Union Party, Dick Clark,. The other, surprisingly, was the Deputy Prime Minister, Neville Edwards.

Dick Clark was the obvious choice as a long-time Euro-enthusiast. With a French mother, bi-lingual, having lived as a child in Paris and later studied at the Sorbonne, he had been a keen advocate of political integration.

He and the President knew each other well personally, and his had been the name which had jumped to Weurmann's mind when the Czech Foreign Minister had made his suggestion. He was in

Brussels regularly, and easily contactable without arousing suspicion.

He had come to Parliament under another banner, but as eurosceptics in the party began to gain the high ground and force a shift in Party policy, he found his principles compromised on every issue touching on European integration, and finally felt he had no option but to resign the whip.

Finding one or two colleagues joining him after a little, it was a short step to the formation of a new party. And as the opposition parties as well as the Government adopted an increasingly eurosceptic stance, there was a considerable drift from them as well, to his fledgling party.

Clark had by and by found himself at the head of a significant group in the House, and the new party the only real home for the votes of committed Unionists in the country at large.

Their weakness was a lack of wider political organisation, and they were unable to field candidates in other than key constituencies around the country.

And at the landslide election, although they held on to many seats because of the loyalty to sitting MPs who had a good record in their constituencies, they lost others, and picked up no new ones at all.

Their strength was their commitment to the European ideal, and the high principle and personal charisma of their leader.

This was the man whom Weurmann invited to meet with him, discreetly, if not clandestinely, in the Presidential Office in Brussels.

'Good to see you, Dick,' he said warmly, shaking the other's hand, 'but we have problems, we Europeans, do we not?'

'Yes, we do indeed,' said Clark. 'These are dark days for Britain. I didn't expect the Prime Minister to go quite so far, I must confess.'

'Dark days for the United States of Europe too, Dick. We need to try at all costs to maintain the integrity of the Union, and prevent Britain's secession.'

'Well, yes,' Clark nodded, 'though I don't quite see how it can be managed.'

'That is why I wanted to see you,' said Weurmann.

'Of course, I'll help in any way I can,' Clark offered. What had you in mind?'

'I expect,' said the President, 'that you and your supporters, and many committed Europeans around the United Kingdom, would like to see the Federal Government do what it can to halt this headlong dash towards secession.'

'Certainly,' said Dick Clark.

'I can say that a request for assistance from such a substantial body of opinion would not go unheeded in Brussels.'

'Request for assistance?' said Clark with a puzzled expression.

'Assistance in preventing the British Government taking such an unconstitutional and illegal step, abnegating their commitments under the Treaty of Berlin.'

'But what could you do?' asked Clark.

'Exercise our federal powers to require the investigation or removal of ministers or officials acting unconstitutionally.'

'Do you mean the Prime Minister?' Clark asked with some surprise.

'And members of the Government supporting him in such an illegal course,' said the President, with a meaning look.

'But how?' Clarke said, stunned. 'They're not going to resign with the mandate they've just been given.'

'Then they would have to be removed.'

'How?' said Clarke again.

'By whatever means necessary.'

'You mean by force?'

'As a last resort – but if necessary.'

'And then what?' asked Clark, incredulous now.

'Then we would require a caretaker government.'

'A caretaker government?'

'Yes, Dick. That is why I have invited you here.'

Clark stood up abruptly.

'Never!'

Now it was the President's turn to parrot.

' "Never"? What do you mean, Dick?'

'What do you mean, "what do you mean"? I mean never! I would never countenance such a usurpation of democratic authority, never mind be party to it!'

'But I am offering to give you the Prime Minister-ship – besides, the British Government is usurping the democratic authority!'

'It isn't yours to give Mr. President!' exclaimed Clark, in anger and dismay. 'And unless I hear an immediate retraction, I'll make sure the Government is clear who's trying to usurp who.'

The President realised they had read Clark wrong, and immediately back-pedalled. He sighed. 'All right, Dick. I just wanted to get your ideas. Perhaps it is crazy – you are right. I was just testing the temperature of the water. I just cannot stand to see any break-up of the Union.'

This mollified Clark a little. 'Nor I – but that's dangerous talk, Mr. President. I don't think you should repeat it. Not everyone is as much a friend to the Union as I am. Others who don't share your strong ideal may not be so tolerant when it gives rise to extremist thoughts.'

'No – you are right. Thank you for speaking frankly, and thank you for coming. I know you will treat our discussion as confidential.'

And Clark took his leave, pacified, but still uneasy.

He could scarcely believe the proposition which had just been put to him. It was flattering, yes, but could the President really have seen him as a man of such elastic principles?

Could he trust Weurmann again after what he'd heard? Would he treat the discussion as confidential?

And yet, as he thought further about it, he felt that Weurmann must have been flying a kite. He couldn't put such a proposal in earnest, and then just let him waltz off back to the UK.

In any case, if he did speak out, the President would simply deny it – there wasn't even any evidence that they'd met. It had all been in secret.

But still he felt uneasy.

Well he might. No sooner was he out of the President's office than Weurmann flipped a switch on the intercom.

'Get on to Edwards,' he said. 'Get him here as soon as you can. But be discreet. Remember this is the Deputy Prime Minister.'

CHAPTER 12

Neville Edwards had just returned to his flat from one of his late night visits to a lady in Camden Town when the phone rang.

'This call is in the strictest confidence Mr. Edwards,' said the Presidential aide. 'Can I assume that you will not discuss it with anyone.'

Edwards was nothing if not pompous and self-important, and retorted in a rasping tone, 'I am the Deputy Prime Minister. I can make no promises without some idea of what it's about.'

'It could be to your personal advantage,' said the aide.

There was a pause.

'That's a different story – fire away. My lips are sealed.'

'The President would like to see you in Brussels in the morning.'

'Well, I'm honoured, but I don't know – things are hotting up here with the Secession Bill...'

'It touches on that,' said the aide, 'and on your personal interest, as I said.'

Another pause.

'All right then – you've baited the hook very nicely.'

'Till tomorrow then.'

'Yes, goodbye.'

Edwards pursed his lips.

'Hmm,' he thought. 'wonder what all that was about.'

But his devious mind almost matched the case. As he ruminated over a glass of brandy before snatching such sleep as he could if he was to catch the first flight to Brussels, he came close to guessing the message in part.

Edwards was the leading europhile in the Government – or at least the leading Government figure wearing europhile colours, for he had no personal conviction extending beyond self-interested opportunism. And as such he knew and was known to the President, and so, like Dick Clark, had some measure of the man.

'He wants to drive a wedge into the Government,' he said to himself. 'If he can enlist me, he knows I can enlist some Cabinet waverers, and he can split the Government and see off or stall secession.'

He picked up the phone and rang Camden Town. 'Cissy,' he said to the sleepy voice at the other end, 'Cissy, wake up! I'm on the move. I've just had a call from the President's Office, and he wants me in Brussels in the morning, so I can't give you your elevenses. You'll have to DIY,' he said with a salacious chuckle, 'but keep it warm for me – I'll come round at night.'

'Well, I don't know exactly,' he said in reply to a perfunctory enquiry from the other end of the line. 'I think he's going to make me an offer he thinks I can't refuse. Perhaps I can't, but I'm certainly going to milk it for all it's worth – and I get to put a knife in the Prime Minister's guts and twist it, if my guess is right.'

Half right as his guess was, even Edwards did not expect the proposition the President laid out.

The same probing preamble he'd used with Dick Clark provoked in Edwards, Deputy Prime Minister though he was, none of the incredulity or protest which boiled up so swiftly in Clark, the leader of a minor opposition party.

The President, feeling as a result that he was on surer ground with Edwards and did not have to be so circumspect, went on straightforwardly.

'If push comes to shove,' the President concluded, 'we will need an interim administration with someone we can trust, and someone the people can trust, at the head of it.'

Edwards' eyes glinted.

'That is why I have asked you here. If we are asked by our friends in Britain to give "assistance", we need to have the key people in place ready to carry on the Government.'

Edwards, suppressing his glee, made a quick calculation here. If he was to play the reluctant debutante to up the ante, now was the moment.

'Will you be asked by your friends in Britain?' he asked, raising an eyebrow.

'That is also why I have asked you.'

'It would be a very risky move for me,' said Edwards.

'I do not think so,' said the President.' We cannot allow Britain simply to opt out. If secession fails, the Prime Minister must fall – one way or another. Then it will be our man in charge.'

'You're risking a lot even talking to me about this,' said Edwards.

'I am taking the risk because I think I am talking to the right man. Am I?'

'Perhaps.'

'But we want a peaceable transition,' Weurmann went on, 'and we would like to think there would be substantial support for such a step. What is your view?'

This is where I play my cards, Edwards told himself.

'Have you spoken to others?' he asked.

'We have other possible candidates,' replied Weurmann guardedly.

'Well, if I say it myself, you are talking to the right man. I can ensure the most painless transition. The Deputy Prime Minister becoming Prime Minister would cause no great upheaval, such as would arise if you installed, say, Dick Francis, the Leader of the Opposition, or for that matter, Dick Clark.'

Weurmann smiled slightly – Edwards was certainly acute. Francis, the Leader of the Opposition, had been the third "possible", but was ruled out initially because he always had to compromise to maintain party unity.

'And I can deliver the "substantial support" you want. Francis can give you less than half his Party, and a war with the few remaining Government europhiles, who might want Europe, but don't want all the social legislation baggage – and the Unionists don't trust him because they see him as trying to ride two horses. He says he's pro-Europe, but he won't let go of the Party leadership because he's so desperately ambitious and wants to be Prime Minister. So he's perceived as more interested in his own career than the Union.'

'They could say you ride two horses,' observed Weurmann.

'The difference is I ride them in the Cabinet – you don't back out of the race when you're on the winning team. The Unionists will back me as "the man most likely to" in the Government. For them the Union is everything. They put principle before self-interest. If keeping Britain in the Union means backing me, they'll back me.'

'I'm not so sure,' said Weurmann, the meeting with Dick Clark fresh in his mind.

'There may be some objection to the means,' conceded Edwards, seeming almost to read the President's thoughts, 'but they care more about achieving the end result they want. When they realise this plan guarantees the future, they'll fall in behind quick enough.

'Even Francis may back me. The last landslide was a major blow to him. It put paid to his hopes of becoming Prime Minister in the foreseeable future. If I were to offer him Deputy Prime Minister he would probably jump at it. That would unite Government and Opposition Europhiles, and the Unionists.

'Getting the Opposition aboard – at least the Leader and a large chunk of the Party – would go down well in Scotland, and for that matter in Wales, where we're not flavour of the month.

'And it would give us a good chance of getting some of the Scottish Government on board.'

'We have some other thoughts on Scotland, and getting them on board will be key. So anything that helps that will be welcome. But we can discuss our other thoughts on Scotland later. 'What about Northern Ireland?'

'They're preoccupied with their own problems,' said Edwards. The situation there may be more settled than before, but the old antagonisms will take generations to work out. Being in or out of the Union is not high on the agenda. They'll be happy enough to stay in – secession would mean even more changes, a shift in the political balance, a different relationship again with the Republic. The people don't want more change – they want more stability. So, not a problem.'

Weurmann was heartened. This man was confident, shrewd, and sounded as though he could deliver.

'I think I am indeed talking to the right man,' he said.

Edwards again saw his advantage. I want five years out of this, he thought.

'Good,' he said to Weurmann. 'I just want to be clear, however. When you talk of an "interim administration", how "interim" do you expect it to be?'

'Well, for public consumption we must say until we can hold elections,' said the President.

'Elections won't do you much good at present – look at the last one. We need time to show the country the benefits of staying in the Union.'

'Yes, I see that. I was not thinking of immediate elections – but perhaps after two or three years.'

'More like ten,' said Edwards. 'Ten years to really create a "feel good" factor.'

'Ten years is a long time in politics,' said Weurmann. 'Perhaps five.'

'Five it is,' said Edwards, with a triumphant inner smile.

He'd cut his deal.

He would have plenty of time to provide for all the comforts of office, and sort himself out a nice little financial package, once he was in Downing Street, he told himself – and who knows, perhaps even engineer his continuance in power.

CHAPTER 13

General Le Blanc's life at Union Headquarters had not been easy for the last few months. Life in general at UHQ had not been easy since it was set up in response to the increasing need for a pan-European force, which could react as a single body to increasingly widespread terrorism around the world, and other common threats.

English and French were the official languages, and all staff officers and most others were expected to have a command of them. Not all did, and even those who did frequently had difficulties with shades of meaning.

To superimpose on this imperfect organisation with uncertain internal communications, the need to plan and execute an invasion of a member state, in complete secrecy, and with a large proportion of the Joint Forces opposed to the action and the precedent it set, Le Blanc had to summon up reserves of diplomacy, in support of his command authority.

But fate had played a part, in the form of the major Joint Forces exercise which had been in the planning for a year.

When President Weurmann had secretly asked Le Blanc to prepare contingency plans for a military solution as British attitudes hardened, it had not taken a great leap of the imagination to realise the potential for diverting this exercise to the end desired.

'Most of the exercise action is in the Channel anyway,' Le Blanc had pointed out. 'And there are landings covered by tactical air support in the existing plans.

'Adding a few parachute battalions will not cause comment at this stage.

'After all, I'm a paratrooper. We can say I wanted my Arm in a higher profile role, out of my natural arrogance and conceit. They'll swallow that!' he said with a short laugh.

For the last three months two planning groups had worked simultaneously. Those working up the exercise did not know even of the existence of the other group. But the other group knew every last detail of their plans for the exercise, and added their own little embellishments via Le Blanc.

But a week before the 'off' they were still not happy with the result.

'There are many weaknesses, General,' they told Le Blanc. 'For one, the British have ships at sea elsewhere, not taking part in the exercise – and the Trident submarines could be anywhere. Then again, if timing goes wrong, and the paras land before the British fleet is blockaded in harbour, or vice versa, the British will immediately be suspicious.'

'Timing had better not go wrong, then,' grunted the burly Frenchman.

'And then the concentration of troop movements on the Channel Tunnel makes us vulnerable there.'

'Not if we move swiftly enough,' said the General. 'The risk is worth it. It's the best way to build up forces rapidly.'

Nonetheless a certain malaise hung over the whole HQ, and dark comments were heard in dark recesses.

Apart from the uncertainties over the plan, there was unease about the Federal Government's course of action in principle.

The planning had been very detailed, and even the names of British unit commanders were listed. Many of the staff officers knew them personally and individually – had drunk with them on joint courses, met their wives, played with their children.

Now they were to suborn them, or disarm them – or eliminate them.

Only the most cynical or most unquestioning could carry this forward without, at the least, nagging doubts.

But, trained to obey, the plans were completed, doubts or no doubts, and it would not be long before they were translated into action.

At the other end of the chain of command, on the other side of the Channel, a querulous private was giving voice to the sense of mystification, which over the next days and weeks became the prevailing feeling in units throughout the UK.

'What the bleedin' 'ell's goin' on, corp?'

'I don't bloomin' know, do I, but they're issuing live rounds, so get your arse into gear and get out there.'

Minutes later the battalion fell in on the square – or such of them as were still in barracks or could be rounded up at short notice.

The CO's Land Rover whirled to a stop in front of the men, in a cloud of dust. The CO climbed on to the bonnet.

'Sorry to interrupt your weekend, but something's come up.

'The battalion will be deployed in its rapid response role for duties in the UK.

'Company and platoon commanders will brief you on assigned tasks as appropriate.

'Meantime, you will prepare to move out with full equipment, and combat ready.

'This is not an exercise.

'I expect all of us to acquit ourselves in the best traditions of this regiment. Good luck.'

He jumped back into his seat, and the Land Rover sped off.

'More of a bleedin' mystery than ever,' muttered the private out the corner of his mouth. 'The Old Man told us sweet F.A. The bleedin' mushroom theory of command again.'

'Shut your face, and get in there and get your kit together. Mr. Lawrence is going to fill us in in ten minutes.'

'Yes, corp.'

'There's something v. strange about this, Jock,' the CO said to the tall, gangling major leaning over the map table with him. 'How come we get orders direct from the MOD on this one?'

'It is strange, sir, and yet the codes were all right. I don't see we have a choice.'

'Of course not. That's why we're moving out. But it's fishy – v. fishy.'

The door swung open after a hasty knock.

'Excuse me, sir. Urgent signal from UHQ. Personal code to you, sir.'

'Thank you, sergeant. That will be all.'

The CO punched his password into the scanner, fed in the signal, and stared at the screen for a moment or two, as if bewildered.

'This says we've to stay put, Jock,' he said.

'How come it's from UHQ anyway, sir? You mean the flap's over?'

'I should think it's just beginning. They say we may get conflicting orders, but are to obey only those on normal command channels or direct from UHQ – I said there was something fishy!'

'Get on to the MOD, Jock. Ask for confirmation of their original order.'

Minutes later the tall major put down a copy of another signal, with a very serious expression.

'Well, Jock?'

'Well, sir, as you say – bloody fishy. In fact, alarming. The MOD say they've taken over direct control of all three services, and orders emanating from UHQ are to be ignored – except they want copies to the MOD for Intelligence.'

'Christ, Jock! That news item earlier about the Prime Minister being "temporarily indisposed" and Edwards standing in – it's a cover!

'It's a coup! Somebody's got the bugger! It's a bloody coup, man! And we're at the shitty end of a power struggle!'

'Steady on, sir!'

'Well, what the hell else would explain it?

'UHQ say don't to anything anybody else says – then the MOD says the same!'

The colonel pulled his chin. 'The question is, Jock, what do we do?'

'UHQ is the supreme command, sir.'

'Yes. But the MOD is the British "supreme command".

'Wait one, Jock – this is all starting to fall into place. It's about this bloody Euro row!

'Surely to God they haven't taken leave of their senses and gone for a military solution!'

'God, they can't have,' groaned the major. 'The original order did say to be prepared for possible action against hostile forces.'

'Yes, but we were thinking Al Qaida or some such – what else could it have been? I mean you wouldn't imagine this scenario in a million years – except in the classroom - a Staff College exercise or something.'

'I don't know, sir – when you think about it, Maggie Thatcher did. When they first talked about political union she said it would "fuel nationalism and risk conflict".'

'Right, Jock. Well, we're not going to be the meat in the sandwich.

'We'll move out as planned – but we'll decide where to.'

'Sir! We can't just go off on our own, off our own bat! With no authority!'

'My authority, Jock!! I'm responsible for battalion training, right?'

'Right, sir.'

'Right! We're going on a training exercise!'

'Where to, sir?'

'Somewhere we can sit tight till we know who the devil's in charge!'

CHAPTER 14

Neville Edwards was 'the right man' - at least insofar as he knew who was who around the Cabinet table. He knew without thinking who he could approach to join him and who he could not.

As General Le Blanc's plans were being finalised across the Channel, Edwards was pondering his moves.

There were two or three doubtfuls it would be too risky to talk to at this stage, but who might side with him when they saw how things were going.

The Scots, the Welsh, and the Irish, were not going to welcome him, but Wales was not a problem, and Weurmann had his 'other thoughts' on Scotland.

He would have opposition enough though, and for that reason, if for no other, he determined that the ministers opposed to him must be well treated, and given time to come round.

Two of the Cabinet at least would jump at the opportunity, and though he'd painted a rosier picture for Weurmann than he was confident would materialise, he was also reasonably optimistic about David Francis, the Leader of the Opposition.

Evesham, the Agriculture Minister, and Boyd from Transport – who along with Edwards were the last pro-Europeans in the Cabinet – were taken completely by surprise, but took very little time to decide to join him. They had no future in the Government after secession, whereas with Edwards they would be at the top of the tree.

Francis was a horse of a different colour. As Leader of the Opposition he had considerable standing. Whilst pro-Union personally, he had balanced the two factions in the Party so long and so successfully when no one else had managed this feat, that he was of a mind to continue.

Besides, he was by no means certain that Edwards and the Union would pull it off, given the resolute mood in the Government, half his own Party, and in the country generally, as the general election had so recently demonstrated.

But within twenty-four hours, during which Edwards met him in person twice and telephoned at least six times, he had begun to be swayed by the Deputy Prime Minister's insistent arguments.

'The President means business,' he told Francis at their second meeting. 'There's no question of Britain being allowed to secede. The future is with me.'

'But there will still be an Opposition.'

'Will there?' said Edwards ominously. He had decided this was make-your-mind-up-time for Francis, and pulled no punches.

'Well, why not?' said Francis. 'And I'll still be Leader.'

Then as the penny dropped and the import of Edwards' retort suddenly became clear to him, he showed some agitation.

'But surely...Parliament...you're not saying...?' he stammered out.

'Desperate times call for desperate measures,' said Edwards – and Francis realised it was now or never, and with some trepidation nodded his assent.

'Good,' said Edwards, simply. ' Now this has to be between you, me, and the President – so keep it under your hat. I'll be in touch.'

He left soon after Francis, rubbing his hands in glee, jumped in a cab, and gave the driver the address of the lady in Camden Town.

The lady answered his knock in a red satin negligee trimmed with black fake fur. She managed half a smile, but was evidently put out.

'What happened to you? I thought you were coming round as soon as you got back from Brussels,' she said petulantly. ' You haven't been round for ages.'

'Been busy, petal. But never mind - I've brought you some lovely choccie-woccies,' he said, holding out a box with four little drawers and a gold bow. Then as she reached for them, he put them behind his back, and leaned back against the wall, so that she had to press herself against him to reach for them.

As she did, he slipped his hand under the negligee and clawed at her, plump and yielding under the satin.

'Not so fast – you know what you have to do for them,' he said with a coarse laugh.

When she'd done it, he rolled over beside her, and with a self-congratulatory grin said, 'You've just screwed the next Prime Minister.'

'Wha-a-at?' she gasped. 'You – really?'

'Scouts' honour. Now when we do it we'll have a detective watching!'

She gave a little scream, then had a fit of the giggles. 'You're teasing,' she said. 'Nev, you are awful! But how? When?'

'By this time tomorrow night – well, officially, Saturday,' he corrected, thinking that even his little Camden Town flower might let the cat out of the bag prematurely.

'But how? Don't they need another election?'

'By the personal invitation of President Weurmann! And no, we don't need an election – the Prime Minister's been a naughty boy, and is going to be made to stand in a corner!'

A suitable corner had been selected for the Prime Minister, and now the plans were being implemented to put him in it, coordinated by UHQ with a little help from some sympathetic eyes and ears in Downing Street.

Timing was of the essence from this point on. It all had to slot together with mathematical precision from this point – the snatch, the press statements, the paratroop landings, the blockade, the Cabinet meeting at Chequers.

From midday on the Friday everything was run by the stopwatch.

Edwards' job was to marshal the Cabinet and make excuses for the Prime Minister at dinner, by the end of which he would be well and truly in the corner.

The paratroops would come in on Saturday morning to secure key points in the Capital and around the country, and at the same time the naval exercise was to end and all ships were to steam into harbour, led by the Royal Navy contingents – but in the event, only they would, and find themselves bottled up and at the mercy of the Union ships still standing off.

Edwards was as nervous as a kitten after he announced the Prime Minister's delayed arrival at the start of dinner at Chequers. What if something should go wrong, and the Prime Minister walked in large as life, Edwards wondered?

It was down to him for the next twelve hours, and he must live by his wits. Sharp as they were, he believed them hardly up to the task of coping with the myriad points of the plan which could go wrong.

There were scarcely any Union troops in position on the ground yet – only the Special Forces unit detailed for Chequers and one or two other advance targets. But though he knew they were out there, he didn't know where, and had no way of contacting them.

But if he was nervous, two hundred miles away so was Weurmann. The weak point was the Tunnel. They had put as many troops as they dared into the area adjacent to it, but had to hold most farther back to avoid making their intentions too obvious.

Shortly there was to be a 'crash in the Tunnel' as an excuse for stopping regular traffic moving through, and troops in the area would be detailed to 'help rescue operations'. But suspicions were going to be aroused.

All depended on ensuring a smooth but rapid flow to and through the Tunnel, as soon as General Le Blanc gave the green light.

The other weak point, Weurmann ruminated, was the Cabinet meeting.

If Edwards did not perform, or word about the Prime Minister got out, or some of the Cabinet smelled a rat, or the Special Forces unit did not get into position at the precise time scheduled, or...or...or....

But by late evening the Union had crossed the Rubicon with the abduction of the Prime Minister. There was no going back now, and whatever happened, it must be made to go right.

Neither Edwards, nor Weurmann, nor many, many others, got any sleep that night.

But hard as the adrenalin was pumping through them now, the President and the new 'Prime Minister' found some relief in the thought that it would all be over bar the shouting, in another seventy-two hours.

There would be a lot of shouting, no doubt, but by Monday night, Weurmann told himself, the UK would again be firmly under the control of the Federal Government.

Meanwhile Neville Edwards basked in contemplation of five years at least in No. 10, and began to turn over in his mind schemes for extending his tenure.

CHAPTER 15

David Wardhope, His Majesty's Secretary of State for Defence, red in the face, dishevelled, but with a determined and murderous gleam in his eye, stalked into the operations room of the underground command centre.

'Good God, sir, where did you come from?' the Army Chief of Staff spluttered, rising from his stooped position over the map table. 'Intelligence told us they'd got the whole Cabinet.'

'Well, I'm glad to say Intelligence got it wrong – but not far wrong.'

'How did you get out, sir?'

' I said I wanted a pee, walked towards the toilet, then kept on walking – right out the front door. Someone challenged me and I just said "I'm one of your lot", told him some of the others were having a bit of trouble inside and could do with some help, and walked on.

'Then I found my car and driver, got in, and drove away.'

'Well, if that's their state of readiness it shouldn't take us too long to sort them out. Well done, sir!'

An Intelligence officer stepped forward. 'No doubt you want a briefing, sir, and of course, we'd obviously like to know your end of it.'

'It's Edwards, and it's treason!' exclaimed Wardhope.

There were gasps round the room.

The Chief of Staff spoke again. 'We realised it must be something like that. The first we knew was when the air exercise over the French coast and the Channel turned north and headed inland.

'At first we assumed they'd mistaken their course, or that we hadn't had full information on the extent of the exercise.

'But ten minutes later they were dropping paratroops in St. James's Park and all around.

'I was in Whitehall, and by a pure fluke, I'd popped out for a few minutes with my aide. When we saw troops heading for Horse Guards', we jumped in a taxi and came here. Otherwise they'd have had us as well.'

'Close shave. Very glad you made it. What's happening now?'

'Well, sir, you can see from the electronic plot. Red areas are enemy forces – I assume they're to be regarded as the enemy. The deeper the shade of red, the larger the concentration of enemy forces in that area.

'Where we have detailed information, that can be brought up on the screen by keying in the number of the area.'

'What's their plan, do you think?'

'At the moment they're concentrating on securing key command, communications, and control objectives – in particular they've gone for airports and the Chunnel, communications centres, Government buildings, some police HQs, telephone exchanges, TV and radio stations, and newspaper offices. Reinforcements are coming in fast, so their force must be sizeable even now – though curiously, they haven't followed quite the same pattern in Scotland and Northern Ireland.'

'What's our response been?'

'Well, frankly, sir, we haven't known what to do. We've been monitoring, but of course there's been no political direction. It's not exactly an invasion by a foreign power, where we would just immediately start chucking them back in the sea – they do have a sort of legitimacy.'

'And what did you say about Scotland and Northern Ireland?'

'Well, they've gone for certain key targets, but seem to be standing off, rather than taking them over.'

'Hmm, curious,' Wardhope mused. 'What about the police?'

'The police have kept a low profile. Can't blame them. There are so many heavily-armed troops on the streets, there's little they can do. They seem to be concentrating on their normal role – which must be keeping them busy, as there's been looting and vandalism in quite a few places.'

'No confrontation between them and the Union troops?'

'Not to speak of, sir. These are UHQ troops acting on legal orders from the European Council.'

'Which is stuff and nonsense,' growled the Minister. 'We still elect our own Government and choose our own Prime Minister.

'The Prime Minister was elected to office in a general election. They've abducted him and usurped power.

'The Cabinet members siding with Edwards have lost any claim to legitimacy by their collusion.

'I'm the only member of the legitimate Cabinet at liberty.

"I intend to stop this attempted coup.

'I represent the majority in Cabinet, the majority in Parliament, and the majority in the country, all of whom have voted for secession.'

'Yes, sir.'

'So – we start chucking them back in the sea!'

'Yes, sir!'

'Order all units not manning fixed installations to disperse from their regular bases, not to their pre-planned dispersal points, but at the discretion of the local commanders.

'Set up communications procedures to ensure they obey our orders and nobody else's.

'Those manning key fixed installations are to defend them. Reinforce them as necessary to enable them to do so.'

'Yes, sir.'

'Then let me have a full appreciation of the current situation, and your thoughts on a strategic plan to restore and maintain the authority of the legitimately-elected Government.'

CHAPTER 16

It was probably a mistake on Edwards' part to allow the captive ministers to associate with each other at Chequers.

Possibly the puppet regime did not wish to appear harsh or uncivilised, or then again it might simply have been due to pressure on accommodation.

Whatever the reason, the erstwhile Cabinet members were allowed the use of the amply-proportioned morning room.

Showing remarkable resilience in the face of the catastrophe which had befallen them and the Government, and being the political animals they were, they lost no time in falling to scheming and plotting.

The remainder of the first day, following the Cabinet meeting, had been full of fears and uncertainties, and they were at first confined to their own rooms with no chance to talk.

The night had been bad for some. Despite Edwards' promise – perhaps because of it, given the dramatic demonstration of his propensity for treachery – a few feared a 2 a.m. knock on the door and a bullet in the head. In vain they argued to themselves the irrationality of this extreme, and sleep only came with exhaustion.

Others were fatalistic, and saw little point in contemplating the deaths which would come to them, or not come to them, regardless of anything they might do.

Some, clear-sighted and looking beyond immediate events, easily persuaded themselves that they had little to fear as, treacherous as he had shown himself to be, Edwards wouldn't shoot himself in the foot by an act of barbarism – certainly not before he had a firm grasp on the levers of power.

And Weurmann, pulling Edwards' strings, was certainly no barbarian, but cultured and sensitive. To the most rational of the captives, who were able to focus on the broader context, this was the most paradoxical aspect of the seizure of the Cabinet.

It was so out of character for Weurmann. The only explanation was that his pursuit of the ideal of a European super-state had become obsessive, or that Edwards had distorted the President's normally well-balanced judgment, fearful of his own inability to carry with him his Cabinet colleagues and the wider political establishment.

But the fears, and fatalism, and bewilderment, of the night were banished by the dawn, and breakfast was served to them in their rooms just as though they were still the VIP guests they had been the morning before.

When they were invited to use the morning room after breakfast, the whole situation began to take on an air of unreality.

But as they drifted in from their own rooms a considerable hubbub arose, as they discussed the previous twenty-four hours.

It was some time before they realised that Wardhope, the Defence Minister, wasn't among them and not in his room.

'The bastard's gone over to Edwards!' exclaimed one.

'Never in a million years,' another retorted. 'You heard him arguing the point in Cabinet and telling Edwards he'd lost. He can't stand Edwards.'

'Who can?' said the first. 'But that hasn't stopped some of them throwing in their lot with him.'

Silence fell at that – there had been a few surprises over who had sided with Edwards, and gloomy contemplation that the popular figure of Wardhope might have joined them. Then incredulous comments began to ripple round.

'I still can't believe that Roy would join him.'

'Or Margaret! Can you imagine?'

'All the gutless wonders, you notice.'

'That's not quite fair, Bob. Margaret has always been keen on Europe – though I'd never have dreamt she'd go this far.'

'Margaret I'll give you, but you can't say that of Roy – or Neil.'

'No – it certainly hits for six the idea that we really know each other's viewpoints even though we're Cabinet colleagues.'

'Yes, and gives us an opportunity,' said Charles Eager, the Home Secretary, always positive, always to the fore, always in the lead.

The others looked at him. 'What do you mean?'

'Well, you heard him,' said Eager.

'Heard what?'

'He gave us twenty-four hours to decide to join him.'

'But nobody here is going to join him!'

'Think about it tactically,' said the Home Secretary. 'It could be very useful – vital even – to have somebody in Edwards' Cabinet.'

'As a mole, you mean?'

'If you like. We don't know what's going on out there, but we know they've abducted the Prime Minister, we know they're holding us, we know Edwards is "taking over" – or being installed. And they seem to have brought troops in, judging by the escorts round here – I did try to get something out of the young lad who was escorting me, but they've obviously been briefed to keep their traps shut.'

'Likewise,' said the Chancellor.

'Anyway – they're obviously very serious about it, and we can assume it won't be a short-run thing. If we also assume there'll be resistance, it'll be extremely valuable to have a "mole" in there, as George puts it.'

'But Edwards knows our views too well. It's not going to be very credible if one of us goes over now in an apparent sudden conversion, like Saul on the road to Damascus.'

'Well, that's just it,' said Eager. 'Someone said a couple of minutes ago that we don't always know each other's real viewpoints. So why shouldn't a closet europhile decide to come out of the closet?'

'Still a bit suspicious that they should choose this moment to do it.'

'Perhaps, but look at it from Edwards' point of view,' Eager went on. 'He's got all his known supporters in tow – why give the rest of us twenty-four hours? In my view he simply wants as many of the real Cabinet aboard as possible – much better PR that way.

'He knows we won't really be on his side, or he'd have spoken to us before. He just wants us any way he can get us.

'He's appealing to any base motives we may respond to – saving our skins, self-interest, megalomania. Edwards has a rich seam of base motives running through him. He probably expects to find one in everyone else. Let's humour him and do the country a favour.'

'It would certainly be a brilliant stroke if we could manage it,' said the Chancellor, 'but I still think it's implausible. Who would we go for?'

'What about you, Charles?' said Shirley Alexander, the Education Secretary.

'Ha, ha! I don't think so – I'd certainly be implausible. Remember I told him he'd only be Prime Minister over my dead body!'

'Whoever it is is going to lack credibility one way or another,' said the Chancellor.

'Why not add a little spice to make the prospect more piquant, then, and sidestep the credibility gap?' ventured Eager.

'More piquant, Charles? What do you mean?'

'Just that I thought – well, er – Lynda might be…'

'…the right bait!' supplied the Chancellor.

Lynda Stalker, never bashful, smiled broadly. She knew she was noted for her looks and her smouldering sexuality, which had earned her the title of 'Luscious Lynda' in the tabloids.

Openly flirtatious, in a restrained sort of way, she showed no false modesty now.

'I'm not sure I like your choice of metaphor, James,' she said to the Chancellor, 'but I think it's something we've got to try, and if I'm "it", I'll give it a go. If the bastards have done anything to the Prime Minister, I'll find a way to finish them – I'll find one anyway.'

'Well said! And you shouldn't find it too hard to get on the inside – Edwards has always had a soft spot for you,' said Eager.

'Ugh!' said Shirley Alexander with a shudder. 'The thought of being the bait for that fish!'

'Quite,' said Lynda. 'But I can see it might work. Charles is right – he's always pawing at me.'

'Agreed then?' asked Eager.

'Agreed.'

'Well done, Lynda!' they chorused.

'Just lie back and think of England,' added Shirley Alexander in a whispered aside.

'Metaphorically, of course,' came the swift rejoinder.

Later that morning Neville Edwards blinked in amazement when Lynda Stalker appeared in the doorway of his office after giving a couple of perfunctory knocks.

A little before, the young Dutch captain had sent word that one of the ministers wanted to see him following his invitation the day before, but without mentioning a name.

He had only a couple of minutes to speculate who it might be.

'They're cracking', he said to his private secretary. 'I knew they would. However, I'll have to keep a close eye on whoever comes over. I can't see any of them having any real commitment – they're merely saving their skins. Still – looks better if we can present a good number of the Cabinet on our side.'

But he did not suspect how little hardship it would be to keep a close eye on the first defector, and his surprise was obvious as she advanced into the room.

'Lynda! I'm delighted to see you. Are you going to join us?' he said, as though he was talking about a trip to the seaside.

She accepted the kiss he pressed on her cheek, though she grimaced over his shoulder. And when he clasped her hand between both of his, she left hers in his a little longer than usual.

'This is going to be easy,' she thought, at the same time deciding not to play the push-over.

'I'd certainly like to talk about it,' she said.

'Of course,' said Edwards.

'I assume I would be in the new Cabinet.'

'Certainly,' he replied.

'I'd like to be in some job close to you.'

'I think I can manage that – but I'm a bit surprised. What about you and the Prime Minister? You were very concerned about him at the meeting.'

'Naturally,' she replied. 'But far more has been made of our relationship than ever was there. Besides, I'm ambitious.'

He smiled. 'But not very pro-Union.'

'As I said – I'm ambitious. I don't want to be buried politically for the sake of some fixed idea,' she said. 'Let's be blunt. You and I are birds of a feather. We fly with the wind – not against it. You get farther, faster, that way. Look at you, after all. You've got the key to Downing Street now.'

And, steeling herself, she gave his hand a congratulatory squeeze.

Edwards puffed up with pride.

'Yes, so I have,' he thought, 'and I'll have you, too.'

When word of Lynda Stalker's change of heart reached the President in Brussels, he felt it could only mean one thing. She must feel as he did, and wanted him as he wanted her.

For her part, she did not know that she did not.

But for the abduction of the Prime Minister and the treatment of the Cabinet, she might have gone to him.

Now, given these acts, authored by him, she knew she never would, never could.

Whether she wanted him or not, her conscience spoke too loud within her to contemplate that ultimate betrayal.

CHAPTER 17

'Sir, wake up! Wake up!'

'What is it? What's the time?' The Defence Secretary reached for his watch.

'Steward's brought you a cup of tea.' It was the Chief of Staff.

'Well, what is it, man? Spit it out! You didn't wake me up for a cup of tea!'

'We're getting reports of some of our units taking over key installations in different parts of the country.'

'Our units? What the devil are they doing?' said the Defence Secretary, heaving himself out of bed.

'It appears they're acting under UHQ orders.'

'Have you tried to countermand these orders?'

'Yes sir, but the UHQ orders were accompanied by large chunks of disinformation. They've been told that a coup by senior officers is threatened, and that they're to obey only UHQ orders under new codes.'

'Damn it! Can't these units see what's happening?'

'The fact is, sir, local commanders must be rather confused. As you know, when UHQ was set up, although we're still in the command chain, Central Ops in Brussels were given the authority to give direct orders to units throughout the Union.'

The Minister slurped some tea – strong, brown, army tea. 'Yergghhh!' he grimaced.

'All right – we have to get out the full story to all units, that they are staging the coup, and that we are resisting it.

'Cut through Edwards' crap. Let them know that ministers were rounded up at gunpoint and are being forcibly held under armed guard.'

'Yes, sir, though that may not be enough,' said the Chief of Staff, as the Minister pulled on his dressing gown. ' It's going to come down to who individual COs believe, and even what their own sympathies are. They could go either way and claim they were following legitimate orders.'

Wardhope nodded. 'This is nightmare stuff, Harry! We're going to have the Army fighting the bloody Army!

'We need to review the whole picture. Let's get to it – and get that steward to make me a civilised cup of tea!'

In the ops room a few minutes later, having hurriedly flung on some clothes, the Minister studied the plot with a group of senior officers.

'What about the RAF?'

'As you know, sir, runways have been knocked out at all important airfields. UHQ troops have converged on several stations, and taken over three.

'Two opened the gates and welcomed them. Same problem as the Army – UHQ orders appear legitimate.

'They've been told runway bombing was ordered at short notice, and in total secrecy, to preclude imminent attempts by those behind the supposed coup to use them.'

'You'd have to be as thick as two short planks to swallow that!'

'The point is, sir, there's great confusion on the ground.

'In some places, local COs have obviously said "bollocks!" and there's now a stand-off between UHQ forces and RAF Regiment airfield defence units.

'Overall it appears they're not disposed to attack military units, but only to contain them at present.'

'And the Navy?' queried the Minister, at the same time reaching for the toast and tea being proffered by the steward.

'Big problems, sir. Of course UHQ knew what they were about. The naval exercise was the perfect blind. The result is, our ships steamed back into harbour, the rest presumably opened their sealed orders, and instead of following them in, stood off.

'They now effectively blockade Plymouth, Portsmouth, Dartmouth, and the Clyde.'

'Yes, we haven't heard much about Scotland. Not the same scenario there, you said?'

'It's a bit strange there, sir. They've attempted to secure military targets – command centres, communications installations etc., but don't seem to have gone after civil ones. Same with Northern Ireland.

'Intelligence suggests they may be trying to enlist the Scots by offering independence within the Union, or at least full self-government, in some form or another.

'There's a substantial majority in Scotland in favour of even more powers for the Scottish Parliament, if not independence. They may be trying to tap support from that.

'We've tried to get in touch with the First Minister in Scotland, but at present he seems to be incommunicado.

'Re Northern Ireland, Intelligence think it may be handed over to the Irish Republic, and left to them.'

The Minister snorted. 'They'll need more than the Irish Army to contain the loyalists if they go down that route. The IRA campaigns will look like a game of pat-a-cake if the loyalists go underground. If I were the Irish Government, I'd hand it back! They'll unleash civil war there.'

'At any rate, sir, they seem to be playing a different game in those parts.'

'All right. Try to establish contact with the First Ministers, and keep me briefed.

'Now, what about ships at sea?'

'About twelve altogether, sir, including two Trident submarines. Again, very confused. Commanding officers are going to have to make their own decisions in the end.'

'What about the Tridents?'

'At the moment they're with us, sir – but the other side would never go nuclear in this situation. They're doing this because they want to keep us in the Union, want our wealth, our expertise, our world standing.'

'Just so – but they don't know that we wouldn't. We're the ones threatened. It's our backs to the wall. If they go nuclear, they lose what they're fighting for. If we do, we gain what we're fighting for.'

A dark frown crossed the face of the Chief of Staff. 'I don't think so, sir,' he said in a low voice. 'You know there would be no winners.'

'It's a card in our hand, Harry. Tell the Tridents to disappear. They're to maintain a listening watch only, and stand by for our signals.'

'Yes, sir.'

'How's the plan coming on?'

'They're flat out on it now, sir. A couple of hours and we should have a framework to work on.'

'Good. Let's get some proper food, then get down to it after breakfast.'

'Certainly, sir,' said the Chief of Staff.

'Your intelligence seems to be good, Harry. You're getting the inside track from some of those compromised units,' said the Minister, over the bacon, eggs, and tinned tomatoes.

'Yes, sir. The ones with the thinking caps probably see it the right way round. The officers are, however, divided in a number of units.'

Wardhope nodded, then said, 'That's wonderful news about the King. They blew that. Any more details yet?'

'Well, it seems he should have been at Buck House, but decided to slip off for a bit of fishing on the Q.T. His detective got a call when the first paras landed, and they buggered off out of it – just the two of them.'

The Minister raised the thick earthenware mug. 'Well, I've never drunk the Loyal Toast in tea out of an army mug before, but I give you – "The King!" '

'The King, God bless him!'

'If he's gone to ground, it obviously means he's having none of it, knew nothing of it. Which means he's with us. How could he not be?

'Now – I'd like to get in more political support.

'As I said, I'm the senior Minister at liberty – unless anyone else went for a pee just after I did.

'However, I should think Chequers is watertight by now, and there's no chance of getting anyone out. But perhaps you could have the cloak and dagger brigade get some of the next rank ministers along for a meet.

'Also key Opposition people of sound views. Shadow Cabinet members and so forth. Most of them will be as outraged as we are. I'll give you a list.

'And if we can get any senior figures out of Scotland or Northern Ireland, so much the better.

'We will carry on the Government as a government of national unity, a coalition if necessary, to unite the country behind us.

'If the King is with us, we can ask him to appoint a new Prime Minister, then form a Cabinet.

'We'll then have right, democracy, and constitutional propriety on our side!'

CHAPTER 18

Neville Edwards pulled nervously at his tie as he looked into the camera and waited for the cue light to turn red.

The auto-cue began to roll.

He put on his media smile, adjusted it, thought better of it, and assumed what he hoped was a frank and confidential seriousness.

The floor manager bit his clipboard in an effort not to laugh outright at this performance.

Red light. Cue Edwards.

The rehearsed serious face slipped with his first words, and the habitual thin-lipped smile and engineered sincerity took its place.

'My friends,' he began, leaning conspiratorially forward over the bony fingers clasped in front of him. 'I have had – for the good of the nation – to be party to a deception on a grand scale, and I want to set out for you now the reasons why this was necessary, and to put the key facts of the present situation before you, to dispel the rumour and uncertainty which is rife.

'The Government had embarked on an unconstitutional course which undermined the whole structure of the United States of Europe, which so many have laboured so long to build.

'The President and Council could not allow this to occur, and the principal advocates of that course to remain at the helm.

'The former Prime Minister' – gasps in the studio – 'and his Cabinet colleagues have therefore been removed, by order of the President and Council. They have come to no harm, and are being treated with strict propriety.

'I have been done the honour of being asked by the President and Council to take over as Prime Minister – but only until such time as the constitutional proprieties are re-secured, and free and fair elections can be held.'

The floor manager muttered aside to his assistant, from behind the clipboard, 'I wouldn't put any money on that – he wouldn't recognise constitutional proprieties in a bowl of alphabet soup!'

'Yes,' hissed the assistant. 'He must think he's talking to the Tweenies if he thinks his audience'll swallow that.'

'Cabinet colleagues,' Edwards continued, 'have been invited to join me, and I am delighted to say that several have.

'I am in the process of forming a Government to lead the country back from the brink of the economic suicide to which my predecessor's policy would surely have led, and in that task, I can count on the support of a large pool of highly-talented people from across the party divide.

Not least among them is the Leader of His Majesty's Loyal Opposition.'

'Whew! That's a bombshell, all right!' whistled the clipboard.

'This epitomises the spirit of consensus which exists to sustain the country at an admittedly difficult time.

'And having alluded to His Majesty's Loyal Opposition, I should re-affirm the allegiance of His Majesty's Government, which remains at the service of His Majesty, whilst His Majesty honours the traditional politically-detached stance of the monarchy.'

The floor manager rolled his eyes. 'A warning to the King now – what next?'

'The President and Council regret the need to deploy troops to ensure a smooth transition to the new regime.'

'It's the only way they'd get airtime on this bloody station,' growled the director in his box.

'However, 'Edwards went on, 'effective policing was felt to be necessary.

'Although the Union's initiative commands substantial support throughout the country, there are dissident elements whose political posture necessitates such precaution.'

Muttered sarcasm aside – 'Yeah – they're called the Prime Minister and Cabinet!'

'It has been necessary to invoke the Civil Contingencies Act and take emergency powers, to ensure minimal disruption to the everyday conduct of affairs.

'No citizen need have anything to fear from that so long as there is no interference with the machinery of government, or the normal commercial and industrial life of the country.

The floor manager said, sotto voce – 'But stick your head above the parapet and we'll blow it away – just what the civil rights people feared when the Civil Contingencies thing came in.'

'I look forward to restoring economic prosperity, which has been undermined by the former Government's intemperate actions, and to working closely with President Weurmann and the Council to ensure the happy and harmonious cooperation of the United Kingdom with the other member states of the Union.

'Good night.'

'And good bloody riddance,' said the director out loud behind his glass window, but paled as Edwards looked up sharply, directly at him. Could the bloody man lip-read? But then he realised Edwards merely wanted a little compliment. In normal circumstances he was no flatterer, but these were not normal circumstances, so he picked up his trowel and laid it on thick.

'Oh, bravo! Yes, excellent!' he said, switching on his mike to the studio. 'Very powerful! Very powerful!'

'You thought it was all right, then?' said Edwards with almost childlike hunger for approval.

'Oh, yes, splendid, splendid!' gushed the director coming down on to the floor.

'And you didn't think I looked too bad?'

'Oh no, not at all! Make-up did a wonderful job!'

Edwards was a little in doubt how to take this, but the assistant floor manager wasn't, and he doubled up in a corner choking back the laughter.

'What a vain old woman he is,' muttered the floor manager as his deputy continued to splutter.

But Edwards' natural conceit reassured him that the director was quite sincere, and as he unclipped the mike and stood up, he felt quite pleased with himself.

He was shown through to Hospitality and offered the customary drink.

Having stood his company for as long as he could, the director had bid him goodnight and was about to show him out, when Edwards said with boyish excitement, 'Do you think we might just go back through and have a look at the tape?'

The director groaned inwardly, but reluctantly turned back to the studio.

After all, he was the Prime Minister, sort of – and look what had happened to those who had stood in his way.

CHAPTER 19

The glass-topped table reflected the light of the log fire on the other side of the oak-panelled room. Carved into the wood beneath the glass, in intricate detail, was a highland hunting scene – a stag at bay, as the hounds circled in.

The King gazed contemplatively at the carving. 'I felt like that for a time, Rory – like that stag. Not cornered physically, but I knew they would be closing in on me. So I just packed up my traps and hot-footed it up here with Johnson.'

'I'm delighted and honoured, of course, sir – if somewhat shell-shocked at the turn things have taken,' said the bearded figure on the other side of the fire, 'but what made you think of here?'

'Well, I had to cudgel the old brain somewhat, as of course I obviously couldn't go back to London, couldn't go to Balmoral or any of the other family haunts, had to steer clear of my known pals. But of course, one is apt to be recognised, so I couldn't just meander about, either.

'I decided I had to go to ground, and I remembered our chat when we sailed on the west coast together, that night the others buggered off to the pub.

'You told me about this place and how private it is – you joked that if you wanted to plot a revolution, this was the place you'd do it – people could come in by sea, or even by air, and never be spotted, you reckoned.

'The revolution has been plotted – but I'm thinking of plotting a counter-revolution, so here I am.'

'And I'm with you, sir' said Rory.

The King slept that night his last full night's sleep for many weeks.

Daybreak found him in the stone-flagged kitchen of the old keep, poaching kippers in butter and milk, as the porridge hottered on the vast cooking range.

Inspector Johnson eyed him blearily, and warily eyed the glutinous mass burping and heaving in the porridge pot.

'Where did you learn this, sir?'

'Oh, one of the estate cottages at Balmoral,' he replied, stirring briskly with the spurtle before again turning his attention to the kippers. 'I used to be friendly with the head stalker's son. His mother made wonderful porridge, and her kippers were out of this world.'

The detective blanched as the King dolloped several wooden spoonfuls into a soup plate, saying, 'Get that inside you, man, and we'll give the buggers what for!'

Rory in a nightcap and nightshirt entered the kitchen, sniffing the air like the Bisto Kids. 'Do you know, I haven't seen kippers done like that since dear old Cook, when I was a lad,' he said, eyeing the pan hungrily.

'Best way,' said the King, 'but they can't seem to get the hang of it at the Palace, so I usually have to have them grilled like everybody else.'

'You're up early, sir.'

'There's work to be done, Rory.'

'Yes, of course – and you were serious about the counter-revolution?'

'Indeed', said the King, sombre now. 'Indeed.'

'Is there not a constitutional problem?'

'Certainly there is. These swine have just driven a coach and horses through 800 years of the Constitution – that's the constitutional problem! Of course, there is a problem in the sense you mean, but I know this country. The country doesn't want this. Won't stand for it.

'I have to take a lead – we don't know who else is out there. It sounds like they've got the whole Cabinet one way or another, as well as the Prime Minister.

'They've cordoned off the Palace – and Kensington Palace, too – it seems, though thank God they don't seem to have gone after any of the rest of the Royal Family. I suppose they must realise we still enjoy the affection of most of the people, and it would be counter-productive.

'But have your kipper, Rory, and then we'll get down to it.'

Round the great oak kitchen table, as they ended their meal, the breakfast bonhomie slipped from the shoulders of the three men – the King, his personal detective, and the bearded Highland gentleman.

In its place descended a mantle of serious purpose – upon the King especially.

'First we must find out what's going on,' the King said.

'Phone or internet will be risky,' said Rory.

'Johnson has a box of tricks or two that will get round that problem. The question is, who to call. Who can we trust? I do have one or two chums who are junior ministers and might be on the loose. We can start in on that line and then play it by ear.'

Minutes later, miniature satellite transceiver set up in the conservatory, the King's eyes glinted keenly as he cradled the handset and spoke rapidly but softly into the mouthpiece.

'What did he say, sir?' quizzed Johnson as the King finished.

'We struck lucky. He's had a visit from some MI5 wallahs – Wardhope, of all people, got away.

'He intends to carry on the Government and is pulling people in to join him. My pal, Spencer, doesn't know where he is, but I've asked him to pass a message.

'He also suggested I could link up with the First Minister here. Apparently when they heard what was going on, the Scottish Government withdrew to the Castle, and are sitting tight. But of course that would just be putting myself into their clutches, as Spencer quickly realised.'

With that, the King, Inspector Johnson, and Rory, returned to the table, spread out a map of the British Isles, and began to plot on it such information as Keith Spencer had been able to give, together with what they had gleaned from radio broadcasts and the net, and pondered what action might be feasible.

CHAPTER 20

Wardhope paced the floor of his combined private office and sleeping quarters in the bunker deep below the Berkshire countryside.

He checked his step and looked up as the door opened. His aide, a young naval lieutenant, ushered in four men.

'Ah! The first round-up! I hope you didn't find the experience too alarming, but we had to get to you in secrecy, and of course we didn't know whether they'd be watching you, or have picked you up, or what.'

The four murmured greetings from behind grave, set faces – the Deputy Leader of the Opposition, the shadow foreign minister, a minister of state from the Home Office, and Spencer, the junior minister from the Northern Ireland Office.

'Order some tea and coffee, Peter,' Wardhope said to the aide. 'And biccies – some of these oat-mealy ones,' he called after the retreating figure. Then apologetically to the rest of the company – 'No chocolate ones, I'm afraid – we're on emergency rations down here!'

Then he continued. 'Well, gentlemen, I don't know how much you know about what's going on.

'Briefly, the PM's been abducted, Edwards has most of the Cabinet locked up at Chequers, or at least had – God knows what he's done with them now. He's announced that he's taking over the country as you probably saw on TV, and has, I'm afraid, the support of a few Cabinet quislings and assorted lackeys and lickspitttles.

'However, we can expect some intelligence on what he's up to from the inside. He gave the whole Cabinet twenty-four hours to decide whether to join him, so they decided to put up Lynda Stalker as a turncoat, to get someone in and get his plans out. Good thinking!'

'Lynda Stalker? Why her?' quizzed the Home Office Minister.

'Edwards has a weakness for women in general, as you probably know – and apparently for Lynda in particular,' Wardhope replied. 'Of course we're checking it out, as it could be Edwards' side installing her as a sort of ministerial double agent.

We've had one or two intelligence traps laid to test her out – but we think she's genuine.

'Assuming she is, it'll be very useful to have a set of eyes and ears in their camp.

'Meanwhile there are UHQ forces all over London and around the country, and they're pouring through the Channel Tunnel in thousands as we speak.

'The Army is fighting the bloody Army, or preparing to, because they're getting conflicting orders and information from UHQ and from us.

'It appears they're trying to drive a wedge between Scotland and England, playing on nationalist aspirations, and may be contemplating handing Northern Ireland over to the Republic.'

Spencer form the Northern Ireland Office shook his head in disbelief. 'They're biting off more than they can chew if they go ahead with that idea,' he said.

'Yes, indeed,' said Wardhope, 'but it's worrying. And the Scottish Government seems to have circled the waggons – presumably waiting to see what happens. So I don't think we're going to get anyone in from there.'

But I've brought you in along with a dozen or so others who are yet to arrive, with a view to establishing a national government to resist the Union take-over.'

He eyed each of them with a steely gaze. 'I trust you're with me.'

Nods and murmurs of assent from the four.

'I hope you can deliver the Opposition, Bryn,' he said to the stocky Welshman opposite who was turning an ancient, battered, empty, pipe between his fingers.

Bryn Thomas glanced sidelong at his colleague, the shadow foreign secretary, pursed his lips, and said. 'I reckon I can deliver the Opposition all right – though its Leader's a lost cause.'

'It seems so,' said Wardhope.

'I reckon he's been made an offer. He was an easy target – no prospect of getting into office for years, since your last landslide, but desperately ambitious.

'I phoned him when I heard about Edwards, couldn't get him, and his wife was being very coy. Of course, we don't get on so well. I'm there to keep the other wing of the Party in the fold, as you know.'

'What do you think the Party will do?' asked Wardhope.

'Oh, I think we can count on it, most of it – eh, Jack?' turning aside to his colleague.

'Yes, I think so,' said the shadow minister, 'with a few exceptions who'll try to ride on the Leader's coat tails. But no right-thinking – or even left-thinking – member could stomach the Union action. It's outrageous.'

'That's good,' said Wardhope, 'though it's a blow not to have the Leader of the Opposition with us – and a big boost for Edwards.'

Tea came in, was served, and the oat-mealy biscuits handed round.

'Where is the Prime Minister, anyway?' asked the Home Office minister. 'Do we know?'

'We're trying to find out. They snatched him in a chopper, that we do know – but we haven't been able to pin down where it went.'

Now Spencer proffered a piece of folded paper to Wardhope. 'This is from the King,' he said simply.

Wardhope and the others stared in surprise.

'Of course, you're a friend of his,' said the Defence Minister after a moment. 'He's been in touch, then?'

Spencer nodded.

Wardhope took the paper, scanned the contents, raised his eyebrows, and eased his large frame upright in the swivel chair.

'Gentlemen – the King has asked me formally to form a government and head it as Acting Prime Minister.'

There was a moment of reflective silence. Then after a moment – 'Well, if we've got the King, we don't need the Leader of the Opposition, do we now?' said Bryn Thomas.

'Congratulations, David!' said Spencer, and the rest joined in shaking Wardhope's hand warmly.

'I don't know that that's the appropriate comment,' said Wardhope, ' but thank you all the same.'

A few hours later the re-convened meeting had grown in number from five to twelve.

Ministers had been assigned their portfolios, and again they sat round expectantly as the now Acting Prime Minister led the discussion.

'Thus far our response has been defensive, and largely ineffective because of that. But we needed time for planning, rather than lashing out in uncoordinated actions.

'The staff have been working flat-out, and General Smith is outside to brief us.'

'What about diplomatic initiatives?' asked one of the new ministers.

'I see no point in parleying with Edwards. That would give him seeming authority, which we deny he possesses, and which he certainly doesn't possess legitimately.'

'What about a direct approach to President Weurmann?' asked another.

'Perhaps. But it's rather like saying to a bully "please stop hitting me". The bully is likely to keep on hitting you until you're thoroughly cowed, or until you hit him back hard and make him wonder if it's worth it.

'They haven't taken this decision lightly. They've decided to subjugate the UK to the authority of the Union. They must have expected resistance. If they don't get it, it's effective acquiescence, and whilst we might resist passively, they will inexorably secure their grip until we can't shake free.

'All the time we're talking, they're reinforcing by land, sea, and air, and I believe our only option in the absence of United Nations intervention is a determined military response.'

'What about the UN?' asked Bryn Thomas.

'We're trying to get hold of Sir Richard Humphrey in New York at this moment,' said Wardhope, 'but we need contingency plans now, because we don't know how the UN will react.'

Then he nodded towards the door, and the secretary quickly slipped out, returning in moments with a surprisingly young general.

'This is General Smith,' said Wardhope, and signalled to him to go ahead with his briefing.

'Good afternoon, gentlemen,' he said, taking his seat and spreading his briefing papers in front of him.

'The Prime Minister has asked me…'

'Acting Prime Minister, General,' Wardhope cut in. 'Let's not forget for a moment that the legitimately-elected Prime Minister is still held – we hope only held – by these traitors.'

'Indeed, sir. I beg your pardon.' Then he continued, ' I have been asked to outline in broad terms the military situation, and a possible response.

'The situation is this. We've been caught completely off our guard. While our troops are reeling in a confusion of conflicting orders, each with an apparent claim to legitimacy, the Union is proceeding with a massive armed build-up.

There's little real fighting at present, except on a local scale where specific installations have been defended.

'However, the Union has already seized a number of key targets. Stand-offs have developed at others – including some where our own troops were persuaded to side with Union forces, initially convinced they were quelling a right-wing coup.

'Because of the difficulty in establishing the credibility of orders, we can't rely on our normal defence establishment. Many units are effectively under UHQ command.'

Wardhope shook his head impatiently – 'How can they be so blind to the real situation?'

'It's not so much that they're blind, sir – it's more the dilemma of who they should obey,' the general replied. 'But because of this we have to plan to create maximum impact with minimum resources.

'We have two key cards to play – a third if we can play it.

'One – they have concentrated their invasion route on the Channel Tunnel. This facilitates a rapid build-up, but also makes them vulnerable. A counter-attack there would have considerable effect.

'Two – we have the capacity to carry the fight to them. The psychological effect of taking it into their own back yard would be massive, and may cause them to re-think

'Three – we have two Trident subs at sea, fully-armed We do not, of course, wish to use them, but they exist to deter aggression, and we should play that card.'

Braithwaite, the shadow foreign secretary, looked sidelong at Bryn Thomas, then said to Wardhope – 'All my life I've been opposed to nuclear weapons. I hope I shall never be asked to sanction that option.'

'I think we could all wish never to have to contemplate such a course,' said Wardhope, 'but what is clear, is that whatever action we take, it's likely to represent a considerable escalation of force.'

General Smith nodded, 'I'm afraid that's so, sir.

'Gentlemen, these are the effective options which are within our capabilities. The decision as to which, if any, to use, is largely political, and so of course a decision for you and not for me.'

The general then retired, leaving a very chastened Cabinet to grapple with the political implications.

CHAPTER 21

The telephone rang in the penthouse suite overlooking Central Park.

The tall figure gazing out over it, high above the Fifth Avenue traffic, whirled from the window and grabbed the receiver.

'Yes?'

'This is David Wardhope...'

'Good God, how did you get away, sir? And how did you get through on this phone?'

Two surprises – they hadn't got the whole Cabinet, and this was still a secure line.

'By being clever, number one, and being very clever, number two.'

'But you'll be monitored.'

'I don't think so – the un-scrambler their end probably went into melt-down after we hooked up our gizmos, according to my signals chaps.'

'What's the situation?'

'Situation is that they've got the Prime Minister, locked up the Cabinet with the exception of their lackeys, and Edwards has effectively been installed by the Union.

'He claims he's acting as a caretaker, but I wouldn't hold my breath waiting for him to give up the reins of power once he gets them in his grasp.

'They've got troops on the ground over a wide area.

'As the only Cabinet minister at liberty - apart from the Judases who've sided with him - I've put myself at the head of the legitimate Government to organise the response. And the King has now asked me formally to be Acting Prime Minister.'

'The King? He's ok then? That's good news. I'm with you, of course. What do you want at this end?'

'I want an emergency session of the Security Council, a resolution condemning Union aggression, and UN military assistance.'

'Very well. Can do, on point number one. Two will be difficult. Point three will take some time, if it's possible at all. I'll do everything I can – but what about our own forces?'

'They have conflicting orders and don't know who to trust, but we'll get them round.'

'It's all in your hands, then. Good luck.'

A noisy babble rolled round the chamber as Sir Richard Humphrey finally rose. But as he peered slowly round over the top of his half-moon specs, each delegation in turn fell silent.

His face was haggard. He hadn't slept more than two hours since the phone call the day before. The intervening time had been consumed first in procedural wrangling over whether he should be allowed to speak, or indeed be allowed to call the special session at all, and then in intensive lobbying of other members.

Edwards had anticipated the move, and sought to have Sir Richard's accreditation withdrawn and his own representative installed.

President Weurmann had instructed Monsieur Giraud, the Union ambassador, to resist resolutely any motions in support of the UK.

That the Council had agreed to meet in special session and hear Sir Richard was the first clear gain for Britain, and the first clear blow for Edwards and the Union.

The ambassador did not wish to let the significance of the moment escape anyone's attention.

When he rose, he brought a hush to the chamber. His face might be haggard, but his eye was steady, clear, and bright, and his voice had all the gravitas and command of a Churchill.

In addition to the Union ambassador, each member state still had its own representative for a transitional period, recognising the reality that the fledgling Union was a Union of former nation states.

Sir Richard eyed each of them in turn.

'In the last few days, the world has witnessed one of the most shameless and deceitful acts of naked aggression ever,' he began.

'The invasion of the United Kingdom by the United States of Europe is unparalleled since the Second World War.

'Already alliances are forming – taking sides on the side of might, or on the side of right – among the oldest and longest-civilised nations of the world. 'Divisions which have already engulfed one nation, and which threaten to rive asunder the stable order which has prevailed in Europe for more than half a century.

'And to what end is that prosperous and harmonious continent brought once again to the brink of a further great cataclysm?

'Is it for right and justice to triumph over oppression? Is it to relieve poverty and suffering? Is it to restore a legitimate government usurped by a tyrant?

'No – it is for none of these. It is to deny the right of the democratically elected government of a great nation to determine the best interests of that nation.'

The Union representatives began to shake their heads, but Sir Richard continued unperturbed.

'There surely need be no more said in this august assembly, conceived out of the ruins of a war which began on that same Continent, and entrusted with the hopes of all nations that they should never again witness or suffer such a man-made catastrophe.

'The aggressors may claim what justification they will – they are aggressors still.

'This Council must condemn them in the most unequivocal terms, and intervene with all possible speed, to achieve a return to the status quo, and the recognition of the rights of legally-constituted governments.'

No sound was heard, and no foot stirred, when Sir Richard stopped speaking, until the Union ambassador switched on his microphone with an abrupt "click".

'As we listen to Sir Richard, we might think ourselves in the nineteenth century. He speaks as though Europe was the Europe of Talleyrand, Palmerston, or Prince Metternich.

'But this is now the twenty-first century, and the EEC, European Union, and United States of Europe, have been fact for over fifty years – proof of the ability of the nations of Europe to live in harmony.

'Until now, when the arrogance of the British surfaces again to say, "No, we don't want to be European".

'But if the legitimate Government says "no" now, it says so illegitimately, because a previous legitimate Government signed the European Constitution and the Treaty of Berlin – the Treaty of Union.

'That democratically-elected Government accepted the harmonisation of laws and institutions, accepted majority voting as in any democratic body, acknowledged the federal authority of the European Council, and acknowledged the higher sovereignty of the United States of Europe.

'In this process, along with the other member states, they became European first, and British second.

'So did the French, so did the Germans, so did the Italians, and the Danes, and the Dutch, and the Belgians. So did we all – Norwegians, Swedes, Finns, Austrians, Poles, Hungarians, Turks, Czechs, and Slovaks, and all the nations of the Union.

'A substantial part of the British establishment accepts this, and the action has been taken in concert with them.'

Sir Richard again shook his head. 'Not the establishment – one quisling and a few hangers-on. There is resistance everywhere.'

'There is some resistance, yes,' Monsieur Giraud continued, 'but if there were not, there would be no need for this action.

'We meet in the heart of one of the great democracies of the world. A federal democracy.

'If Texas, or Florida, or California, sought to secede from the Union, with all the economic and social disruption entailed, the Federal Government in Washington would act as necessary to ensure the interests of the nation at large were protected. Indeed it did just that a century and a half ago.'

Shaking his head slowly and deliberately this time, Sir Richard said, 'Not an analogous situation.'

'But it is analogous,' retorted the Frenchman. 'Since the Treaty of Berlin, the United States of Europe has been a federal union, and its constituent members acknowledge the federal authority of the European Council.

'Sovereignty resides in the European Council. The so-called secession of the United Kingdom has no more legitimacy than would an act of secession by Texas in the United States.

'Now, given the fact of it, a police action has been necessary, and that is what we are witnessing.

'To portray it as Sir Richard does, as Europe staring into the abyss, is to exaggerate and over-dramatise in the best traditions of Churchillian rhetoric, and we may dismiss it as such.

'In conclusion, I propose that no action is taken by the Security Council, as this is an internal matter, and any action would constitute interference with the internal affairs of the United States of Europe, which is contrary to our founding Charter.

When he sat down, after some more in this vein, the tide of debate ebbed and flowed for two hours and more, but the Union ambassador carried his argument – even those most favourably-disposed to Britain could not gainsay it.

The United States of Europe had been constituted as a sovereign body by the Treaty of Berlin, and relations between constituent states and the Federal Government were unarguably 'internal affairs', the Security Council concluded.

Sir Richard wearily gathered his papers, closed his case, and oblivious of the rain, and the protestations of his driver, walked all the way along East 42nd Street, by Grand Central, and on up Fifth Avenue to his apartment.

CHAPTER 22

Two parallel mental struggles were going on in the commanding officers' cabins of two Trident submarines, though they were three thousand miles apart.

One glided beneath the polar ice away to the north of Norway, the other lurked in the Atlantic deeps a thousand miles from land.

In command of one, Captain Andrew McCormack, forty-eight years of age, married, three children, 26 years service, graduate in politics and international relations.

In command of the other, Captain Jonathan Easson, forty-four, single, 27 years service, Britannia Royal Naval College, promoted captain at the youngest age of any officer in the Royal Navy in modern times.

Beneath the ice, Captain McCormack lay on his bunk staring at the deckhead above him. A sheaf of signals he had just tossed aside as he flopped on to the mattress, balanced precariously on the edge of his desk.

He had read each again and again in the hope that the balance would tip one way or the other, and relieve him of the necessity of making a decision – but to no avail.

His bunk was not now the comfortable refuge from the loneliness of command, where usually he could pull about him thoughts and images of wife and children, family and friends, to ease the isolation and the burden of responsibility.

Now he tossed on the horns of a dilemma, almost glad to continue tossing, knowing that his decision could decide the fate of a country, a continent, and countless millions of his fellow men.

Not that he believed he would be called upon to press the nuclear button in the present crisis, or ever – just that where he placed his support would be pivotal to the military balance, and to the political posture of the two key players. On the verge of sleep, as a reaction to mental overload, he dreamily questioned the reality of this high-tech world he inhabited. This mental struggle had been begun by a signal received by satellite, he thought to himself – and what was this signal, after all, but a mere disturbance of the airwaves, pulses in the ether reaching from the UK out into space, and back to him in his elemental home.

Suppose they were a freak of atmosphere; suppose they were the game commands of some teenage hacker; suppose they came from, and not just via, space itself – a close encounter of the fourth and final kind; suppose there was no one out there really and it was all in his imagination....

And then a stark dream picture, exact in every detail, of the submarine's missile fire control console, formed before him in his half-sleep, the red firing switches in the centre. He seemed to see his own hand descending on to them, and with a cry he jerked back to full wakefulness.

Rubbing his eyes, he sat up and moved to the desk, then spread the wad of signals before him.

The first had been from UHQ.

This had told him to ignore all orders from lower on the command chain, and given a unique code to identify their special orders.

He had asked for clarification and been told there had been a coup attempt, and he could expect conflicting orders and disinformation. The original order had been repeated.

He received all this with frank disbelief.

Then came Wardhope's signal – in effect, 'lie low, maintain radio silence, obey my orders only' – and he knew something was happening.

Ignoring the radio silence, he asked for clarification of this in turn, was told the Prime Minister had been abducted, the Cabinet seized, and Union troops had invaded to install the Edwards regime.

He felt like he was back at staff college, dealing with some fantastical exercise, with situations stretched to such absurdity that they lost credibility – yet this was supposedly for real.

He decided his only course was to drop out of sight and try to get more information.

Certainly there seemed to be a coup, but who was mounting it?, he asked himself

A right-wing military coup might just work like that, he thought – seize the Prime Minister and the Cabinet, seize the national command centres, and get the services on board. Then the Federal Government moves in to counter it and re-establish the Government, putting in a caretaker Prime Minister in the interim.

On the other hand, a coup or assumption of power by the Union would go like the situation presented by Wardhope and the MOD.

He couldn't work on so little information, so he had his radio operators tune in to whatever news broadcasts and web chat they could pick up from the UK or other countries.

It gradually became clear that the Union had acted to forestall secession, but where did that leave him and his command?

This was the problem he now wrestled with over the pile of signals and news reports spread across his desk.

I'm officially under the operational command of UHQ, but I command a ship of the Royal Navy, he told himself.

Under the Union's Common Defence Policy it makes sense for national fleets to be under UHQ command, he reasoned, and the UK of course has its own representatives at that command.

But if the UK chooses to secede from the Union, it should be able to withdraw its forces from UHQ control – clear enough, if the Government is intact.

The scene now, however, is that one minister claiming to represent the Government is issuing orders.

Is he a legitimate authority, McCormack asked himself? If not, who is? Surely not an invading force? And yet, they represent the Government of the Union, to which the UK gave up sovereignty by the voluntary act of her own Parliament.

His head spun. Can she then resume sovereignty? Certainly that was the nub of the issue.

And then he came back to the clear expression of the country's will in the election which had confirmed the Prime Minister in power. The people manifestly wished to recover sovereignty.

He wasn't a politician – he shouldn't have to decide this – but he was going to have to.

And then there was the balance of power issue. The Union had France's nuclear capability on its side – though surely it would never use it. And yet, and yet....

Meanwhile the UK had the two Tridents at sea - though their sister ship had been caught in the blockade, he realised – and possibly also some left-over RAF nuclear hardware, though this was now so outdated it would never reach its target.

So he and Jonathan represented the only big stick available.

He wondered what Easson was thinking now. He must be facing this same dilemma, but was he making such a meal of resolving it? Probably not.

They knew each other well, had been together on the Perishers' course in the Clyde for aspiring submarine commanders, had each passed with distinction, but with their rather different command styles very much in evidence.

His own was teamwork-oriented, egalitarian, democratic within limits – Jonathan's, encouraging competitive individualism, authoritarian, autocratic. But both ran efficient ships.

Jonathan would see this as black and white – but which was black, and which was white?

It would be good to talk, he felt, but that they could not. For ultimate security, the Tridents often didn't know each other's location or tasks, and didn't communicate directly.

If they acknowledged the standard line of command, McCormack told himself, they were effectively on the Union side, and whether used or not, the deterrent threat they represented was at the Union's disposal, with nothing to counter it. Therefore the Union could steamroller the UK if it chose.

But on the UK side, they would represent a counterpoise to Union might out of all proportion to their size. They would never be used – but again, the threat was there.

That was it, he decided. He had to go with Britain, with the will of the people. What must they be feeling now, under an occupation force for the first time in a thousand years? He had to go with the MOD, which was miraculously ahead of the game, and deserved some support to help it stay that way. And he had to go with the Royal Navy, so effortlessly sidelined by the Union. In short, he had to go with the under-dog.

With deterrent power more balanced, he said to himself, the politicians would have to come up with a political solution, and the prospect of a military 'final solution' would recede.

Far out in the Atlantic, Captain Easson had indeed faced the same dilemma, following the same initial confusion. But as Drew McCormack had surmised, the issue to him had seemed much clearer.

Not that he had not looked at the moral dimension, or agonised over the implications and ramifications of his decision.

He thought, in his turn, of Drew McCormack, and wondered about Drew's reaction, rightly guessing that he would give himself a very tough time, before coming down on the opposite side.

They did get on after a fashion, these two very different characters, but their relationship was based on shared experience and mutual respect rather than any real liking.

For his own part, he did see it in black and white.

He had had an order from UHQ. It was his duty to obey, he said to himself, as it was his legitimate command authority. His not to reason why – he was a sailor, and didn't have, couldn't have, the full perspective on the events in the UK.

But from the perspective he did have, he adduced the argument for himself that the UK Parliament had ratified the Treaty of Berlin, effectively giving sovereign power to the Union. The Union was acting to prevent an illegal act and in defence of the Treaty, and he, under the command of UHQ, was bound to follow orders so legitimately-based, he told himself.

Not that he didn't grieve for the fate of the UK, and on a personal level worry himself to sleep about his parents and sisters in Derbyshire.

From the reports he had they should be safe enough, he thought, far enough from the scene of action – but would they try to get to him through them? Surely not? It wouldn't be British – but then was he being British? He allowed himself the unaccustomed luxury of a little self-doubt. He must arrange to have his family brought out – that is, if they would go.

But he knew he would do his duty regardless. They had role-played these situations in the classroom countless times – what if the order came, and you had to push the button, knowing that the enemy had either struck, or would get in a strike, and your family and friends would be on the receiving end, etc.?

Some men had tears in their eyes as they struggled with these doomsday decisions even in training sessions, he recalled.

He had found it straightforward. He loved his family, but he knew he would follow orders.

CHAPTER 23

The vast bulk of the Castle rock towered massively above the City just as it had for centuries. The batteries and battlements of the Castle itself rose in silhouette against the western sky, the great looming fortifications seeming to shield and protect the paradoxically tiny, ancient, chapel, like a great nut its secret kernel.

Atop it all flew, defiantly, the Union Jack, and beside it the Saltire, as though daring all enemies to test again the rock's impregnability, fabled from days gone by.

Far below, in the world of men, the Union's special envoys looked out from the grand hotel which dominated the City centre.

'I was here for the Edinburgh Summit in '92,' said the principal envoy. 'I expected to have these talks in the Palace, where we were then – it was splendid.'

'The problem is it's the King's Palace,' said his Scottish host, 'and the King doesn't appear to share the Union's position. As for fitting the occasion,' he added cryptically, 'I wouldn't be too concerned about that. It's not so much of an occasion for some as for others.'

The envoy eyed him quizzically, trying to read the significance of this remark.

'And besides, ' said his host, 'the Palace is right beside the Parliament, and they're not shaping up as Union allies either, with the Scottish Cabinet barricaded in the Castle, and half the MSPs likewise in the Parliament.

'But we're better leaving them be, unless you plan to smoke them out, or bomb them out, which just might be a tad counter-productive,' he said with heavy irony.

The window they stood at looked out on to Princes Street, with the soaring monument to Sir Walter Scott in the foreground, and beyond, the Castle, huge above the national Gallery.

The little group gazed up at it.

'Of course we won't do that, and they know it,' said the envoy. 'So like the sieges of old, no doubt they will just sit tight, and nobody will get to them unless they choose.'

The Scotsman gave a wry grimace, 'Yes – meanwhile they dominate the area, and if occasion demanded, there are enough troops and hardware there to drop a few shells in awkward places, as well as keeping everyone's watch on the dot in Princes Street!'

Then with a telling glance at the special envoy, he went on darkly, 'And in the past, as long as the King held Edinburgh or Stirling, the usurper's power was still in question, though his armies laid waste the land!'

The principal envoy winced, then with a last, long, reflective look, said, 'Certainly a more potent symbol of defiance is hard to imagine.'

The envoys were there because Weurmann's 'other thoughts' on Scotland had begun to unravel before they were halfway knitted up.

For the intelligence was right – the Union's grand scheme was indeed to detach the Scots from the UK with the carrot of full independence.

Edwards, power-mad as he was, for his part had been quite sniffy at the idea that Scotland would not be part of his fiefdom if the plan went ahead.

He loathed the Scots in general, and in particular the jumped-up self-importance, as he saw it, of their 'pathetic little parliament'. He had already indulged in some enjoyable quiet contemplation of how he would clip their wings when he came into his own.

'But why?' he'd quizzed, with open-mouthed incredulity when this was first mooted by the President.

'What is it you say in England? "A lot of sheep country up there",' said Weurmann. 'It will be strategically difficult if we face real resistance. Much better to get them on our side from the start.'

'But with David Francis and the Opposition in our camp – well, he has so many cronies up there we have every chance of keeping them on-side anyway,' Edwards argued.

Weurmann was openly sceptical. 'They don't like being governed from Westminster, and, if you will forgive me, my friend, they will like it less from what I hear, when you are Prime Minister.'

Edwards positively snorted. 'They don't like being governed from Brussels either! I can deal with them!'

'You make my point for me,' retorted Weurmann. 'If we can avoid having to "deal" with them, that is much better. We will have enough to "deal" with.'

Though the argument had gone on and on, Edwards had seen that he was on a hiding to nothing, and grudgingly dropped the point.

But it wasn't long before Weurmann knew he too was on a hiding to nothing, with his plan to recruit the Scottish Government and Parliament intact.

Attempts to sound out the First Minister and others had fallen on stony ground. Weurmann's aides of course couldn't be entirely candid about their brief when they were received in Charlotte Square.

Ostensibly they had come to discuss fisheries policy, but over lunch strayed off into apparently informal chat about attitudes on this and that.

'Interesting, this idea of "independence in Europe", ' was the opening gambit. Then later, 'And what does Scotland make of the Prime Minister's secessionist stance? If the UK were out of the Union, where would that leave Scotland?'

'Out of the Union too, obviously, as we're part of the UK,' was the First Minister's tart reply.

'Might some not be tempted to go a different route?'

The First Minister fixed the two aides with a stony gaze, 'This is a democracy – we've just had a general election!'

When a similar theme emerged over dinner, following another two frustrating hours of formal discussion on fisheries with no substantive progress, the First Minister knew there was a hidden agenda. He had been a politician too long not to be able to smell a red herring.

Still, through the woolly diplomatic double-speak, and treacly, affected, bonhomie of the aides, he could form no clear idea what that agenda was.

But he formed it quickly enough when the paratroops began to drop on London, and David Francis phoned minutes later with an unequivocal proposition which revealed the Union's hand.

And he made his decision.

Perhaps he should have gone underground. Perhaps he should have gone to the Holyrood Parliament. But if they were putting troops in and he might himself be grabbed at any moment – as he felt was likely after his equally unequivocal reply to Francis – he decided to go for the nearest point with his own soldiers around him. The Castle.

Weurmann ground his fist into his palm at news of this setback. He began to feel he'd been seriously misinformed.

When all communication was rebuffed, with a steadfast refusal by the First Minister and the Parliament to negotiate under duress, Weurmann took a new tack.

'If the elected representatives of the people will not negotiate, we will negotiate with the people direct!'

And so the envoys had come to Edinburgh to address a convocation of the great and the good, and the not so good, in the absence of any formally constituted authority.

So all the while, in the street beneath their window, cars had been coming and going with delegates to the hurriedly organised conference.

When the envoys made their way at last into the hotel's ballroom, some hundred or more were assembled under the chandeliers.

News-watchers could recognise amongst them some churchmen, a judge or two, a handful of lesser-known MSPs, some council conveners, businessmen, media faces, union leaders, party activists.

The envoys mounted the dais, and a hush fell on the select company.

The principal envoy tapped the microphone.

'Good afternoon, ladies and gentlemen,' he said in a distinctly middle-European accent. 'Thank you for coming.'

'I represent the European Council. I am here to discuss with you the constitutional implications for Scotland of the current action undertaken by the Council to prevent the secession of England.'

He was interrupted by a florid, white-haired figure, almost before he had taken a second breath. 'That's a very different statement you're making to those made on radio and TV. You speak of Scotland and England, but until now you have always referred to the UK.'

One of the platform party leaned forward to whisper to the envoy, identifying the speaker as a senior judge.

'I do speak of Scotland and England, and indeed of Northern Ireland, Lord Duncan,' agreed the envoy. 'And intentionally so.

'In the circumstances of today, with emergency powers in force and the temporary suspension of Parliament, the normal decision-making process is unavailable. So we have invited you here as a representative group of decision-makers in Scotland to explore these topics.'

A clergyman in the front row harrumphed.

'Is this Euro-speak for "thrust a unilateral Union decision upon us of what's to be done with Scotland", as you have done in England?' he asked abrasively.

'Reverend sir, I realise that emotions are running high. This has been a turbulent time. But let us use dialogue and work together,' the envoy rejoined icily.

A voice from the back called out, 'Is that what you're doing with the Prime Minister and the Cabinet? Is that what the paratroops are doing in London?'

'I repeat – this has been a turbulent time, but for that reason, we wish to explore options for Scotland which will avoid force,' said the envoy.

Another voice called, 'And if we agree on these so-called options, how can they be given effect?'

'They can be given effect under the Civil Contingencies Act.'

'And if we don't agree?'

'The indications are that there is likely to be strong support for this solution.'

'Aye, and if there isn't, the Union army will be marching up the Royal Mile, as well as Whitehall.'

'If there isn't, why would all those present be here?'

His audience grew restive at this, and shouts rang out around the room.

'Because you've come to talk, we've come to listen, that's all!'

'Because our elected representatives are holed up for fear they'll be abducted, too!'

'Because we want you to know how we feel about Union duplicity!'

The envoy swallowed. He could see he was in for a rough ride – not at all what he'd expected.

'Why should we want to be just a state within the Union,' shouted another from the back of the room. 'We were marginalised in the UK before devolution. In the Union we'd be so marginal you'd need a telescope to see us.'

'Not so, not so, there are checks and balances, a Committee of the Regions...' the envoy tried to reassure them. But he'd lost control now, and from all sections came a flood of critical comment.

'I've been a supporter of independence in Europe – until now,' said one. 'Now I wouldn't touch the Union with a barge-pole. The Council's attitude to dissent is "disagree and we send the troops in". How can the rest of the member states feel secure ever again?'

This produced applause, and a chorus of supporting shouts.

'As soon join the old Soviet Union!'

'Aye, and look what happened to it!'

'You've shot yourself in the foot – even the pro-Europeans are deserting you.'

For some time the envoy struggled on.

The closest he came to support was from one delegate who warned, 'I don't like this any more than anyone else – but if we turn down this offer today, we'll have the troops in tomorrow.'

But this was immediately shouted down.

'Sell out just to save our skins? Never!'

'This is Edinburgh – not Vichy. No collaboration!'

'But we are not the enemy,' pleaded the envoy.

'Aren't you? Tell us who is then. The Government? A Government elected by a huge popular majority?'

'You're the ones dropping paratroops on London! You're the ones with the tanks in Whitehall!'

'We did not know you felt so much part of the United Kingdom, still,' said the envoy.

'Well, ye ken noo!' roared a voice bred on the terraces of Hampden Park, in what was almost the last word of the conference.

'Why didn't you warn us?' the envoy asked bitterly of his host, as they left the conference room.

'We did,' he said simply, 'but you didn't want to be told – that is, your people didn't.'

'We were not briefed to expect that! We have been made fools of, laughing stocks!' he said, his bewilderment and chagrin turning now to anger. 'They will see – they are not the only fish in the sea!'

Back in his hotel room that night he made some calls, and by the time he went to bed, he was again relaxed and optimistic, in spite of the events of the day.

He had heard the answers he wanted to hear from one Scot at least, and arranged a secret rendezvous for the following night.

They might yet fulfil their brief from President Weurmann to detach Scotland politically, he mused, as he sipped a nightcap of rare single malt.

CHAPTER 24

It was dark moonless night in the Kent countryside, and the small group in night camouflage were no more than shadows as they glided across the fields.

They moved soundlessly, almost as one man, and left no trace of their coming or going.

Two miles away, under a blaze of arc lights which turned night into day, endless columns of men and equipment surged out from the platforms of the Channel Tunnel.

The engine noise of trucks and tanks and heavy guns rose at times to a deafening roar. Tracked vehicles left a pattern on the tarmac approaches, and rutted and churned the fields beyond.

It seemed chaos to the casual observer, but everywhere were marshals with light-wands, guiding, directing, allocating holding areas.

And beyond and far away a constant deep murmur of men and machines on the move, pushing on out through the perimeter of the Tunnel bridgehead, heading north and west towards their objectives near or far.

Huge stockpiles of supplies rose monolithic against the bright glow of the lights.

Around the whole area a heavily-armed defensive perimeter had been set up. Infantry were dug in round a three hundred degree arc which circled from the coast in the east, around and in front of the landfall area, and back to meet the coast to the west.

Offshore could be seen the dark silhouettes of a naval task force running under doused lights – two aircraft carriers, with the folded wingtips of fighters and the rotor blades of helicopters still dimly perceptible against the sky, and scuttling round their huge bulk, half a dozen frigates constantly patrolling.

Helicopter gunships criss-crossed the area a few hundred feet up, dropping down occasionally to train searchlights on something half-seen in the dark beyond the arc lights.

In the midst of all this ceaseless activity, two muffled thuds from far beyond the perimeter made some of the marching figures look up.

And those who did saw in surreal progression, like a dance in slow-time, the body of a traffic marshal rise into the air, doll-like, still clutching his light-wand, and rising behind him a Land rover with bodies spilling out, and on the ground below, showers of earth and stones raining down, and the crater where the marshal's dais had been.

Two hundred metres away a towering pile of crates lay scattered like toy building blocks where another shell had landed.

Two more thuds in the distance seconds later dropped one shell almost on top of the first, and the second half a mile away.

Seconds more and the sky to the north lit up like day. A thunderous roar arose, and the organised chaos of the marshalling area became chaos indeed, as the unseen gunners – happy now with their ranging shots – laid down a carpet of shellfire a mile and a half wide and half a mile deep, across the bridgehead.

The scene went dark, as lights were cut to deny the gunners any visual reference, or were blown to pieces in the onslaught.

Now tanks and guns on the perimeter opened up in reply, and from seaward came the flash and crump of naval guns, and the roar of jets being scrambled from the carriers.

Eight shadowy figures detached themselves from the deeper shadow of a small group of trees, and slipped noiselessly between slit trenches where soldiers covered their heads with their hands and mumbled long forgotten prayers.

They smiled with grim satisfaction at the gunners' accuracy, the barrage always just to the north of them, spreading panic throughout the area as men sought cover, and marshals sought to disperse massed fleets of vehicles and armour, all in the chaotic dark.

It was easy, really, to get to the Tunnel mouth.

Once there they split into four teams, making off in crouching runs to their assigned tasks.

The river of men and equipment issuing from the Tunnel had ceased to flow, and more than one of the black-clad figures swallowed hard to think of the massed troops just inside the entrance.

No margin for error, now. No communication with the other teams.

Everything down to drilling, and practice, the second hand on their watches, and total confidence in teamwork.

But working swiftly, professionally, within ten minutes they were retreating again.

Still the barrage rolled, and the fierce response from ship and tank and field gun made deafening reply.

Men and machines were on the move again. They might find safety in dispersal – there was none in staying put.

And then all the roar of the guns was drowned by a tremendous explosion at the Tunnel mouth. A great tongue of flame flashed from the exit, and the earth was shattered.

When the rain of concrete debris had ceased, and dust and smoke settled, there was no ordered structure to be seen marking the tunnel's exit to the upper air – only a jumble of reinforced concrete, tangled metal, cabling, signs, and dangling lights.

And beneath it the screams of those buried alive, and beneath that, the silence of those buried in death.

The Government guns fell silent, and in moments so did the answering voices.

In that pause, those who looked around, looked into a hell they had only imagined. Peace-time soldiers many of them – drilled and trained, yes – but never called upon before to bear arms in earnest.

A few veterans had seen something of it – in Bosnia, Iraq, Afghanistan, or UN missions in Africa, but for most it was new and terrible.

Whole companies caught in the open, bodies lying on bodies, torn limbs, blasted faces. Men burned beyond recognition, crushed beneath vehicles, buried under rubble.

And the injured, the terrible injured. Unimaginable injuries. Maiming, disfiguring, blinding injuries.

And even in that twenty-minute barrage, there were those who ran screaming round, shell-shocked, minds maimed by the carnage and the terror, though their bodies were whole.

Now it began again, after the lull to let the bombers find safety for themselves in the shadows whence they'd come.

This time the barrage crept forward, pulverising all in its way, pausing in its progress as it ranged across the Tunnel mouth to complete the burial rites of those below, ashes to ashes, dust to dust.

CHAPTER 25

'God! God! God! This should never be!' President Weurmann shouted aloud in anguish. 'All those lives! All those young men!'

'We have knocked out many of their guns and inflicted many casualties, sir,' said the Italian colonel, Weurmann's military aide, across the desk.

'I do not want to know about that. I do not want to know about people being killed. It is no satisfaction to me if we have an eye for an eye.

'But it means now it is absolutely essential to keep the UK in the Union, or we will have "Fortress Britain" across the Channel – not just "Little England" as we had before. All trust will be destroyed now. Cooperation would be impossible.'

'The problem we have now, sir,' said the aide, 'is that it will take months to repair the Tunnel.'

'But that is only one route,' said the President. 'We have been sending in troops by air. Surely once we secure key ports, we can reinforce by sea?'

'Yes, sir. It is just that it will be a much longer build-up. The British will be able to consolidate, and what we hoped would be a quick police action is likely to become a protracted campaign,' the aide replied.

'And that is just on the military front,' muttered the President. 'The political dimension is also crucial. It is clear we have been badly advised. Edwards' judgment was hopelessly wrong about likely resistance.'

'Have you tried to get Lynda Stalker again, Jacques?' he quizzed the other aide. 'Why will she not speak to me? I do not trust Edwards any longer. If I could get her over here, I am certain we could rely on her judgment much more than his.'

The aide raised an eyebrow.

'All right, all right!' said Weurmann impatiently. 'That, too! And to see her safe.'

'I think...' said the aide, then thought better of it.

'Well? Out with it! You think...?'

'I think that she does not want the personal involvement, perhaps.'

Weurmann sighed. 'I know that, of course. But if she was here, perhaps I could change her mind. Her Prime Minister is out of the way, so why will she not come to me?'

'Perhaps that is why,' said the aide gently.

Again the President sighed, then snapping himself out of this melancholy thought, he turned back to the briefing.

'And anything more about Scotland and Ireland?' he asked. 'The conference in Edinburgh was certainly inconclusive.'

'As you say, sir – inconclusive. Most seem to favour remaining in the UK – perhaps another instance where we have been badly advised.'

'What about the nationalist fervour and all the independence proposals we heard of?'

'That really defines the split, sir. There is probably a majority for devolution, but not for independence. However, as I said, we have had interesting discussions with the nationalists. They have long argued for "independence in Europe", as they phrase it. We feel we could do with them what we have done with Edwards...'

The President snorted. 'You mean totally misjudge it and head down the slippery slope to war there, too?'

'With respect, sir, in Scotland we can be more open. We would be working with a properly constituted party – not a closet faction within a party, which Mr. Edwards represented.'

'Yes, but we would have to back them with soldiers again,' muttered Weurmann.

'We will have to back our action with soldiers there now anyway, sir. And by using the nationalists we might tap the support of a sizeable minority and make the job much easier.'

'In either case it defeats the object of detaching Scotland with the people behind us. It seems we have indeed misjudged, and the Scots are British first, and Scottish second.'

'Well, at least "British" before they are "European", sir.'

'And Ireland?' he queried.

'Ireland is good news, Monsieur Le President,' Jacques.

'I'm glad something is,' grunted the President. 'Tell me.'

'We think the Irish Republic will agree to take over Northern Ireland.'

'Are we sure that is good news?' asked the President. 'Are they not worried about the loyalists?'

'They're concerned, of course, but feel they couldn't withstand the likely nationalist backlash at home if they didn't take the opportunity to unite Ireland when it was offered.'

'Good,' said Weurmann. 'That is something.'

'And it does put pressure on the British rear, sir,' said the small dapper Italian, and gives the Irish the problem. To that extent it eases things for us.'

'Yes, and gives us one less outpost of empire to deal with – on balance I think it will benefit us. But I wonder....'

No one found out what the President wondered, for as he wondered, a siren broke into a pulsating wail in the corridor and red lights flashed on Weurmann's desk.

'What is it? Fire?' said Carlo, after the first start of consternation.

'No,' said Weurmann, 'more serious!'

He opened his desk drawer, took out a pistol, and pushed it into his pocket.

Seeing the President's reaction, the Italian nervously unbuttoned the holster at his belt and took a grip on the butt of an automatic.

At that moment the door burst open and a man rushed in, gasping and wild-eyed.

The colonel drew his pistol and raised it.

'No! No! Carlo! He is staff! What is it? What's happening?' he said to the breathless secretary.

'Air raid, sir!' he gasped.

'Air raid?' the aides chorused.

'They cannot be so crazy!' exclaimed the President, as he was ushered through the door towards the stairs.

But his bodyguards, hard on the heels of the secretary, were already pushing people towards the door.

The small group moved quickly down the concrete steps which led to a basement bunker..

Ahead and behind them staff scurried earthwards clutching file boxes, computer disks and tapes, and communications equipment.

'We have not planned for this,' growled Weurmann darkly.

' Now we will plan!,' he said over his shoulder to his entourage, as they hurried down. 'They think they will scare us, but...'

115

'Sir! Down!' yelled the colonel, staring in hypnotic terror through a large window which, at this level, looked out over the rooftops of Brussels.

In the second's pause between the colonel's shout and the violent push in the back from a bodyguard, sending him forward and down, he glimpsed...

'What did I see?...Missile?...Surely not?'

But a missile it was. An astonishing sight. A sleek, black, finned missile – coming, it seemed, directly at the window, not 200 metres away.

Then – in that last fraction of a second, as everything went into slow motion, and he knew he would die – knew they would all die, knew the bitterness of the thought that the Union would die, his life's work die – as his fascinated gaze locked on the nose cone of the missile, frozen, spellbound, hypnotised by its headlong flight, all still in that second – it turned sharp right and zoomed off.

And he found himself sprawled on bruised knees on the concrete landing a few steps below the window, not dead, the bodyguard half on top of him, the other aides tumbling round.

Before they could react or pick themselves up, a deafening explosion erupted, but from some way away - then the building shook, the window blew in, and glass and plaster rained down on them.

'We weren't the target, then,' said the colonel, shaken, picking glass from his hair. 'They've used this building as a waypoint for the guidance system. Anybody hurt?'

Two of the party were streaming blood, and the President limped from the fall. It seemed a long time till they got to the shelter of the basement area.

'What did they hit?' the President called sharply as they entered the secure bunker.

Another military aide pointed to the wall map of the city. 'The Radio Union building, here, sir.'

'What damage?'

'We're still waiting for confirmation, sir. The top four floors have been blown away, but we only know of one person injured – a night security man, hit by debris.

'Get me the...' – and then another huge explosion rocked the building, lights flickered, computer screens went black, secretaries screamed and clasped each other, gazing apprehensively up.

A long minute later a phone rang. The aide picked it up and listened. 'Thank you – keep us advised.'

Turning to the President's group he said, 'The stationery stores – unoccupied at this time of the morning, other than security. They don't think anyone's hurt.'

'The damned British,' Weurmann spat through clenched teeth. 'They make a joke of everything – even war. The stationery store! What do they call it – "Brussels bumf"?

'They will see. They cannot bomb themselves out of the Union. They cannot bomb themselves free of "Brussels bumf".'

CHAPTER 26

'That should make them think in Brussels, Harry,' said Wardhope with a grim smile, as he studied the screen in the ops room. 'What's the latest on casualties?'

'We've only heard of one or two dead, sir, plus a few injuries from flying glass and debris.'

'Excellent! I think we've achieved the effect we wanted.'

'Yes, sir, and we seem to have turned off the flow of reinforcements with our strike on the Tunnel. The Tunnel itself is cut off semi-permanently, of course, but we've slowed down or even stopped the build-up by other means.'

'Yes, bad business, the Tunnel, but it had to be done. I'll tell you, Harry, and I'll tell no one else – I've had bad dreams about that. Haunting. Reminds me of Churchill, and his recurrent nightmares about Gallipoli, the bodies in the sea, floating face up.

'I dreamt of moving hands, stretching skywards from the rubble, the shattered concrete – all those men, buried there, the screams of agony, vain shouts for help, dying moans. Churchill was never free of it. I wonder if I shall ever be.

'But I do feel it had to be done. I think we can see the evidence of its success, as you say. I'm convinced the determination and ferocity of our response has taken them by surprise and forced them to take stock.'

'I'm sure you're right, sir. It's not just the blocking of the Tunnel – they've been forced to review how vulnerable they are in their air and sea landings, in view of our determined opposition. As you said, I don't think they expected it. That's giving us time to consolidate, and to work on persuading those units who don't know which orders to follow that they should be taking ours.'

'How's that going, Harry?'

'Commander Millwood is coordinating, sir. I'll ask him to come over. John – brief Mr. Wardhope on the latest picture, if you would.'

'Certainly, sir. At present it's a three-way split in the Army – one third with us, one third against us, and one third "don't knows".

'The Air Force picture is much healthier – they didn't take kindly to their runways being bombed, and most smelled a rat.

'Unfortunately the Navy is mostly blockaded. That at least has made clear to COs which side is which, but a breakout would be well nigh impossible, and tremendously costly in men and ships if attempted.

'The bad news is that one of the Tridents seems unconvinced.'

'So long as she's just unconvinced, and doesn't actually go over, we can handle it,' said Wardhope.

'Yes, sir. And we do have half a dozen frigates and other subs around the globe. They're now steaming back for the most part – but we may have trouble with some.'

'We must play the King now,' said Wardhope. 'You liaise, Commander, and coordinate that, too. As we discussed, get COs or senior officers from the wavering units, and possibly even those on the other side, and set up a meet with His Majesty. When they realise he's with us, they should come round.

'They'll have to go to him – he doesn't want to come in here, and I suppose he's right. That way he remains mobile, and can establish another centre of resistance if they somehow take us out.'

'It'll be a big job getting everyone there in secret,' observed the commander.

'Get ten or a dozen up there, Commander, and let the old boy network do the rest. There'll be a domino effect when we get a handful of waverers over to us.'

'Very good, sir. I'll get right on to it.'

'Anything else, Harry? Cabinet meeting shortly – Emergency Cabinet, I'm calling it. "War Cabinet" seemed to take us too far down the road, though God knows we could end up there very quickly.'

'Yes, sir – one other thing. We're getting reports that the Irish Republic is moving troops up to the Border with the North.'

'What? No representative conference like they tried in Scotland, to lend respectability?'

'Not that we're aware of, sir. They must have a more pragmatic view of Northern Ireland, and realise it would be hopeless.'

'Well, they've failed in Scotland. Thank God the First Minister was having none of it – and he's been quite pro-Union up till now,' said Wardhope. 'At the least, they've failed to harness any democratic support and get some sort of legitimacy that way. That's one piece of information we can thank Lynda Stalker for.

'But what about our troops in Ireland?'

'We're having a bit of difficulty with them,' said the Chief of Staff. 'They do seem to be buying the UHQ line.'

'So they're going to let the Irish Army walk in? That would be madness – there'll be a bloodbath! It'll be civil war! The whole situation will be reversed. The Army will be seen as supporting the nationalists, and the loyalists will be fighting them instead of the dissident IRA.

'I think we'd better get someone sound over there to get round unit commanders and get a couple over to meet the King. And liaise with Ms. Stalker to keep us as well-briefed on Ireland as she can.'

Minutes later he was in the chair at the meeting of the Emergency Cabinet.

'I've deliberately kept this Cabinet group tight, gentlemen.

'The situation is so difficult and so volatile that we can't afford leaks.

'I know you all, and have confidence in your loyalty.

'To my colleagues from the Opposition front bench, I would just say that whilst we have had our differences, and no doubt will have them again, I know you are all of the highest personal integrity. I would only ask that if at any point you feel we can't continue to work together, you'll come to me and say so.

'There can be no compromise with the integrity of the Cabinet. It's crucial we work together, and that any dissent is expressed openly and can be discussed.

'We shall be almost wholly concerned with the conduct of the resistance to this invasion, and the restoration of legitimate constitutional government.

'I'm gradually building up a full Cabinet to run other affairs, and we shall just have to leave them to get on with it as best they can.'

Then followed a briefing from the Chief of Staff on the military scenario.

'The Tunnel had to be closed, gentlemen, and we've closed it.

'In Brussels they now know we're not about to lay down our arms in the face of aggression, and we're prepared to carry the fight to them.

'We're consolidating control of our own troops all the time.

'But Scotland and Northern Ireland present unique problems, and we shall have to play a waiting game there for a little.'

As the general went on, the mood of the meeting became increasingly sombre, and as he sat down, the Acting Prime Minister took up the theme.

'As you see, gentlemen, the United Kingdom is in a dire situation – not only disunited from Europe, but now having to face disunity within its own borders.

'Whilst our response to the Union has been unequivocal and positive, it nevertheless represents an escalation of the conflict. Their response may lead to further escalation – and it could spiral into full-scale war.

'The seeds of civil war have been sown in Northern Ireland, and there's division in Scotland, and England too.

'I believe we must hold our ground and continue our vigorous response, but we're staring into the abyss – let's not deceive ourselves - and we don't want to fall headlong in.

'I've asked the Chief of Staff to look at the possibility of getting the Prime Minister out, and even the Cabinet.'

'Do we know where he is?' interjected a minister.

'No, we don't. Nor do we know for certain where the Cabinet is.

'We've been trying to find out via Lynda Stalker, but for the moment they're keeping her away from the most sensitive information.

'However, if we can pull it off, we will again have the elected Government - or at least its leader – in control. The people will back that.

'Concern for the Prime Minister personally, and outrage at the way he's been treated will, I believe, tap a huge wave of sympathy across party divisions.

'This is a medium to longer-term strategy, but will perhaps calm things down a little.

'The Union can't proceed, surely, against huge popular resistance – and the people are with us, right across England, and

Scotland too, in the main. Though unfortunately I don't think there's much chance of us getting the First Minister out – but nor can the Union without creating even more of a backlash. All they can do is use their special forces to make sure he stays put, and so far they've managed that.

'His strength is also his weakness – in the Castle he's secure, but too visible to spirit out of it. He's effectively been sidelined – or sidelined himself – it's been too easy for them to cut his communications.

'Probably a wrong decision, if an understandable one, to dig in there – not enough troops in the Castle to do more than guarantee his personal safety, and his Cabinet's. And most other Scottish units – the ones we've managed to convince so far at least - are on the front line trying to contain the Union advance, and too much needed there to assist.

'But Ireland is a rather different story.'

CHAPTER 27

The garrisons in Belfast and Derry were distinctly jittery.

The Irish Army's concentration along the Border was plain for all to see. From Donegal to Dundalk, infantry, armour, and air support were plainly in view.

Intelligence reports indicated large-scale troop movements all across the Republic, suggesting they were pushing everything up to the front line.

This was in complete contrast to the UHQ Special Forces, who had slipped in quietly in the North, taken their objectives, and kept a low profile as they held them.

The officer commanding the Belfast sector drove down into South Armagh to take a look at the Irish build-up at first-hand, and returned in little doubt about the Republic's intentions.

His problem, in common with all the other commanding officers around the country, was who to believe – MOD or UHQ.

It wasn't even a question of belief any more, he told himself. It was a matter of decision. His decision.

It was a question of legitimacy and who was in the right. UHQ were defending, if you like, the integrity of the Union – the MOD the right of self-determination and sovereignty.

Like the others, he was finding he couldn't stay out of the politics of it.

But it seemed to him that sovereignty had in truth been surrendered by Parliament in ratifying the Treaty of Berlin.

Undoubtedly the general election had given the Government a mandate for their secessionist policy, but surely that should be worked out democratically in the Council and the Union Parliament?

UHQ were implementing a Council decision to prevent unauthorised secession.

He rang his opposite number in Derry.

'What do you think, Alex?' he queried, after re-capping his own thoughts.

'I have to say, I've been on the swither, too, Roger,' said the other. 'But in any case, I don't see what we could do about it if we wanted to. The Republic has troops all long my front from

Ballyshannon to Lough Foyle. Presumably they're under UHQ command, and are waiting to see which way we go.'

'Yes,' said his colleague. 'One thing's for sure – they're going to come in one way or another. It's only a question of whether they come as friend or foe.'

'I don't know,' said Alex. 'The problem on their side is that when they cross the Border, they'll be both friend and foe as far as the people are concerned. Nationalists will welcome them as friends – loyalists will oppose them as bitter enemies. Some will fight to the death, and all the progress towards peace will be wiped out at a stroke. '

'Circumstances alter cases, though,' said Roger. 'The Irish forces will be coming in as an arm of UHQ under orders from the Council of Europe, not as the instrument of the Irish Government.'

'The means might be different, Rog, but the end'll be the same – all Ireland under the control of Dublin, even if it is within the Union. And en route to that will be blood-letting the like of which has never been seen – even in Ireland.'

'If they're going to come here in strength, they'd do better to send neutral troops – Danes, Poles, or whatever,' said the other. 'From what we know of the Special Forces task groups, they seem to be mainly Dutch.'

'This is my point, Rog. I think UHQ are wide awake enough to know they're asking for trouble sending Irish troops in. They may just be pushing them up to the Border to contain the situation, afraid of a counter-attack on this front, as well as in England.'

'So you think they're waiting to see what we do, on the basis that we'll arouse less immediate opposition even if we side with them, as we're here already, and won't have to fight our way in?'

'Yes, I do, and it's easier for us to link with those already on the ground. My other thought is that we're on our own in this. There's no way we can be backed up from the mainland. The MOD obviously has its hands full at the Tunnel preparing for a break-out. London's a lost cause from the sound of it, and Union reinforcements are pouring in again. They'll need everything they have to contain that.'

'And yet,' said Roger, 'as soon as we declare ourselves, we're going to be the target of one side or the other in a way we haven't been for years – and that's not in the interest of either side.'

'No,' said Alex. 'We also run the risk of becoming targets for the Union Special Forces.'

'I think some determined fence-sitting is the order of the day,' said Roger, ' at least until the situation clarifies.'

'Agreed,' said Alex.

And now a stalemate developed, with Irish troops playing a waiting game on one side of the Border, and the British Army – or at least its senior representatives – playing the same game on the other side.

When Wardhope's emissary got there he was entertained to a courteous but non-committal hearing, and he soon realised that the senior commanders were not going to be shifted from their ground – or rather their fence.

His next tactic was to try his arguments with the unit commanders, though this had to be done with a measure of subterfuge as the sector commanders had positively refused to allow a direct approach.

Before the whistle was blown on him and he was put back on the boat under close escort, he had found a solid loyalty to senior officers which he had seldom encountered.

Perhaps, he surmised, this was due to the boilerhouse atmosphere in Northern Ireland, where soldiers from top to bottom of the hierarchy sweated out their tours together.

However, he did persuade a couple who were either more questioning or less decisive than their colleagues to join a "fact-finding group with several other unit commanders" – that is, the group being assembled by Commander Millwood on Wardhope's orders, for the secret meeting with the King.

But the report which Wardhope received soon after the liaison officer's return was not optimistic about the Government's chances of holding the Six Counties.

And Wardhope became even less so, as reports began to come in of the breakdown of law and order all across the Province.

Determined fence-sitting was not in the make-up of loyalist leaders, or loyalist paramilitaries, or for that matter the loyalist community at large, and "No surrender!" rang out again in strident tones across the land.

The all-too visible threat on the Border was anathema to them, and their ire was turned on Catholics, nationalists, and republicans, as of old.

A swelling tide of violence surged through the two communities, and engulfed them both, as revenge was taken in kind for each violent act, an eye for an eye, a tooth for a tooth, a life – or several – for a life.

As rumours spread about the Republic being given a free hand in the North, this was no longer about sovereignty, secession, or constitutional propriety – it was the eruption again of that molten mass of bitterness and division, still seething deep beneath the old crater which had smoked away harmlessly enough for a decade or more.

So now the Army was dragged in, like it or not, in its old role of trying to maintain some sort of order, offer some sort of protection to the community, contain the reviving paramilitary action and counter-action.

And trying to be on the fence, even-handed between the two factions, they quickly came to be seen as on the other side, from whichever side they were viewed.

And from there the protests, and the violence, and the armed confrontations, began to spiral ever more rapidly downwards, towards civil war.

What price now Good Friday?

CHAPTER 28

'Don't you see Dugald? This is just the opportunity we've been waiting for! said McIan.

Dugald took a last long pull from the flattened cigarette end he held between thumb and second finger, before stubbing it out on the rim of a beer can, and letting it fall with a final hiss into the dregs inside.

He wore a tartan shirt, tartan trews, and a Glengarry bonnet. A perfect single eagle's feather rose from the great silver cap badge, distinguishing him as the Chieftain of the Scottish Liberation Army. But the bonnet was pushed to the back of his head, contributing to a dissolute appearance. The head beneath was balding and red, and such hair as there was, was lank and greasy, and ragged around the ears. But still he was an impressive figure, well over six feet tall, even with his head hunched down between his massive shoulders.

'We get legitimate, and get power, both in one stroke!" McIan continued.

The Chieftain fingered the blinds, and adjusted them to allow only the merest opening, through which he peered as though fearful of discovery.

The light filtering between the slats of the blinds revealed McIan's clean-cut intelligent features, a high forehead, dark curly hair, and steel-rimmed glasses. He, too, wore the tartan shirt, trews, and Glengarry.

His face was characterised by a dark intensity, as he spoke again in his measured, educated tone.

'Their agenda isn't our agenda, Dugald, but it is a means to our end.'

'We want an independent Scotland, not a puppet state!' Dugald expostulated, spinning on his heel to face him.

'But we won't be a puppet state!' McIan retorted. 'They simply want Scotland, on its own, disconnected from England and the rest of the UK. Why should they want to run us? They want to hand it to us. "Independence in Europe"…that's what they see.'

'Now you're talking like the SNP! Why fight for independence from a union of four countries, just to become part of a big one? Does that make sense to you? It doesn't to me!'

'SNP be damned!' said McIan. 'I'm just saying that that's what the Union see. They've seen this slogan "Independence in Europe'. As far as they're concerned a nationalist, is a nationalist, is a nationalist – end of story. They have so many nationalists across the Union, they can hardly tell red from blue, never mind tartan.

'The First Minister made his big mistake turning the Union down out of hand, and his second rendering himself impotent by holing up in the Castle – very symbolic and all that, but easily contained. As we know, big mistakes are second nature to that lot.

'Now the Union's turned to us, we can't make the same mistake. You've got to give it a go...even just for the arms and cash. We can use them as a source of arms and equipment, and dump them later. They won't care if we secede or not – we're small fry, and only important to them just now as a diversion.'

'We give nothing a "go" till I say so!' snarled Dugald.

'That's why I'm here talking to you. But I'll tell you this – if you don't take this chance now, there are others who will.'

'Oh aye? Who? Are you threatening me?' he said, hauling himself up to every inch of a massive six feet six inches, the tip of the eagle feather now brushing against the beamed ceiling.

'No, Dugald, of course I'm not – but if you're seen to pass up this chance of power, how will you explain that?'

'I don't give explanations – I get them!' said the other fiercely. 'And I want one now – who's pulling your strings? You've never fronted up to me like this in your puff! Why now?'

'I just see the chance!'

'Aye, but what chance is it you see? Maybe all you've got in your sights is power for yourself! Naked ambition. The main chance. Maybe you'd like to wear the feather yourself?'

'Look, Dugald, you're the cornerstone of the SLA. You've kept the show on the road these three years while the Government's been gunning for us, and neither MI5 nor the SAS have got on to us. We want you up there as always – but maybe, just maybe, I'm saying – maybe you're an underground leader.'

'We've always been underground – and effective because of it.'

'Yes, I know that, but this could be a whole new era. Above ground! Legitimate! Walking the corridors of power hand in hand with Weurmann! But it's going to need new strategy, new tactics. Maybe you just don't like the daylight.'

'You are threatening me!' Dugald roared, baring his teeth and grabbing the other by his shirt front.

'Look, they're doing the same in Ireland!' he said, trying to push away from Dugald's grip. 'Only there, they're offering it to the Republic' He waved his arms helplessly.

'I know that, but that's just the difference – nationalists want to break with England and have a united Ireland. We want to break with England, but we don't want to join up with anybody – and we're not bloody going to! Got it?' he said, thrusting his face right into the other man's.

Then he thrust McIan away so hard that the other stumbled and fell back, hitting his head on an oak beam with such force that his glasses fell on to the stone floor and broke.

McIan looked steadily at the Union envoy through the one good lens of his glasses, squinting with the other eye through the criss-crossed sticky tape now holding the broken shards together.

'I can't deliver the Chieftain,' he said levelly, 'but I can deliver the Army – with me at its head.'

'From what I hear of the …"Chieftain"…you must be a brave man to think of crossing him,' the envoy smiled sarcastically. 'Of course, I don't mind who is in charge – just whether you can deliver.'

'Whether or not I'm a brave man, I'm a rational one. Dugald is a great fighter, and a leader who can inspire – but he's not a thinking man, and he's blinkered.'

'How will you get them to follow you, if he's the one who inspires?'

'He inspires the hearts – I will inspire the minds.'

'And how will you deliver the country?'

'We have command cells in place the length and breadth of Scotland, and in the islands. Trained, ready, communications in place. Most cell commanders are committed, thinking individuals – they'll respond to logical persuasion.'

'And you can work with the Scottish Liberation Party?'

'If they can work with us,' he said, straightforwardly.

This was the best bit!, thought McIan. UHQ intelligence must be really lousy if they didn't know the Scottish Liberation Party was the public, democratic face of the Scottish Liberation Army.

'What do you need from us?' the envoy asked.

'Weapons.'

'What sort of weapons?'

'Rifles, machine-guns, handguns.'

'Ok.'

'Rocket launchers, anti-tank weapons.'

'Ok''

'Shoulder-launched surface-to-air missiles.'

'Harder – but ok.'

'Money.'

'How much?'

'A lot.'

'How much?'

'Ten million.'

'Ok''

'A month.'

'We'll see – what else?'

'You keep the regular army off our backs. For the most part, they don't seem to be getting involved. We need you to keep it that way.'

'I can't promise all units will obey UHQ orders – we're having problems with that elsewhere. But they are not actively opposing us in Scotland, perhaps because we have not targeted them. They are waiting to see what happens, I think. And the UHQ troops who came in to secure key targets can give you some assistance.

'Anything more?'

'Keep the First Minister bottled up and cut his communications. Ditto the Parliament.'

'It's already in hand.'

'I think we can do business, then,' said McIan.

CHAPTER 29

You could still fly transatlantic out of Glasgow, and Wardhope's special envoy did it that way.

He had been roused from his bed at his seaside retirement home on the Solway Coast in the wee small hours, to the great alarm of his wife and daughter.

Sir Terence Davies himself, in a long and distinguished diplomatic career, had had too many two a.m. calls to be more than mildly surprised, and that mainly because he was now retired.

He had been retired for five years. In that time, he had had the odd Government job, heading an inquiry here, doing a report there, but now devoted most of his time to writing and brown trout.

The two a.m. messengers this time brought him a lengthy brief from the Acting Prime Minister.

Wardhope's choice was easy. Sir Terence's sympathies, he knew from his own spell at the FO when they had worked together, lay in the right place. He was the former ambassador to Washington and had lent support to the election of President Main, who was more pro-Britain and pro-NATO than most. And he lived a hop, step, and jump, from the one place you could still step on a plane and get out – part of the Union's strategy to woo the Scots.

He dressed leisurely in his old tweeds and fishing hat, while his wife and daughter, well-practised in the art of hurried packing, threw some things into an ancient leather travel bag which had seen more international hotspots, hotel rooms, presidential palaces, and air miles, than most.

Waving aside the messengers' offer of an escort, he fixed his trout rods to the roof rack of a battered old Volvo, kissed the ladies, climbed into the driver's seat, and smiling out of the window at the little group, said, 'Now I'm disguised as a potty old fly fisherman. If they're controlling the border, no one's going to bother about me.' And with that, he drove off.

They were controlling the border. They had gun emplacements on either side of the road in front of the "Welcome to Scotland" signs, and all vehicles had to negotiate a chicane of concrete blocks and razor wire.

He wryly recalled all the jokes about the Scots setting up machine guns at the border to keep the English out. There was tragic irony in the scene before him now.

Union soldiers were stopping all vehicles as they wound through the road blocks. Some were being directed to lay-bys for random searches.

'Good morning. Where are you going?' said a young officer in the infuriatingly excellent English of Northern Europeans, as the Volvo rolled to a stop.

'Fishing,' he replied.

'You cannot come here just for fishing – things are dangerous now, you know. You have fishing back where you have come from, no?'

Adopting the cantankerous but forgiveable manner, which is the privilege and the practised art of the elderly, he tapped the soldier on the chest and said, "Look here, young man, I've been fishing the Kirtle Water, man and boy, these sixty years, and I'm not stopping now for all this political claptrap.'

The soldier looked uncertain at first, but then laughed – 'But why so early?'

'To catch the first rise of fly as the sun comes up, of course!'

'Ok, sir,' and he was waved on through.

From then on it was all plain sailing – or rather, flying. They obviously did not want to alienate the Scots, and so it was business as normal at the airport, and he saw nary a Union soldier after the border.

But he did see a surprising number of men in tartan shirts and trews. They loitered in groups of two and three around the airport and its approaches. Some carried heavy batons, and more than one had an ominous bulge beneath his shirt at the belt line.

They wore Glengarry bonnets pulled low over their brows, forcing them to stand tall, hold their heads erect, and look at passers-by down the line of their nose in an arrogant and menacing manner.

As Sir Terence made his way to the departure gate, he puzzled this over. They couldn't be soldiers, as none of the regiments wore tartan shirts. Besides, they didn't have the trained or disciplined look of regular forces. More like irregulars - and he should know, he'd seen enough of them in all parts of the worlds.

Then he recalled the bulletin he'd heard on one of the underground radio stations which had begun to spring up, trying to get out information on the real situation in the country, and counter the disinformation and black propaganda campaign Edwards was waging through the regular media.

This station had carried reports of the Scottish conference. The Union appeared to have made little headway with this direct strategy, and none at all with its mainstream approach to the Parliament or the Scottish Government. And now there were stories of insidious dealings between Union envoys and fringe groups of militant nationalists.

He'd previously heard talk of the "Scottish Liberation Army", a shadowy grouping of extreme nationalists, but thought of it as representing a mere handful of the lunatic fringe, if it existed at all.

Was this what he was looking at today – now adopting a bold public posture, instead of lurking in the shadows?

But he had no more time to speculate, as his flight was called for the last time. He made his way aboard the 767 – for once breaking his promise to himself that he would never cross the Pond on two engines.

He settled back in his seat, refusing all offers of boiled sweets, in-flight movies, stereo headsets, hot towels, and strong drink – though he did permit himself a croissant and a cup of coffee mid-morning – as he focussed in earnest now on the task ahead.

He changed at Boston, and by the time the plane circled in over Washington, he felt the glow of easy confidence which came from being in command of his brief.

An official from the State Department met him at the foot of the steps, not without a ripple on the surface of his polished urbanity at the sight of the fishing hat and old tweeds.

Sir Terence graciously explained and, after a quick change in the airport VIP suite, was whisked off to the White House without further formality.

'Sir Terence', said the President warmly, stepping from behind the desk in the Oval Office, in front of which sat another man.

'Glad to see you again. You remember that night at the Convention after I got the nomination? Boy, that was a night!'

'Indeed I do, Mr. President,' said Sir Terence, and with a twinkle added, 'though there are quite a few who don't, I imagine!'

'There sure are! There sure are!' laughed the President.

'Now, you know Secretary of State Buchholz, and I thought it would be a good idea if he sat in with us.'

Sir Terence shook hands with cold formality. Their paths had crossed before. 'And the President knows it,' he said to himself. 'What's more, he knows that I know he knows it. This isn't a good sign.'

Notwithstanding, the President ushered them both to a suite of easy chairs arranged round a low table, and rang for a steward to bring coffee.

'Well, Sir Terence,' he began, 'a difficult business.'

'A bad business, Mr. President. Briefly, we on the UK Government side...'

'That begs the question right away, Sir Terence,' Buchholz interrupted, ' – namely, who are we to recognise as the UK Government?'

Sir Terence looked at the President. The President looked at his hands.

If this was to be the tone of the conversation, Sir Terence thought....

But the President, having allowed Buchholz to strike home the barb, now let Sir Terence off the hook. He turned to the Secretary of State saying, 'Chuck, I think in talking to Sir Terence we can deal off the record with the situation as it is, without prejudice to any position we may decide to adopt officially.'

Then to Sir Terence, 'We know what side you're on Sir Terence. Please go on.'

'Thank you, Mr. President. There is no question as to who is the legitimate government. It's the government elected by the people. I should not have thought, Mr. Secretary' he said acidly to Buchholz, 'that in the "Land of the Free" that could be called into question.

'Indeed, that is one of the main points of my remit. We simply seek to defend our right to implement democratic decisions.

'The decision to secede was democratically arrived at. There is a clear consensus in favour of it. The Union's action in invading is a recognition of that consensus. If it did not exist, they would have no need of such a draconian measure.

'They have attacked with considerable vehemence, and it is partly to ask for assistance in countering this that I have come.'

'Seems to me you've countered it quite dramatically in the Tunnel, and carrying the fight into their back yard,' said Buchholz laconically.

'It was essential for us to show rock-solid resolve at that point,' retorted the envoy.

The he continued, 'Mr. President, to maintain our position militarily against the considerable forces deployed against us, we need help.'

'That's a hard one, Sir Terence,' drawled the President. 'You and I go back quite a ways, and you know I'm a friend to Great Britain, isn't that so?'

'Indeed it is, Mr. President.'

'I've always acknowledged the "special relationship" which exists between our two countries, and I still do. We could have no stauncher ally than the UK, and you could have none stauncher than the United States, in the face of a common enemy.' Buchholz here pulled a face behind his hand. 'History has shown that, in two world wars, in Korea, in the Cold War, the Balkans, Iraq, Afghanistan.'

'Yes, Mr. President.'

'But we're not talking about an enemy here – and certainly not a common enemy. We're talking about a fight among friends. As desperate and vicious a fight as it has become, it's still, to us, a fight among our friends.

'We're very willing to use our good offices to get our friends to stop, and help them get back into good grace with each other, but more we cannot do.

'You must see clearly that we would be interfering in what is, now, the internal politics of the United States of Europe.

'Besides this, how could we reconcile any partisan assistance with our NATO membership? The Union forces and our own are the core of NATO, and the British are a key component in the Union role. It would be NATO fighting NATO.'

'It's NATO forces fighting NATO forces at present, ' put in Sir Terence.

'Why, yes, and we see our role as trying to re-establish harmony between natural allies, and not escalating the problem by throwing in with one side – certainly not militarily.'

Sir Terence pursed his lips and nodded his head, acknowledging that there was no more to be said on this issue.

'I would then like to come to my second point,' he said.

'We know you will have had approaches from Mr. Edwards and President Weurmann. They will, of course, seek United States' approval and recognition as a way of legitimising their position.

'We trust you will not accede to that, representing as it does a clear usurpation of power.'

'That's a hard one, too,' said the President, cocking his head on one side and pulling his chin. 'We can understand and sympathise with your position. I was a state governor before I became President, as you know - and state governors and state legislatures are always very jealous of their powers and prerogatives. Naturally enough, they try to limit the encroachment of the Federal Government on their preserve. So I know where you're coming from – but the Federal Government has its duty, too.'

'Thank you, Mr. President, but with great respect, I don't think the situation is quite analogous. Britain is a nation-state. Part of the United States of Europe, yes, but she now chooses to withdraw from that, by dint of the national will as expressed in the recent general election.'

'Well, I see the argument, of course, Sir Terence. But I've gotta tell you – Chuck here has had his people on to this at the State Department, and the international lawyers are coming up with the word that you signed your sovereignty away in the Treaty of Berlin.

'The answer I'm getting is that your Parliament, having signed away sovereign authority, can only resume it with the unanimous agreement of all the other member states and the Federal Government, and that it's acting beyond its powers in legislating for secession – so I don't see that there's a whole hell of a lot we can do.

'The only thing we have a beef with, Sir Terence, is their use of force. But then, if they'd knocked politely at the door, I don't suppose they'd have gotten in.'

Sir Terence continued to argue, skilfully and forcefully, for almost an hour – but being the skilled diplomat he was, he knew he'd had his answer in the first ten minutes.

He put in a rueful call to Wardhope in the UK, using a special link, and relayed the outcome of his discussions.

'If President Main doesn't want to know, it looks like we're on our own,' said Wardhope dejectedly. 'Sir Richard is still bashing his head against a brick wall at the UN.'

Two hours later Sir Terence was back in the air, heading for home, an incongruous and disconsolate figure, in ancient tweeds and a fishing hat.

CHAPTER 30

Away in the north, the dark chop on the surface of the sea loch which lapped up to Rory's ancestral keep, with its royal guest, was broken by the slim black stalk of a periscope.

It scanned 360 degrees, then slid silently back beneath the waves.

Minutes later the dark whaleback shape of a submarine parted the surface.

Even while the water streamed off the shadowy hull, three inflatable boats were launched from the casing.

Minutes later, a dozen black figures dragged them up over the sand on the loch shore, deflated them, and hid them beneath overhanging bushes on the margin of the beach..

They looked back a moment, but the waters of the loch had closed over the secret visitor, now gliding seaward again through its deeps.

The shadowy figures, almost invisible beneath the bushes, paused another moment to make sure they were unobserved.

Then, one at a time, they moved swiftly from the cover of the undergrowth, flitting between the stunted, wind-bowed trees edging the fields which swept down to the beach. Light reflected from the grey-white bark, glinted dully on automatic weapons slung over the dry-suits of some.

They moved from the trees to the shelter of a dry-stone dyke, and followed the line of it, crouching low, pausing every 50 metres to look and listen.

Now, beyond the rising ground in front, the old keep came into view, a faint reflection of starlight on its dark slated roof, the high-pitched gables rising in stark silhouette against the midnight-blue sky.

As they moved forward, a chink appeared at the base of the tower, then flung a wide pool of light across the home paddock, seeming to illumine their stealthy advance, before waning to a chink again.

Rory stood before the iron-studded door.

The leading shadow moved again and motioned to the others.

A mallard called up by the castle wall. Another answered along the dry-stone dyke.

Rory strode forward, peering, then swept the length of the wall with a powerful torch.

The beam came to rest on the first two figures.

The foremost stood up, reached for his weapon – pushed it to his back, and smiled a tight-lipped smile.

'Good evening, sir. Commander Wilhurst. All clear, I trust?'

'Yes, Commander. Welcome. How many of you?'

'A dozen.'

'Come in, then. There probably isn't a soul for miles, but then again, the wood may be full of poachers.'

'My chaps would give them something to think about, if so.'

'So would your duck call – a strangely nasal mallard, that one!'

Shortly after, they stood round the fire warming themselves – outside by means of the crackling logs, glowing and spitting in the great stone hearth, inside by means of a fine single malt produced by Rory.

Then he said to Wilhurst, 'I imagine you would like a private word with my guest, Commander?'

'Yes, please.'

'Through here,' said Rory, leading him out of the great hall, followed by a few puzzled looks from some of the group.

'Good evening, Commander,' said the King, striding forward with a smile as Wilhurst entered the small sitting room. 'All went smoothly getting here, I hope?'

'Yes, thank you, sir.'

The King briefly introduced Inspector Johnson and then said, 'Very well, Commander – to business.'

'I have a briefing for you from the Acting Prime Minister, sir, ' said Wilhurst, ' but it's sketchy, because the situation is still extremely confused. However, Mr. Wardhope's main concern on the military front is that service units don't know which orders to obey – they've been getting orders from UHQ, and now they're getting conflicting orders from the MOD. They simply don't know who to believe.'

'Yes, I can see that must make Mr. Wardhope's task very difficult,' nodded the King.

'He thought that you could play a crucial role, sir, as he said in the dispatches arranging this meeting. Your endorsement of the MOD will legitimise it in the eyes of the unit commanders.

'He would've liked you to come back with us, sir, but I gather you're not in favour of that.'

'Too risky, I think. I don't mean to me personally, of course. I'd be delighted to come back with you, but if I stay put, we then have at least two centres of resistance, widely separated. This one is totally secret, whereas they know exactly where Mr. Wardhope is. They just can't get at him – unless they loop the loop altogether and drop a nuclear bomb down the chimney..

'No,' the King mused, 'he's safe inside, but can't come out, whereas I'm safe outside for the present , though I can't "come in". But I can at least move around.'

'Makes sense, sir,' said Wilhurst with a nod.

'Of course, we'll need some more hardware to set this up as an alternative command and control centre. Need to get a few more bods in, and all that. Can do?'

'Can do, sir, if that's the decision,' said the Commander. 'Deep water right in to the head of the loch. Well away from shipping routes, and even fishermen. 'Those fishermen there are, are used to seeing subs around on exercise. Could hardly be better.'

'Very good,' said the King. 'Now – how many chaps have you got through there?'

'There are twelve in the party, sir. Eight are COs of various units – six from across England and Wales, and two from Northern Ireland, where we're having a particular problem convincing the troops.

'The others are seamen petty officers to handle the boats, and myself, of course.'

'And they don't know who they're meeting?'

'No, sir – not a clue. We felt that was the only way to ensure security.'

'Good-oh! I like surprises!' said the King, rubbing his hands in anticipation.

'Just one more word, sir. The petty officers and myself are armed to deal with any security threat which might arise.'

'Do you anticipate any, Commander?' asked Johnson, his eyes narrowing.

'Not really, Inspector. But all of these chaps are on the swither between UHQ and us. There is therefore an outside chance of some heroics.'

'You mean attempted hostage-taking?' said Johnson.

'Or worse,' said the King, knowing that the others would be too tactful to mention it bluntly.

'Better have the body-armour, sir,' said Johnson. 'Just in case.'

'Certainly not,' said the King. 'The day an officer holding the King's Commission decides to put a bullet in me, I'll be happy to give up the ghost.

'To be King is something, still,' he said, and made ready to test the proposition.

Commander Wilhurst returned to the hall and briefly addressed the officers gathered there, now with their dry-suit tops rolled down around their waists, and beginning to perspire in front of the blazing fire.

The three petty officers had discreetly retired to the corners of the room, unobtrusive, but alert.

'Could I have your attention, please?' said Wilhurst. 'We asked you to undertake this trip in great secrecy.

'In just a moment, you'll know why, and I trust your doubts will then be resolved.'

He turned towards the door.

'Gentlemen – His Majesty the King.'

There was an audible gasp as the King appeared in the doorway, the glint of the firelight highlighting the well-known features.

The officers snapped to attention, as much as they could snap in dry-suits and rubber overboots.

'At ease, gentlemen. Stand easy,' said the King.

'How are you all? You've had quite a journey for landlubbers! Anybody green about the gills? No?' and he moved from one to the other, chatting and shaking hands.

'Please sit down, gentlemen,' he said at last.

'I gather you've had a tricky time of it – piggy-in-the-middle between UHQ and the MOD.'

Nods and muttered assent ran round the group.

'So what's the problem?' he asked, inviting a response by a pause, and a look from man to man.

'The real problem has been the disinformation, sir,' ventured one. 'Manifestly, Union forces have been in the driving seat, and UHQ is the normal command line. One has therefore tended to believe that such an open and coordinated attack has been, as they claimed, in defence of the Government.'

'The MOD, by contrast, has been rather disorganised,' chipped in the officer next to him. 'It's been issuing contrary orders, and of course claimed to be representing the Government – but then "they would say that, wouldn't they?" if UHQ claims were true.'

'Very well. I do understand the difficulty, gentlemen – but the position is straightforward.

'My Prime Minister has been abducted, my ministers placed under house arrest, the country invaded, and a puppet regime installed.

'They've reaped this reward because they've been true to the mandate wholeheartedly given to them by the country at the general election, to take us out of the United States of Europe.

'This naked aggression is being resisted by the only loyal minister who escaped when the Cabinet was seized. It is your job to assist him.'

And looking round the room, he said with intense feeling, 'I trust I have your support.'

'Yes, sir!' they replied, as one man.

To be King was something, still, after all.

Thirty-six hours later they were back with their units, and their units were back with the MOD. There was indeed a domino effect, as Wardhope had predicted.

Within days he was finally in effective command of ninety per cent of UK forces, and the conflict entered a new phase, with battle lines clearly drawn.

CHAPTER 31

If Wardhope needed any convincing that he must use the forces he had won over in real earnest, that conviction arose now. Stories began to come in of rape, torture, and summary execution.

He stared in dismay at the first such report to come to hand.

A Union infantry unit, re-grouping after the Battle of the Tunnel, had commandeered a girls' boarding school, complete with the sixth form girls.

They had been stripped naked and tied to their beds in the dorms.

The unit had lost many men in the bombardment, and the girls were raped repeatedly and brutally in a sort of revenge attack.

Word got out to the villages around, and soldiers from the unit began to disappear, before turning up in ditches with pitchforks and billhooks driven through their private parts, having bled to death.

And then 'death squads' began a campaign of retribution in the villages by night, hauling men from the arms of their wives, and to the accompaniment of screams from their horrified children, shooting them in front of their families.

This was of course stopped, as soon as word got back to senior commanders.

'We are not a marauding army of occupation!' they stormed. 'We are not barbarians! We're here to underpin the authority of the Union – legitimately. This is Federal territory. These are not the enemy – they're citizens of the Union, just as we are....'

'Tell that to the boys buried in the Tunnel,' muttered the collective voice of the fighting soldiers, under its breath.

At any rate, the damage had been done. Panic ran ahead of the advancing Union forces, and resistance hardened.

Even Wardhope, distasteful as it was to him, had to take the advice of his intelligence officers to make propaganda capital out of these and other atrocities.

All this resulted in great trains of refugees moving northwards from Kent and Sussex and the Home Counties, to join with streams already on the move out of London, in scenes reminiscent of Bosnia or Kosovo in the 'nineties.

But it also resulted in a fiercely determined resistance movement going underground and inflicting substantial damage on Union convoys, supply dumps, communications centres, and such targets.

'I want these resistance chaps given every support,' said Wardhope to his staff. 'Weapons, ammunition, communication equipment, organisational assistance, training – whatever's needed. That type of guerilla action is just the thing to slow the Union advance.'

Gradually a team of liaison officers was put in place, and in areas controlled by the MOD, resistance cells were set up systematically, armed, equipped, and trained, and command and control structures put in place.

Defensive bunkers and weapons caches were built at strategic points, and briefing sessions held on a regular basis.

If and when Union forces did penetrate to these areas, they would find their opponents dug in for the long haul, certain they could maintain their secret network and operations for as long as there was a job to do.

After all – this was their home turf.

The girls' school incident and other similar events played their part in deciding the 'don't knows' among the regular forces.

The gangling major was on the verge of convincing his CO that they must accept orders from UHQ, as this was the legitimate command line.

Then word reached them of Union troops shooting six old men in a well-known pub in the garrison town they had so recently vacated.

The pensioners had taunted the soldiers, and had obviously penetrated to the quick, for all six had been left in a pool of their own blood around the domino table.

'I'm sorry, Jock, I've had it with all the "correct line of command" stuff, though you very nearly had me over. I know what's right and what's wrong.

'Sometimes a soldier has to do things he doesn't like because orders are clear, and he has no choice. But what we're seeing going on is wrong, and we do have a choice.'

'I'm with you now, sir,' said the major. 'Instant convert after the Red Lion shootings – and apparently in Kent they've been quite literally raping and pillaging. Not our type of fighting at all – more like the benighted Balkans of old.'

'You were there, of course.'

'Yes, indeed, sir. With the UN. Ghastly! Ghastly! And a fat lot of use we were. I'm certainly not going to sit back and watch that all over again here, let alone join the other side.'

'Ok, Jock. Let's get on to the MOD and tell them we're on their team. Get them to task us, and let's get to work.'

'Very good, sir!'

Meanwhile in towns and cities in the Midlands and North, refugees from the South were being welcomed and made as comfortable as possible.

Old army camps were opened, tented villages sprang up, caravan sites – normally empty at this time of year – teemed with people.

Schools, church halls, and community centres were full to overflowing, and the spare rooms of many a private house boasted new lodgers.

A ragged front line began to form, from Gloucester to Oxford, to Bedford and Cambridge, and on to Lowestoft – though as Union troops began to pour in at the ferry ports at Harwich and Felixstowe, this eastern section was pushed back north-westwards to The Wash.

To the north of this front line were the British – millions of them refugees, displaced from homes and families, but the more defiant for that. The remainder, whose homes were still behind the front line, were determined to hold it, and not to suffer the fate of their guests from the south.

To the south were the Union forces, increasingly sensing that victory – where they had victory – was empty.

They had come, as they saw it, to help the people throw off a Government embarked on a relentless course to secession, with all its consequences – economic and political - for Britain and the Union.

But the people threw them off instead, fleeing before them, or staying to defy and harry them.

The front line firmed and became more defined, as more and more military formations fell in along it under the direction of Wardhope and his staff – entirely cut off now in their underground command post, but in command nonetheless.

And the Union advance began to grind to a halt.

They still indeed held pockets in strategic locations around the country, but these came under increasing pressure as UK forces re-grouped under MOD command.

Weurmann viewed the line on the map at UHQ with consternation.

'What a little bit we have, and at what cost,' he said ruefully. 'And what a big bit is left.

'We cannot fight our way from town to town. We hold London – but the British have left it behind.

'I begin to feel what Napoleon must have felt when he got to Moscow at last – but I will not retreat.'

'No, sir,' said General Le Blanc at his elbow, ' but we are approaching a stalemate, and if we do not maintain momentum, that is the best we will achieve.'

With an anguished grimace, Weurmann posed a rhetorical question to the empty air. 'Do we even want to govern there, if we have to fight every centimetre of the way?'

'That is a question for the politicians, sir....' said Le Blanc.

'No, no, General. It's all right. I was just musing out loud. What options do we have militarily?'

'Attrition, sir. Cut off supplies. We more or less command the sea as it is, and have much of the prime agricultural land under our control. If we can secure Scotland and Ireland and cut these off as supply routes, we can make life increasingly difficult.'

'Too long a timescale – they could survive indefinitely on the remaining territory.'

'Terror, then, sir.'

'What do you mean "terror" ?'

'Indiscriminate bombing and shelling. Harassing the civilian population. Random horror and atrocity.'

'General! General!'

'Legitimate strategy in all-out war, sir. Break their spirit.'

'That has been tried on the British before – read your history.'

The General paused, looked straight into Weurmann's eyes with a cold, dead, expression, and said – 'And there is a nuclear option.'

'No, General! There is no nuclear option!'

'A credible threat to use it is all it would take, sir.'

'And if they call our bluff?'

'Then one clear demonstration that it is not bluff.'

'Mein Gott!' said Weurmann, reverting to his native tongue in despair at the General's apocalyptic proposal. 'Das konnen wir nicht tun! Niemals! Niemals!'

'Sir, you ask me for results, but you ask me to fight with one hand behind my back.'

Weurmann merely stared, not looking at the General, but numbly looking into the abyss.

He abhorred nuclear weapons, and had campaigned against them since his political coming-of-age.

Now he recalled how that day at the Wall, as he swung his heavy hammer, he had felt he was also striking blows for peace and an end to the Cold War.

He could scarcely comprehend this present reality, that he was calmly being advised to pull the nuclear trigger if it came to it.

He waved the General away and, as the door closed behind him, buried his face in his hands.

CHAPTER 32

Probably the reason why Neville Edwards found it so hard to run the country was that it was hard for those he came in contact with to see him as anything other than a traitor.

Even the ministers who had sided with him felt that at bottom.

Indeed, he felt something of it himself.

From the moment it became clear a defence and counter-attack was being mounted against the Union – against him and his paymasters – on the political front as well as the military, he had become a lame duck.

'If it hadn't been for these bloody thickos letting Wardhope get away, it would have been a very different picture,' he ranted to the Agriculture Minister, Evesham, one of his co-conspirators. He was indeed the only one in whom Edwards felt he could confide, and even then thought to himself contemptuously what a half-baked individual he was – what a half-baked bunch altogether.

Agriculture, for God's sake! The one Union policy he really had no time for was the Common Agricultural Policy, and this chap supported it! Then a bone-headed boy-o of a Welsh Secretary, and the bloody Transport Minister.

There was at least one light in the darkness, he told himself, in the form of the Minister for Women – though he wasn't sure it wasn't just her form he went for. Big tits – and boy, does she know how to use them to full political advantage!

With that blouse open one button too many, she can get anything she wants out of the stuffiest old codger of a permanent secretary. She could probably get anything she wants out of me, come to think of it, he mused. But she has a bit up top, too.

The rest of his Cabinet and junior ministers were recruited from wearingly ambitious and politically amoral rookies, for the most part.

He had certainly expected to be able to recruit better calibre people than these, but somehow many of even the most pro-European MPs declined his invitations. Why, he couldn't fathom.

The europhiles had been happy enough to propel him upwards as their voice in the Cabinet. Now they muttered about 'not the decent thing', and seemed prepared to abandon the great leap forward into Europe for the sake of conscience. Bloody public school types!

Evesham was droning drearily on about something as he reflected on all this, and he hauled himself back from a brief fantasy about the low-buttoned blouse.

'After all,' Evesham was saying, 'what could we have expected? We didn't expect the whole army, navy, and air force were going to fall into step behind us, or lay down their arms when requested. So I don't see that Wardhope has made such a big difference.'

Edwards returned to the ranting tone with, 'Of course he's made a difference! The bloody MOD wallahs would be faffing about like headless chickens without Wardhope's political direction! They would've done what we told them or else done nothing, if it hadn't been for that shit!'

'We were always going to get opposition,' said Evesham. 'We knew that.'

'Yes, but we expected to be on firm ground to fight it. Now it feels like we're on shifting sand!'

Evesham was meanwhile thinking to himself, 'What a pathetic quisling Edwards is turning out to be. He expected it all on a plate, and now it's come to a fight, he hasn't the guts. Bloody grammar-school types – they're all the same.'

Downing Street had been a problem, too. The staff he inherited were so sullen and disobliging he wondered that the Prime Minister had put up with them. He didn't quite recall them being like that when he'd called at Downing Street as a minister in the past – but anyway, he'd changed the lot, he boasted to the lady in Camden Town.

The new lot weren't much better, he confessed, and began to feel that they looked at him askance.

In Whitehall, he and his ministers found it difficult to get things done. It wasn't that the civil servants were obstructive – or at least, weren't openly so. There just seemed to be a terrible inertia, impossible to overcome, so that one had to accept the pace and manner of the civil service machine, or move not at all.

And then, he sometimes felt as though some of the permanent secretaries and some of the other senior civil servants had their own agenda, and that it was moving a step or two ahead of his, and not subject to the same inertial forces.

Even the Cabinet Secretary seemed to be being economical with his cooperation.

'We're going to have to take action to improve credibility and public acceptance,' he acknowledged to his inner circle at a late evening meeting at No. 10, two weeks into his 'premiership'.

'Weurmann and his sidekicks are leaning on me to deliver more support.'

'Meanwhile Wardhope is doing his damnedest to undermine what we have,' said Williams, the sometime Welsh Secretary. 'But it was a feather in your cap to pull in the Leader of the Opposition.'

'Yes, it was, if I do say so myself,' Edwards said with a nod, and a smile of smug self-satisfaction. 'But we still need to underpin our position. Too many bloody rookies – we need some heavyweight ballast. Something to give us bottom.'

'We've worked right through our original list,' said Evesham, 'and really only the Leader of the Opposition came up on that trawl.'

'At least we landed a big fish,' said Edwards, ' and if we can land one, we can land another couple. We need to shoot our nets again and go for another haul.

'What I propose is this – that Lynda and I...' turning and glancing significantly at her. She leaned towards him, nodding attentively, and the collar of her blouse fell aside momentarily. He stammered on, 'th...that Lynda and I go down to Chequers and see if we can't persuade some of our former colleagues to join us. As a recent convert herself, she may be able to sway one or two.'

This did not meet with immediate approval, however. Several objections were raised.

'Surely if they didn't come over within a few days, they won't now?' said the one 'rookie' admitted to the inner sanctum, who was still smarting over the implication that he lacked 'bottom'.

'Some may have grown tired of bread and water by this,' said Edwards with an unpleasant smile. 'Not everyone bears the martyr's cross happily. And if the Union hadn't tried their ridiculous scheme in Scotland, we might have got some of the main men from there – but of course they're all half-tempted by the prospect of greater glory if Scotland goes it alone. But we still might convince some of the others.'

'But if the others come over now, just for their own comfort and convenience, what use are they to us?' asked Lynda, playing devil's advocate.

'And could we trust those who did?' wondered Evesham.

'It's the name that matters,' said Edwards, ' not the substance. It's window-dressing, PR. And of course we'd keep a close eye on them. If we could get, say, the Chancellor, or the Home Secretary...'

'Ha, ha, ha!' laughed Evesham, somewhat disloyally, but unable to contain himself. 'The man who said you'd have to go over his dead body to become Prime Minister! I don't think you've much of a hope there!'

'...as I was about to say,' continued Edwards, giving him a withering look, 'if not them, at least one of the popular or high-profile ones. Then people would take note.'

Having determined his own course, Edwards wasn't in the habit of being deflected by the opinions of others. He'd stated his intention, and the meeting was drawn to a close.

As they rose to go, Edwards touched Lynda Stalker on the arm, saying, 'Could you just hold on for a word about arrangements for Chequers?'

She hung back as the others said their 'goodnights'.

'Like a drink?' he asked disingenuously. 'I'm having one.'

'Thank you,' she said after a momentary hesitation, but eyeing him closely as he turned to ring for the butler he had just employed.

'Let's go through to the sitting room – more comfortable,' he said.

For the first time since she'd 'joined' Edwards' camp, she almost lost command of herself. For it was there she'd sat with the Prime Minister, and there he'd slept against her breast on the morning of the landslide victory – so short a time ago, and yet such an age.

But as he led the way across the landing, and ushered her to the long, low settee, she rallied herself with an effort. He waited while the butler poured the drinks and served them, then settled on the settee beside her.

'Actually, tomorrow's not really a problem. My car will pick you up at eight. It's just that – well, it seems a bit silly you going off at this time, just to come back first thing. I thought you might like to ...to stay here.'

It was that fatal hesitation – 'to...to stay here', that gave away his intention. Realising immediately from the expression which passed across her features like a black cloud that he'd overstepped the mark, he added hastily, 'The guest rooms are all lying empty...far too big a place....' But she already had her bag in her hand, and was heading for the door, the pink gin abandoned half-finished on the side table.

As the door slammed behind her, Edwards downed his Scotch, poured another, and downed it, too.

On the other side of the door, Lynda Stalker walked along Downing Street in a flurry of emotion. A thin smile spoke of her satisfaction that Edwards had so thoroughly taken the hook she'd baited for him – but the set of her features a moment later denoted her determination to keep him at arm's length. Then as she thought of Edwards sitting on that settee, anger flashed in her dark eyes. But finally, as she recollected once more that close and tender quart d'heure on the morning of victory, her eyes moistened and her lip trembled.

Back at No. 10 Edwards went downstairs, pulling on a high-collared trench coat, and slipped out the back door into Horse Guards, with barely a nod to the policeman on duty.

His personal detective knew better than to follow him when he took this route, which led from his high office of state, to a nondescript bed-sit in Camden Town, and the lady of easy virtue.

CHAPTER 33

'No – they cannot! This is wrong! It is so wrong!' stormed Weurmann, tearing up in a rage the pages of the dispatch which had just reached him and flinging them from him to flutter to the floor. 'This is against everything! This is not the plan!'

He stalked from end to end of the oak-panelled room, jaw set, eyes wild, pounding his forehead with the heel of his open hand, fingers tensed with the rage of despair which shook him.

'This is what we fight against – this spectre of nation against nation, like for a thousand years, two thousand years, in Europe!

'Europe is for peace! It is for harmony! It is for working together and prospering in peace!'

His aide, Jacques, just touched with his toe one of the torn fragments on the floor, and nudged it towards another, jigsaw-like, stealthily almost – afraid to be caught in this rushing flood of anger bursting forth from the President, squinting down his nose to see what terrible intelligence the paper contained.

'…and the Governments of Norway, Sweden, and Spain jointly declare that unless the military intervention in the United Kingdom is immediately terminated and troops withdrawn, they will…'

'They will what?' wondered Jacques, alarmed, but shrinking back against the panelling as Weurmann, still mouthing distraught imprecations, surged past where he stood.

The other torn scraps of the dispatch had swooped under the huge mahogany conference table as they fell, the print too small for Jacques to read from there.

'Sir…' he said hesitantly, but Weurmann didn't pause. 'Monsieur Le President, what is it that has happened? What do they say?'

Weurmann appeared not to heed him. By degrees he seemed to focus his mind on the room, on the group of advisers, on the Commissioner who had brought the dispatch, on Jacques, but still seemed unaware of the question.

'What do they say?' the aide said again.

Weurmann fixed him with baleful eyes. After long moments he raised his eyebrows and opened his eyes wide. 'Say? What do they say? They say they will secede also, and stand with the British!

'It seems we are not all Europeans after all. We are nation states again, changing partners, changing alliances, like always in Europe.'

'Sir, they are just four out of thirty states,' ventured Jacques. 'They are no match if it comes to that.'

'No match? This is a community, not a "match"! If this split comes about, all will take sides. "Stand with the British" means "fight with the British". Then before we know it, France is fighting Spain, Denmark is fighting Norway, Germany is fighting Poland – I tell you, this is the Doomsday scenario!'

The President pulled up now in front of the Commissioner, still standing by the head of the table.

'What do they say, these ministers? Senor Perez is a moderate man, a committed federalist. Why does he do this? He does not love the British as British – only as Europeans.'

The Commissioner paused, choosing his words. 'They say we have all misjudged. They include themselves. They are shocked, taken aback, like everybody, that the British people will come out on the streets for this – for anything.

'They think before it is the Government which is against a federal Union. Now they see it is the popular will.'

'No!' said Weurmann. 'The people do not fight against being European. They fight against being invaded.'

'And we should have known it,' replied the Commissioner. 'They have not been invaded for 1000 years. Senor Perez says Mr. Edwards misread it catastrophically – or else has simply used us for his own megalomaniac ends. Edwards said they would not fight the policy. Maybe they do not, but they fight the action.'

Weurmann turned to the military staff, seated at one end of the table. 'And you, gentlemen – what are your thoughts now?'

'It is very bad on the ground, sir. We do not know how much of the British military is with us, how much against. Some who obeyed UHQ orders at first, now do not. The British are consolidating their resistance.'

'The King is with them, and that is much in Britain, still,' said another.

'We see only skirmishing again now,' continued the general, 'but soon we must get another counter-attack. The British like surprises. They like to do the thing no one thinks they will do – like the missile attack.'

Weurmann stroked his chin. He moved to the table, placed the fingertips of both hands on its polished surface, leaned forward on them, and as he stood, appeared to study his reflection in the surface.

Then he raised his eyes, looked slowly round from one to the other, and finally said, 'There must be a Summit, gentlemen. We must decide together how to proceed.

We must be united! We must act as the United States of Europe – not as France, or Spain, or Germany, or Italy! We must speak with one voice!'

A few days later Jacques intercepted him as he made his way to his office.

The aide had been tasked with arrangements for the extraordinary session of the Council – still usually referred to as a Summit, out of habit.

'They will not come, sir!'

'Who will not come?' thundered Weurmann.

'Spain will not come. Norway and Sweden will not come.'

'Why will they not come?'

'They say they have declared their position. They fear for their personal security. They fear they may become hostages to secure their country's cooperation.'

'Ridiculous!'

'They point to the action against the British and say it is not ridiculous. At any rate, they will not come.'

Weurmann and Jacques surveyed the preparations for the special session, which were well in hand in the large chamber below the gallery where they stood.

Four vacant places round the table would be a potent symbol of the split which had developed. And in this new scenario with two camps developing, when members did take their seats in the Council, each would have a store of uncertainty and mistrust of his colleagues, wondering which side each other would support.

And yet it could still be reckoned in weeks, not even months, since all had been unanimous

The spectre of disintegration of the whole Union now arose before Weurmann as he looked down, and a haunting lethargy pervaded his whole being, so that he had to lean against the rail which ran round the gallery, finally putting his head on his hands on the rail.

He remained like that for some minutes, unmoving.

Gradually work slowed and ceased on the floor below them, as first one, then another, then the whole company of workmen, organisers, and officials, gazed upwards at the picture of utter dejection which the President's posture portrayed.

Jacques touched his elbow.

'Monsieur Le President.'

'Yes, yes,' said Weurmann, straightening – and as he did so, he enveloped himself again in his habitual cloak of dignity and authority. 'Yes, I know. I am merely pondering.

'Britain must be brought into line for the sake of all, and the cohesion of the Union. If the doubters will not come to me, I will go to them.

'I will go by private jet. I will be able to see all three before the Summit. If necessary they can return with me.'

Jacques looked doubtful, and voiced his concern – 'If you fail, it will be a very public failure.'

'If I fail, it will be a very public failure whether I go or not. But there remains an opportunity to succeed, and while there does, I will not give it up!'

CHAPTER 34

The President's private jet touched down on the tarmac at Oslo on an unusually grey day.

It rolled to a half-stop on the runway, turned on to the taxi-way, and lumbered slowly to the apron.

A tractor scurried up with the steps as the whine of the engines died.

The door swung heavily open and Weurmann stood at the top of the steps with a smile ready.

The first thing he noticed was that there was no band, the second, no guard of honour, and the third, the grave faces of the two lone figures in dark suits at the bottom of the steps.

So this was his welcome to Norway now! This had never happened before – not to him. Before, whenever he had landed, it had been to the clash of cymbals and the clatter of the honour guard's salute, the red carpet, and the beaming heads of state.

Of course, before the Treaty of Berlin, the Council Presidency had rotated bi-annually, each member state taking it in turn. Then the President had been the head of government, or head of state, of the members.

Pomp enough in those days – in Maastricht, in Edinburgh, Copenhagen, Brussels or Dublin, in Madrid or Nice, Lisbon or Florence, or wherever.

As he made his way down the aircraft steps, all this rushed through his mind. How in the early days of the permanent Presidency, member states, still jealous of their former sovereignty and independence, would send foreign ministers or even officials to greet him on visits. Then as the powers of the Presidency increased and the balance shifted, the heads of state came personally to greet him, and bowed the head, if not the knee.

Now, as he returned the stiff handshakes of the two grim Norwegian diplomats at the foot of the steps, he felt the wheel – here at least – had turned full circle.

'The Prime Minister will see you this evening, sir,' said the senior of the two, rather bluntly.

'This evening!' the President exclaimed in spite of himself. 'I must be in Stockholm this evening, and Madrid tomorrow morning!' he said icily, drawing himself up.

Inwardly he thought, 'My God! Have I been so wrong, to be treated like this?'

He felt he didn't even much mind for himself, but for the Presidency itself, and all that great edifice of the United States of Europe, more than half a century in the making, now, at a blow, brought so low, at least in the eyes of one member.

As the limousine sped from the airport towards the city, there were no crowds, and only two out-riders. They even stopped at traffic lights, to the curious gaze of pedestrians on the crossings.

From time to time he was recognised, fingers were pointed, and surprised calls of recognition rose up – and then angry fists waved at him through the glass.

And he noticed another thing, ominous and defiant. He had been vaguely conscious of something else amiss at the airport, but only now as he approached the Parliament buildings did he realise what it was.

No Union flag flew anywhere – instead the blue and white and red of the old Norwegian flag flew, it seemed, on every building and every street corner, defying him he felt, defying all he had dreamed of, and worked for, and built.

Since the Nationalities Act had finally passed on a majority vote two years before, national flags of member states were no longer used, except on national holidays and for special celebrations, and only the Stars of Europe could be flown officially.

As he looked, he thought of those other United States, and of Old Glory, and then of that confederate flag raised in defiance of it a century and a half before, leaving that great Union riven in two, that flag a potent symbol still in the Old South.

Then, even more ominously, he thought of the likeness to it of Norway's blue, and white, and red.

And early next morning as he returned to the airport, it seemed as though there were twice as many, streaming stiffly in the wind.

His ears rang still from his meeting with the Norwegian Prime Minister, one of Europe's venerable elder statesmen, only hours before.

'We have been occupied by foreign powers throughout our history,' Weurmann had been told. 'And still within the memory of many of our old people, occupied by one of the worst oppressors the world has ever known....'

Weurmann felt again the old hurt, deep in his being, that all Germans of his generation knew. The weltschmerz which came of the barbarisms of that mean and pathetic figure his suffering nation had let grasp corrupting power. 'Will we never be allowed to forget?' he groaned to himself, as the Prime Minister went on.

'Britain succoured us in occupation, and helped liberate us from it. We shall never stand by to watch her subdued by force.

'Yes, we voted to veto her secession. Yes, we agreed to install an emergency government. And, yes, we recognised that a policing action would be needed in support.

'But, no, we will never countenance occupation against popular resistance.'

He laid an old hand on Weurmann's arm. 'We were wrong, my friend. We misjudged. We were misled – perhaps too eager for the fulfilment of our dream, of your dream. And so the dream fades, and the nightmare threatens.

'We supported the political union of Europe to end war – supporting war to sustain the Union negates its whole raison d'etre.

'We were wrong before, and you are wrong now. Go back, my friend, and say so, and pull us back from the brink!'

In Stockholm, too, next day, national flags were flown as defiantly as any confederate banner – and this time, crowds.

Crowds waiting at the airport on his arrival, and swelling all along his route through the city.

News of his whistle-stop visit to Norway had dominated the evening news, and his visit was anticipated.

This crowd was vocal and demonstrative. Fists were waved, flags were flourished, individual shouts and coordinated chants rang in his ears.

And now he was being told the same in Sweden – not in the eloquent tones and measured words of that wise old Norwegian he had always admired, but in the popular revulsion which the crowds in the capital made manifest.

Everywhere in the city were banners condemning the invasion, and reviling him personally – and yet even in that Weurmann saw a part-fulfilment of the ideal. Here were Swedes, daubing messages in English, to him a German.

' "Nation shall speak peace unto nation",' he thought – and then the doubts flooded in again, 'or are we indeed building a Tower of Babel, as the Prime Minister once said?'

The Swedish premier was just as resolute and determined as Weurmann's old friend in Norway.

Chin jutting below the lean face and the short blonde hair – yes, blonde still, for this was one of the new young bloods of Europe, almost the next generation even to Weurmann, one who had grown up with the European ideal – he confronted Weurmann with stolid opposition. For the scene unfolding across the sea was no more his ideal than it was his Norwegian counterpart's, 30 years his senior.

In vain the President pressed him to attend the summit. Even his personal assurance of safe conduct drew only the tight-lipped reply, 'I do not think it wise' – accompanied by a cynical wrinkling of the eyebrow.

So when he landed at Madrid in the early hours of the next day he expected little, and got less.

The short, balding Spaniard who sat across the table from him was uncompromising.

He demanded the immediate cessation of fighting, withdrawal of troops, and an undertaking to restore the status quo.

And then he told the President that Spain would make no further contribution to the Federal budget until these conditions were met, and would withdraw all Spanish delegations and officials involved in Federal affairs.

And finally, in a sonorous voice, he added – 'And I have to tell you, senor, that Norway and Sweden join Spain in these demands, and this action.'

'But I have just spoken with them!' exclaimed Weurmann, 'And they made no such demand or threat!'

'But I have spoken with them since, retorted the Spaniard.

It was a dejected Presidential party which alighted at Brussels in the late morning.

For all his stern injunctions to himself to maintain his presence, Weurmann's head hung low as he crossed the tarmac to the waiting cars, and he barely acknowledged the greeting of the staff there to welcome him.

'Bad trip?' quizzed his driver laconically, looking in the mirror – almost the only one of Weurmann's staff these days to talk to him as a man instead of a President.

'Bad trip, Hans,' he replied. 'Schrecklich! Schrecklich!' and he slumped back into the leather upholstery, and closed his eyes.

CHAPTER 35

Wardhope in his underground HQ received the messages within five minutes of each other.

One was an intelligence report that a flotilla of five frigates flying the Spanish ensign had detached themselves from the blockading force in the Channel, and moved out into the Western Approaches.

The other was a signal from a submarine patrolling in the North Sea, reporting a sighting of five warships lying fifty miles east of the Goodwin Sands – three Swedish and two Norwegian.

A little later that morning a further dispatch arrived via Gibraltar – now part of Spain, having been ceded by Britain in the Treaty of Berlin. But Britain still leased naval dockyard facilities, and the white ensign was seen there regularly.

The dispatch came from a Royal Marine helicopter assault ship, which had been exercising in the Mediterranean, and put in to Gib for some shore leave just before the paratroops dropped on London. There it had been interned by the Spanish while the captain wrestled with the dilemma over whose orders to follow, and held when he refused to obey UHQ.

But that morning two Spanish naval officers and a senior diplomat from the Foreign Ministry had appeared at the foot of the gangway and asked to come aboard.

Courteously ushered into the wardroom and given coffee, they nonetheless had to endure the captain's torrent of protest about the internment, before they were able to make clear the purpose of their visit.

'Captain,' the diplomat said calmly, when that gentleman paused to draw breath, 'we are not here about the internment, though I am happy to tell you that you will be free to leave port very shortly....'

'Very glad to hear it – never should have been held in the first place – I don't know how you have the temerity...' retorted the captain, getting into his stride again.

'Captain,' the diplomat interrupted, 'can you get a message to Mr. Wardhope in London?'

The captain stopped and looked from one to the other. 'A message to Mr. Wardhope? Well, yes, I suppose so.'

'This is top secret, Captain,' said one of the officers. 'Can it be sent securely?'

'Yes, it can, but what...?'

'Top secret, Captain. You will see the message – you and your operator only – but we cannot discuss it.'

Wardhope was nothing if not an optimist, and a determined fighter, but if he had not felt overwhelmed by the mighty power ranged against him, he had certainly felt beleaguered.

So the third important dispatch of the morning was as invigorating as it was unexpected.

For it announced, in slightly odd though still entirely comprehensible phrasing, that Spain, Norway, and Sweden, having protested to the President with no obvious effect, now wished to demonstrate solidarity with Britain by practical military support.

Each was already taking steps to withdraw forces from UHQ control, and deploy them in readiness to fulfil any supporting role the United Kingdom might request.

'Yesss!' shouted the usually undemonstrative Wardhope, punching the air. 'Weurmann won't go on with it now!'

He believed that the real significance of the offer lay not so much in the military dimension, as in the threat to the cohesion of the Union, before which he felt the President would give way.

The 'Spanish Dispatch' – for so it became known – asked for direct communications and military and political liaison to be set up.

Wardhope's great frustration had been that neither he, nor his staff, nor the Emergency Cabinet, could come and go, and so had had to conduct negotiations through third parties.

Physically they were prisoners of the Union, which now held Berkshire along with most of the southern counties. But the very fact that they were directing events from within enemy territory did add something to the grim satisfaction felt in the success of their operations.

But to now have allies on the outside – powerful politically and militarily - was good news indeed.

'It would be good news for the Prime Minister too,' Wardhope thought, and wondered as so many times before over these weeks, whether he would know anything of the grim events unfolding. Wondered if - hoped - he was a prisoner still. 'Surely to God they wouldn't kill him,' he thought. 'And for sure, I could do with his advice.'

Now, acting on the new developments, Wardhope quickly put in place arrangements for military attaches and special envoys to be sent to Oslo, Stockholm, and Madrid.

'Their surface ships will complement our submarine capability nicely,' observed the Chief of Staff. 'We've several subs out there, but only a couple of ships, whereas they have a very useful surface presence.'

'How would you use them?' Wardhope queried.

'To stop or at least harry Union troop-ships, to prevent further build-up of their forces.'

'We don't want to go in for sinking troop-ships, General,' said Wardhope, taken somewhat aback. 'Weurmann seems undecided whether to advance or retreat, and that might well goad him into action. It would also alienate public opinion in the Union.'

'You must of course make the political judgment, sir,' said the general, 'but from the military standpoint it's imperative we prevent further reinforcement. If we want to weaken the Union grip then sink 'em we must, if they come out of port. And we must sink them in port, too, if we can, to deny them the ships.'

Again he thought, 'If only the Prime Minister were here too, the burden would at least be shared - if we could only find him we might even get him out.'

Then turning his attention to the general again, he said, 'If Weurmann really is undecided, sending a thousand men to the bottom of the sea would soon make up his mind,' said Wardhope.

'But which way?' said the general.

'I meant it would spur him on,' replied Wardhope.

'It might make him leave off,' said the general. 'We gather he was very distressed when we blew the Tunnel.'

He wasn't alone,' grunted Wardhope, with a shudder.

'Of course, sir, but at any rate, he may feel the price is too high.'

This could be true, thought Wardhope. For all there had been a lull in the fighting and the advance, the influx of reinforcements had stepped up again. It could only be for a new push, and perhaps this was indeed the way to weaken Union resolve.

After all, considering Norway, Sweden, and Spain had come right over and were now openly allying with the UK, others must be wavering and wondering.

So the order went out to the submarines, and the request to the new allies, to attack all Union troop-ships and heavy transports.

The Spanish frigates steamed into the Channel from the Western Approaches, and the Scandinavian flotilla ghosted in and out of the North Sea fog banks to threaten the east coast ferry routes.

And beneath the waves, the Royal Navy slipped into the Straits of Dover to prey on the shipping there.

The first twenty-four hours made clear to each side what the other's strategy was going to be. The guessing and uncertainty were in the past. The lull was over.

A requisitioned ferry, carrying eight hundred men and their equipment, was sunk by the first torpedoes fired in earnest by a British Submarine since the Falklands War.

Less than a hundred men survived, as she went to the bottom within minutes.

The frigates pressed home attacks on other troop-laden ferries, before breaking off to engage Union warships steaming up the Channel to seek and destroy the marauding submarines.

Air power was added to the equation from the carrier groups in the Channel, and from land bases in France, Belgium, and the Netherlands, and on the other side from those RAF bases in Government hands.

At evening, an air-launched missile tore through the side of a Spanish warship, penetrated the magazine, and blew to smithereens the ship and all who sailed in her.

Wardhope received the flood of dispatches and intelligence reports with a grim demeanour, becoming quite distraught at the news of the troop-ship – even though it was the other side's – and the Spanish frigate.

' "The other side"!' he said to himself. 'I still can't think of them as "the enemy".'

Bryn Thomas sat across from him late that night. A strange affinity had sprung up between the two in the short time they'd been working together, in spite of their very different backgrounds and former loyalties, and the Welshman was becoming something of a confidant.

Wardhope passed the latest sheaf of dispatches across the desk, and watched the other's countenance take on the same grim aspect that he himself had worn all that day.

'This is bad, David, bad,' said Thomas.

'It's all-out war, Bryn,' said Wardhope. 'And that poor bugger at their mercy,' his thoughts turning to the Prime Minister again.

In Brussels Weurmann addressed the Council at the end of the second day. 'Gentlemen, we are at war. We face our one-time partners as enemies on three land fronts, on the sea, and in the air.'

Blow and counter-blow in the Channel had continued for forty-eight hours, and at the end of it, seven thousand men had perished.

Six troop-ships had been sunk, and three warships. How many planes had gone down wasn't clear, but several.

Added to that was a grim total of wounded, and a heavy toll of equipment.

'Further rifts are appearing between member states,' said the President, ' and there is now a real possibility of the collapse of all that we have worked for.

'It must not come to that – it shall not come to that! We must meet this threat with absolute resolve!

'We must crush the United Kingdom now, once and for all, before the others have time to mobilise fully. Then Spain and the others will have no cause to fight for.'

A visible shock wave ran round the room.

Many had expected this, but in the event, it still came as a shock.

Others had not believed that Weurmann would really go down this road.

But all perceived that a change had been wrought in him over these weeks – a change which boded ill for all opposed to him, and gave little comfort even to his supporters.

CHAPTER 36

The Chieftain of the Scottish Liberation Army mysteriously disappeared from the scene soon after McIan's meeting with the Union envoy. In spite of his great personal following, any opposition to his successor melted away when McIan announced that volunteers would be paid.

On the back of this pledge the new Chieftain - for McIan now assumed the role - launched a recruitment drive, paying a bounty to cell commanders for every recruit they brought in.

This was too good for extreme nationalists to think twice about, and with unemployment in Scotland above the national average, too good for many who were simply out of work to think twice about, whatever their political sympathies.

Tartan shirts, trews and Glengarrys began to appear on every street corner, in every public place, and every public meeting.

They were hardly challenged, even when they added Sam Brownes and long heavy clubs to their uniform.

It wasn't clear what their role was, and having no clear role, they pursued their long-standing bent for harassing English people.

The committed extremists began to revel in the open assertion of their nationalism, and those recruited from the ranks of the unemployed and the downtrodden began to revel in the assertion of themselves.

Harassing became beating, and beating became driving people out of their homes and burning their houses.

But the parallels with the Brownshirts and Blackshirts of the last century became too close and painful for the average Scot.

The more the SLA strengthened its grip and the worse its excesses, the more determined the country became that it wasn't going to allow this latter-day fascism to take hold on it.

With the political machine of the Scottish Liberation Party grinding relentlessly into gear and arrogating to itself many Government functions, the people began to rebel.

Vigilante groups sprang up around the country to combat the SLA menace, and before long, SLA 'soldiers' found it politic not to go out in groups of less than four. Some who did ended up hanging upside down from lampposts.

The vigilante groups began to coalesce, and finally came together as the League of St. Andrew, which was, in truth, a strange coalition of militant Christians, democratic nationalists, Englishmen touched by the growing campaign of terror and oppression, decent, honest, ordinary citizens with no stomach for what was being done in the name of Scotland, and the Rag, Tag, and Bobtail, of left-wing politics.

And as they became more organised, they won the backing of the Scottish Parliament, under siege behind the barricades at Holyrood.

Nonetheless the SLP, backed by their military wing, began to levy arbitrary and instant 'taxes' on the English in Scotland, and siphon off the revenue to fund their operations.

But this became self-defeating as more and more English people were driven out or fled. So the SLP widened the net and started trying to collect from every household – by force if necessary.

As the Scots have never been noted for their willingness to part with cash, Scot began to fight Scot, while the English clustered into tight enclaves – virtual ghettoes – for self-defence, but defended, too by Leaguers, as those in the League of St. Andrew became known.

Confrontation and even pitched battles ensued, and by and by the country split on east-west and north-south lines.

By and large, the SLA controlled the west and north, and the Leaguers the south and east.

Then the Second Declaration of Arbroath – declaring Scotland independent within Europe – coming on top of the levies, provoked sporadic violence on each side of the divide, as well as across it.

Population movements began across this front line, as English people tried to get into safe areas, and extreme nationalists fled north to escape the extreme wing of the League.

In Brussels, Weurmann was angry. Very angry.

'What have we achieved by all this?' he said hotly to the Union envoys on their return from Scotland. 'Almost nothing! We should have sent troops in there, too.'

'But Mr. President, they are at least now so involved with their internal politics and fighting that they do not have time to become involved elsewhere.'

'Perhaps, but we fight to keep the UK in the Union, and only dealt with Scotland separately because we thought we could keep one part at least in, or two with Northern Ireland. So what has become of this "independence in Europe" that was supposed to unite Scotland?'

'That was one party only, we know now – but before, we thought it was most Scots.'

'Why do we not work with that party, then?'

'They did not like the idea of being governed from Westminster, and originally did wish a partnership with the Union, but we have frightened them. They think if it does not work, the Union will send paratroops into Edinburgh, like into London.'

'But do they work with the Scottish Liberation Army?'

'No – with the League of St. Andrew...'

'Who go against separation?'

'Yes, the nationalists feel closer to the mainstream democratic parties, who were against us. So we were forced to work with the militant SLA, and the Scottish Liberation Party – but they have now declared "independence in Europe", so it seems we get there in the end.'

'But declared it with oppression and violence and ethnic cleansing! It seems Britain is to be the new Balkans,' said Weurmann despairingly. 'You think they live in harmony, because they live under a central government. But loosen the grip of that government and the country fragments. All that repressed nationalism, just waiting to erupt!

'This will be the future of the Union, too, if we do not press home our policy. If we loosen the grip of the centre now, it will all fragment.'

He turned away from the envoys and stared ruefully at the blank wall of the bunker where he now spent his days, as did Wardhope, in another bunker, not so very far away.

CHAPTER 37

In still another bunker, the Prime Minister woke to shouts and banging, and the rattle and crack of small arms fire.

He peered round in the dark. All hell had broken loose outside, but all seemed unchanged in the room – the chair, the table...

The shouts and crashing noises came closer and the firing intensified.

Now with a sense of anticipation, the adrenalin pumping, his heart racing, he pulled on his trousers and threw his sweater over his head.

He was still pushing his head through, when the door splintered in with a great crack and two figures smashed through the wreckage.

He backed instinctively against the wall, then somehow knew it was all right.

A powerful torch flashed in his face.

A voice behind it rapped out, 'Prime Minister!'

'Yes'.

'Come with us, sir! Move! Now!' and a hand grasped his elbow.

All three ducked through the shattered door, shying to one side or another to avoid the splintered wood.

They were in a corridor. Thirty metres ahead it opened out in a large hallway.

The flash of automatic weapons silhouetted black-suited figures at the end, firing out into the wider space of the hallway.

Answering fire illuminated the hallway, and again silhouetted the figures at their side of it, in a strobe-like effect.

Now the Prime Minister and his escort darted to the right midway along the corridor, and down four flights of stairs.

The Prime Minister assumed it was a fire exit, but the four flights puzzled him.

'So either this is the basement chamber of horrors, or ...what?' he mused.

And then a hand was pushing down on his head to protect it, and they were through a trap door and into a tunnel.

Two were behind them now, back along the tunnel – perhaps the two from the corridor, having covered their retreat, the Prime Minister thought.

He could just make them out, paused for a moment inside the trap-door, again silhouetted by flashes of fire beyond.

The trap-door slammed shut and the figures became invisible, but their running footsteps could be heard, gaining on them.

There were battering noises from the trap-door behind them.

Then the Prime Minister was hauled into a side chamber by his escort, and the two following flung themselves in, too.

Seconds later there came a tremendous roar, shockwaves from a blast behind them distorting their features for a few split seconds in the flash which lit the tunnel.

'Good one!' murmured one of the new pair. 'That should cork it up good and tight!'

'Where are we?' asked the Prime Minister, for the first time feeling he had breath to spare.

'Old communication and supply tunnel, sir. Been out of commission for years. We don't reckon they knew about it, or if they did, believed it was unusable.'

'What was that place?'

'An old regional command centre, sir.'

'Whereabouts?'

'Norfolk.'

The section leader interrupted. 'You'll be briefed shortly, sir. Dust's settled. Two and three, move out ahead! Four – with the Prime Minister! I'll take the rear.'

They turned into the tunnel once more, and moved off at a run.

'I'm too old for all this excitement,' gasped the Prime Minister, as he was pushed along at the double, bent low in the dripping tunnel.

'You'll do, sir,' hissed back the granite-faced soldier who grasped him by the elbow and propelled him towards the dim light in the distance.

'Not an oncoming express, I trust,' said the Prime Minister, breathless again, gesturing towards it.

'Blimey!' exclaimed the soldier. 'You'll do all right! Banged up there on your own for weeks, not knowing what the heck's going on, getting busted out in the middle of the night with all hell let loose around you, and you can still joke! You'll do, sir! You get my vote next time! The bastards!'

'Thank...you...very much. I suppose...I've already been hit...by my express train. Thoroughly derailed....' The Prime Minister gasped.

'But we're getting you back on the track now, sir, eh?' grinned the soldier, showing white teeth in the black-daubed face. 'Save your breath, though, sir. Keep going. We're not clear yet.'

The three other soldiers in the group kept pace with them – two in front, one in the rear, through the endless tunnel, towards the faint gleam ahead.

'Where am I going?' the Prime Minister asked.

'Dunno, sir. We hand you over at the tunnel exit.'

It was a long tunnel, but the end came.

At the end, it surfaced in a nondescript concrete blockhouse – one of many, apparently identical, partly sunk in the sand, on the edge of a beach which swept away to right and left, as far as the eye could see.

In the blockhouse was a naval commander, and a soldier dressed like the Prime Minister's rescuers, and like them, wearing no insignia.

'Good morning, sir,' the soldier greeted the Prime Minister, then to the men, 'Well done, chaps!'

'We say "goodbye" here, sir,' he said, turning back to the Prime Minister. 'The Navy's looking after you now.'

'Good luck, sir,' said his escort. 'You show 'em!'

'Many thanks – we'll meet again, I promise.'

'Right, sir. Got to get going,' said the naval commander, looking anxiously at his watch. 'We're going for a boat trip, and the tide's turned.'

'Wait a moment - surely someone can brief me now?' said the Prime Minister.

'We have a sub lying off, sir,' replied the commander. 'You'll be fully briefed there, and we have a doc on board to give you the once-over, but we must get moving. Put these on, please.'

'One thing – Lynda Stalker – is she with Edwards?'

'Appears to be, sir. The papers are saying she's involved with him personally.'

The Prime Minister visibly slumped at this response, and his heart sank within him. It had been the thought of her more than anything which had enabled him to get through the dark days of his captivity. That, the searing jealousy he felt over her liaison with the President, and a determination that Weurmann would never succeed on that front.

The commander, handing him a thick sweater and trousers, had to cajole him roughly to put them on. Then he held out a dry-suit and helped the Prime Minister struggle into it, finally pulling a lifejacket over his head.

'Ready for the off, then, sir? This way.'

And the commander, now also in dry-suit and lifejacket, laid a gentle but firm hand on the Prime Minister's arm, and padded off down the Norfolk beach, beyond which the first gleams of morning cast pale reflections on a darkly moving sea.

The Prime Minister looked shoreward from the inflatable dinghy which had been waiting at the water's edge, and saw in the faint glimmer of the early dawn many men, beginning to move out of defensive positions in the dunes around the blockhouse.

He could dimly make out his four rescuers and the unit commander, looking after him as the boat moved swiftly away from the shore.

Turning to seaward, he was in time to see the waiting submarine surface – first periscope and snort mast, then conning tower with markings blacked out, and finally the curving bulk of the hull, breaking the surface like some great leviathan.

He was free, but his fight was just beginning, and now he must fight it with a great empty place inside.

CHAPTER 38

Deep beneath the waves the submarine ran silently up the North Sea, then west at Duncansby Head and John O' Groats, and through the Pentland Firth.

Round Cape Wrath she threaded her undersea course, then south again to the great sea lochs of the Scottish coast.

The Prime Minister slept sound in his cabin through the constant hum of the engines and the electronic singing of a hundred instruments.

It was a dreamless sleep, a sleep removed from the near edge of fear which had shadowed him each night of his captivity, bringing troubled dreams, and little relief from the harsh reality of his days.

In the early hours of that same day, when he had first clambered on to the broad back of the submarine from the inflatable dinghy which had brought him from shore, he had felt himself slipping into a half-conscious state.

For weeks now, he realised, he'd kept going on nervous energy, taut with dread uncertainty. That and the vision of Lynda.

The news of her defection, and the release of the fear and tension of captivity that rushed in now that he was with his own side, behind his own lines, among friends once more, dissipated that sustaining energy, and he'd all but slumped into the strong arms of the sailors who helped him below.

He was half-dragged, half-carried, through the cramped gangway to the sick-bay, where a young surgeon-lieutenant bent over him anxiously. But the doctor didn't take long to reach the conclusion that there was little wrong with him that rest and sleep would not put right.

As he held out a draught to help sleep on its way, murmuring a few reassuring words to his patient, the Prime Minister, half-insensate though he was, reached up and pushed his arm away.

'Wait!' he said in a commanding tone. The doctor paused.

Then more weakly the Prime Minister said, 'I want to know where we're going.'

The commanding officer, who had been hovering in the doorway of the sick-bay, took a step forward, looking inquiringly at the surgeon-lieutenant, who nodded.

'I'm Commander Briggs, sir, in command,' he said to the Prime Minister in a quiet, steady, voice. 'We're heading for the west coast of Scotland, going north about – round the top of Scotland.'

He turned to the doctor. 'Clear the sick-bay, please, Simon,' and as the doctor ushered the last orderly out, stepped out himself, and closed the door, the captain bent close to the Prime Minister.

'I'm sailing under sealed orders direct from the Ministry of Defence, sir.'

'The Ministry of Defence?'

'It's a long story, sir, better told when you've rested. I have a full briefing for you. My orders are to be opened then.'

'Open them now, Commander. I want to know where we're going.'

The Commander gave him a long look, then drew from his pocket a sealed envelope. As he tore it open, he said with a quick smile, 'Even in this electronic age, the old ways are sometimes the best. I've been carrying this inside my guernsey for forty-eight hours, and I don't mind saying I'm glad to be rid of it – it has rather jaggy corners.'

He glanced over it, then with a surprised but serious look, said, 'We're taking you to see the King.'

'The King?'

'Yes. sir.'

'The King! God bless him!' said the Prime Minister almost drunkenly, lowering himself back on to his bunk from the elbow he had propped himself up on, his eyelids flickering and closing, and his head lolling to the side.

Commander Briggs opened the door, revealing the young surgeon-lieutenant waiting in the gangway, still holding the sleeping draught.

'I don't think he's going to need that,' the captain said, with a backward nod at the inert form behind him.

Tinned tomatoes had never tasted so good as they did that first breakfast aboard the submarine. Flanked by two eggs, crisp bacon, and fried bread, he positively relished them.

He'd slept through the whole of that first day, not without one or two brief but anxious examinations by the doctor. But in the early hours of the next day he awoke refreshed, alert, very thirsty, and ravenously hungry.

When he called for a second plateful, asking if there was by any chance black pudding to go with it, the doctor felt he could dispense with a further medical examination.

However, when breakfast was finally over, the doc did an examination as a formality, and finally released his charge from the sick-bay to the custody of the wardroom, and shortly after, to the privacy of the captain's cabin, where Commander Briggs set about the briefing.

He listened intently as the tale unfolded – the incarceration of the Cabinet, Neville Edwards' role, his speech to the nation, Wardhope's escape, the paratroop landings, the confusion amongst UK forces, the military actions around the country, the battle of the Tunnel and the strike on Brussels, the attempts to disaffect Scotland and hand over Northern Ireland, and the spectre of civil war there, the schism in the Union and the new alliances, and the dread cost of the naval actions in the Channel.

A black tale indeed – as black a tale as could be told.

As the Prime Minister listened, first his eyes flashed with anger, and occasionally started with surprise, then as he thought of Edwards' treachery he became furious, then gloomy in contemplation of the support he'd nevertheless managed to attract. And then as he listened to the catalogue of war, he became anguished and despondent.

'My God! Has it come to this?' he muttered to himself. 'And I myself have brought all this on the country! Have I been so wrong?'

Then more audibly, looking at the captain as if for answer, 'It's not worth this! I wanted us out, yes. I wanted Britain to be British – but in partnership with the rest of Europe, not at war!'

'Sir, the people are with you,' said the captain emphatically. 'They voted for you in millions.'

'But now they're fighting and dying in their own country – and fighting and killing each other, too!' said the Prime Minister.

'Sir, I'm a sailor, and I don't take much to do with politics, but you can't be wrong! You put your view of the case to the people, and the people's answer was to send you to No.10.

'Now we're witnessing a demonstration of what you and others have been warning us of all along. The federalists always intended political union. But even they conceived it would be a Union of more or less willing partners.

'Now they've created a monster, and the monster will consume us – consume them as well – unless someone takes a stand.

'That's what you've done – what the country has done – taken a stand'

'Thank you, Commander,' said the Prime Minister, raising himself from his dejected posture. 'Certainly if ever there's a time to take a stand, it's when the enemy is seeking to destroy you whether you stand or whether you submit.'

And Lynda's voice floated into his consciousness – the trite but pregnant phrase it carried in the sitting room in Downing Street that morning after the election, taking on even more significance now – 'This is it'.

'This is it,' he reaffirmed to himself, and despite all, vowed not to give up the fight.

But was she really on the other side now? A gut-churning thought struck him. Had she given more than her body to Weurmann that night in the chateau? Or worse still, had she given herself to Edwards? It all stacked up against her on any objective view – but yet he was loath to believe it of her.

There was a tap at the cabin door, and the first lieutenant pushed his head round it. 'One hour to the rendezvous, sir.'

'Thank you No.1,' said the Captain. 'We're finished here. I'll join you in the ops room shortly.'

CHAPTER 39

'You've what...?' roared Neville Edwards down the telephone which had woken him from sleep in the early hours. 'You've lost the Prime Minister...?'

The room reverberated to his angry, incredulous expostulations.

'What the hell are you talking about, man...? What the hell have you done? You mean he's dead...?

'Well that's something – not dead, just gone! Tell me, then! Tell me!'

At the other end of the line, the Prime Minister's chief jailer vainly tried to convey the story of the Prime Minister's rescue, but made little headway against the tide of vituperation and invective from Edwards.

Finally demanding a detailed written report, and that in the next hour, he slammed the phone down.

Propped on one elbow, he stared fixedly at nothing in particular for fully five minutes.

Then wearily he hauled back the bedcovers, and swung his feet to the floor.

The call had come in the wake of the explosion in the tunnel in faraway Norfolk, when the guard detachment realised they'd lost their chance to recapture the bird who'd flown.

And so Neville Edwards was abed and asleep.

The kimono he'd thrown about him rustled fussily against the black silk pyjamas, as he made his way into the kitchen, mechanically switching on lights as he went.

Staff made a bleary-eyed appearance, in response to calls from the private secretary who'd first taken the message at Downing Street.

In the pantry of the flat atop No. 10, he made himself a mug of instant coffee, and tipped into it a large measure from a bottle of cooking brandy on the shelf.

He drank this down, then without bothering to rinse it, refilled the mug, this time only to the half-way mark, but with brandy alone.

This, too, he drank down, then moved off unsteadily in the direction of his private office.

Ignoring the bustle outside, he went in and shut the door.

Picking up the telephone, he pressed the key code which would connect him on a direct, secure line to President Weurmann in Brussels.

'Mr. President – Matthias – you may already have heard – the Prime Minister was seized from us an hour or so ago in a special forces operation.'

Stunned silence at the other end told him the President hadn't already heard. Then came the flood of questions and the rising anger, with which he in his turn had accosted the captor-in-chief, and to which he could only mumble replies.

'...we don't know where he is...no, nor who's got him, in point of fact...we've rather assumed it's his own side, but I suppose it could be a third party...'

There followed a long, rapid-fire monologue from the other end, in the course of which Edwards once or twice whitened, and quailed visibly,

'Yes, I realise that,' he said finally. 'It does muddy things...well, yes, I suppose so...puts the captain back on the bridge, yes...but....'

Here he was cut off, and stood for a moment, looking blankly at the telephone receiver.

There was a scrabbling in the dark outside his window. It turned out to be pigeons, but a shudder shook him. He called out impatiently, in a voice in which he failed to disguise a note of panic, to the bodyguards he knew would be outside the door, in sudden need of the reassurance of their physical presence.

In the President's suite in Brussels there was much to-ing and fro-ing of aides and advisers, and as the sun rose, a tense round-table conference was under way, and recriminations were flying.

'We were hopelessly deceived in Edwards,' the Foreign Minister was saying.

'With respect,' said the UK Commissioner, 'it's not in fact his fault that the Prime Minister has escaped. That's an operational matter...'

'Operational be damned!' said the Foreign Minister, his voice rising angrily. 'You try to excuse him because you stand or fall together - you recommended Edwards in the first place!'

The Commissioner rose in his place, knuckles white as he grasped the edge of the table and leaned forward threateningly – 'I resent that! Withdraw that remark!'

'Or you'll what?' sneered the Foreign Minister.

'I was asked by the Council to prepare a short-list of possible pro-Union candidates. The Council committee chaired by you deliberated at length on the three names I put forward, as you well know!'

'Yes, but we deliberated on your brief, and that put Edwards forward as clear favourite.'

'So it's my fault that the Prime Minister...?'

'Gentlemen! Gentlemen!' the President interjected. 'We will resolve nothing this way! Nevertheless it has been clear almost from the outset that Edwards was at best an unfortunate choice. The question is, what do we do about it? The British people are against us for the most part, and the armed forces likewise.

'Our ground troops have suffered one heavy defeat, and are facing local reverses around the UK every day, and we are taking heavy losses in the Channel since the intervention of Norway, Sweden, and Spain.

'Scotland and Ireland seem to be pursuing their own agendas....'

'But that does weaken England's position,' the Foreign Minister interposed.

'But does not strengthen the Union's,' retorted the President. 'It is in fact another instance of the fragmentation that is currently threatening its whole structure – Norway, Sweden, Spain, rumblings from others, and now Scotland and Ireland, unshackled after hundreds of years, go their own way.

'Perhaps it is not surprising – having cast off one yoke, they are reluctant to come under another. But that is not as we planned it, or as we were advised,' and here he looked directly at the two men opposite, who could not meet his gaze.

'And then we have the King – no surprise perhaps that he should oppose us in principle – but that he should step into the political arena was again something entirely unforeseen.'

'How could it be foreseen?' muttered the Commissioner blankly.

'There's never been any real interference from the monarch for a century past.'

'And now we have the Prime Minister free, who knows what may ensue,' said Weurmann, ignoring him.

'It is a potent mixture – the King, the Prime Minister, and popular resistance. We must act immediately before it explodes in our faces, and we must act with a fist of iron to achieve a victory before the whole Union comes down about our ears.

'Norway, Spain, and the rest will fall into line when Britain is brought back under Federal control.'

But if truth were told, this was said more in hope than expectation, with the memory of his whistle-stop tour fresh in Weurmann's mind.

And now these three dissenters were throwing in their lot with the UK – if it could still be called the 'UK', becoming fast disunited as it was.

This could indeed be the end for the Union if he did not show resolve, Weurmann told himself. The clock could be turned back not fifty years, but 250 years, when Europe was a continent of warring nation states, characterised by an ever-changing series of alliances, constantly changing partners in a grotesque and bloody game of international musical chairs.

And now reports began to come in of events surrounding the Prime Minister's escape, giving rise to fresh concern among the President and his aides.

One sketchy report suggested the Prime Minister had been taken off by submarine.

Certainly there had been much activity on a usually deserted Norfolk beach only two or three miles from his prison, and a submarine had surfaced briefly.

'See!' Weurmann exclaimed. 'They are running through our defences in areas we are supposed to control!

'Whatever they were doing there, Prime Minister or not, they have a submarine operational in coastal waters,' he said accusingly to a naval staff officer.

'We cannot be certain nothing will slip through our blockade on a 2000-mile coastline,' the officer protested, 'especially a submarine.'

'If it can slip through your blockade, it can also blow a hole through it. If it blows a hole through it in the right places, the Royal Navy will be back on the high seas,' said the President. 'And what then? No Tunnel, no control of the sea, no control of the air. It will become a war of attrition, and the British have proved themselves at that before.

'Our only course is to smash resistance now. Now, before it is too late. The British are still reeling, scattered, confused, but they are re-grouping.

'We have only a brief time before they do. When they are re-grouped, victory will only be bought at great cost.'

'And then,' he said ominously, 'there are the Tridents. Where are the Tridents, Admiral? Do we know that, yet?'

'Yes and no, sir. One has just come over to us – Captain Easson in command....'

'Well, that is something,' said the President.

'...but we do not know where the other is, and we do not know if they know what is happening.'

'Well of course they know what is happening! Otherwise they would be talking to us!

'After all, they're meant to be under Union command. The other Trident must be on their side, or sitting on the fence – but wherever it is, it is on the loose and a serious menace.

'I never thought I'd say it, but thank God for Jacques Chirac and his nuclear policy– otherwise we would be facing nuclear blackmail, and no answer to it.'

'God forbid!' said the UK Commissioner involuntarily.

'God forbid, indeed!' echoed the President.

But one person in the Union camp was very happy that day – Lynda Stalker had seen the formal report of the Prime Minister's escape as it came in later that morning, and had had difficulty in containing her delight.

For hers was the glory, having provided the intelligence for the special forces, hard won at some risk to her cover, but pulled off successfully in the end.

CHAPTER 40

The captain stepped back from the periscope and turned to the Prime Minister . 'Want a look, sir?'

The Prime Minister grasped the handles of the periscope, and stooped slightly to peer through the eyepieces.

A wonderful panorama of sea and sky and mountains was spread before him.

He stepped back with a little sharp intake of breath. It was wonderful, but almost too much – too much space, too distant a horizon, too much freedom.

For weeks – how long was it? – his whole existence had been bounded by four walls, a table, a chair, and a bed.

Even since his release he had been in the tunnel, in the blockhouse, in a small rubber boat in the dark, and in the cramped confines of the submarine sick bay, then a tiny cabin.

But now he bent forward again, this time eager, and finally exultant, like a child vouchsafed a glimpse of fairyland.

Limitless sky above, limitless sea beyond, and between, the grandeur of range upon range of rocky peaks, here plunging steeply into some long sea loch, there sweeping down to a low shore, and inland marching away to the horizon, in lines of ever-deeper shadow, whilst the clouds rose above them in banks, then marched off to form great streets in the sky.

He drank all this in with a greedy gaze, swinging the 'scope round 360 degrees.

'Magical!' he breathed to the captain, still at his shoulder.

'Indeed, sir,' said the captain, divining something of his feelings, and then, after a pause, 'but do you see the yacht?'

'The yacht?' the Prime Minister straightened to look at him questioningly, then bent to the periscope again.

And there it was. Surprising he hadn't noticed it before, he thought. He'd been so awestruck at his first glimpse of the outside world that his eyes had gone straight to the horizon.

Now he saw the small ketch quite clearly, some three or four miles off, and with the flick of a switch, indicated by Commander Briggs, he zoomed in on it.

It was sailing steadily, and so probably had not seen their periscope. He could see the helmsman, and another figure standing in the companionway, elbows braced either side of the hatch, scanning the sea with binoculars.

'Is that it, then?' asked the Prime Minister.

'We think so, sir,' then to the radio operator, 'Give them a call now.'

'Aye, aye, sir. Flying Fox, Flying Fox, this is Yellow Welly.'

'Yellow Welly, this is Flying Fox, good to hear from you, channel eight, over.'

'Flying Fox, this is Yellow Welly. Have you been fishing? Over.'

'Yellow Welly, this is Flying Fox. We've been fishing, and we've caught a whopper, over.'

'Yes, that's our man,' hissed Briggs with satisfaction.

'Tell him to heave to until we join him.'

The radio operator relayed this, as the captain turned again to the Prime Minister. 'The drill is that you go aboard the Flying Fox for your meet, sir. We'll stand by submerged to await your further instructions as per our special orders.'

' "Once more unto the breach...." then, Commander. I must say, it's good to be back in action. It's been grim knowing that God knows what-all was going on around me, and unable to do a thing about any of it,' he said, as the captain escorted him back to his cabin to rig himself out for another wave-tossed transfer by small boat.

A few minutes later he was again in the inflatable, powering over the white crests for the last 200 metres to the rendezvous.

The figure with the binoculars braced in the companionway of the yacht loomed larger, and presently the features resolved into the instantly recognisable physiognomy of the King.

In a minute or two more he was stretching out his hand to help the Prime Minister up the boarding ladder and over the guardrail, and then wringing his hand with unusual warmth.

'Your Majesty...' said the Prime Minister with a breathless smile.

'I gather you've been through it over the last few weeks, Prime Minister. I'm heartily glad to see you at liberty, and indeed looking as fit as ever.'

'If I ever was, sir,' said the Prime Minister, still out of breath.

'And now,' said the King, 'if it's not too presumptuous of a "constitutional monarch", we must put our heads together and decide what's to be done. I've only presumed because you were incommunicado – or worse, for aught we knew – and a "prince amang the heather" seemed a useful insurance for Mr. Wardhope, in case they managed to shut him down. But now I'm rather involved, and would like to see it through.'

'Absolutely delighted to have you involved, sir. It sends a very clear message about who's who and what's what in this whole debacle.'

'Well, hopefully. My feeling is, if the Sovereign's not for sovereignty, then who is? But I know the people are with us for the most part, as my gut feeling has always told me – and the election made it manifestly obvious.'

As the ketch hove to, riding the foam crests whipped up by a stiff breeze funneling down the sea lochs, Rory waved a welcome from behind the wheel in response to the King's shouted introductions.

Then the King and the Prime Minister went below to the saloon. Two armed sailors stayed aboard the yacht as the inflatable skimmed back to the submarine, which was again in the deeps below, twenty minutes after first surfacing.

At the same time, the Flying Fox got under way again to give the outward impression of any other cruising yacht on any ordinary cruise.

Inspector Johnson was in the galley juggling a whistling kettle, six mugs, and a packet of chocolate digestives. And soon the only interruption to the flow of grim-faced and serious talk around the maps and charts spread on the saloon table, was the rustling of the biscuit packet.

An hour went by and the Inspector relieved Rory at the wheel. Then Rory relieved the Inspector, and again the Inspector relieved Rory.

At the end of that stint, the King and the Prime Minister emerged into the cockpit, eyes bright and smiles playing about their lips, but serious and focussed, too.

Rory looked at them, questioning. 'What've you come up with?'

'A very bold stroke indeed,' said the Prime Minister, 'if we can pull it off. You would have to go back to 1743 and the Battle of Dettingen to find a British monarch giving such a lead – that was the last time the King led his army into battle.'

'Good luck to you, then, sir. I wish you well, and am glad to have been of some assistance.'

'You don't get out of it that easily, Rory, I'm afraid!' laughed the King. 'Your country needs you – and the Flying Fox!'

Meanwhile the Prime Minister had stood aside to have a word with the two sailors, who after a surprised pause, pocketed the sealed envelopes the Prime Minister passed to them, and muttered into their radios.

Within minutes the submarine broke the surface, the inflatable came back alongside, the sailors dropped down into it, and with a smart salute, cast off, leaving the King, the Prime Minister, Rory, and the Inspector, aboard the Flying Fox.

CHAPTER 41

The Prime Minister had been impressed with the boldness of the stroke he had proposed in the heaving saloon of the Flying Fox, of going in person to the emergency Summit in Brussels and bearding the lion in his den. But he had been totally unprepared for the King's response.

Although enthusiastic about his own idea, the Prime Minister became immersed in problems about the timescale, secrecy, security, proper briefing, and so on, when the King suddenly interrupted the litany of difficulties.

'I've got it!' he said. 'By George, I've got it!'

The Prime Minister looked up.

'We just go! Now! In the Flying Fox!'

'But....' Said the Prime Minister.

'No, don't you see? It's perfect! They don't know where you are. They don't know where I am. We just drop in, like good fairies on wires in the panto. With no escort we arouse no suspicion. No one will give us a second glance!'

'But I hadn't thought of you going, sir. It's risky. You could end up as a hostage.'

'So could you.'

'Yes, but there are others who can take over from me.'

'And there are others who can take over from me!'

'But we need briefing.'

'What for, dammit? The situation is as plain as day. What's been done needs to be undone, and what's been undone needs to be done up again.'

'But the Flying Fox...'

'Rory will consider it an honour – won't you Rory?' the King fairly hollered up the companionway.

Rory smiled over the top of his storm collar as the rain from a squall shower dripped from his visor, and gave a cheery wave – having heard not a word.

'There you are!' said the King. 'Told you so!'

The Prime Minister smiled. The boldness of the stroke – mad and Quixotic though it might seem – appealed, and grew on him.

It suited his mood. From the time of his release, fear had gradually been replaced by anger, and after overcoming his initial exhaustion, he had been seized by an aggressive urge to get right into the thick of it and punch a few noses, metaphorically at least.

'We don't even have to touch port!' enthused the King. 'Rory's had the yacht stuffed to the gunwales with supplies anyway, in case we had to fly the coop at short notice.'

'All right, I'll go for it!' said the Prime Minister decisively, with a boyish grin.

The sea had been his great love from childhood. He'd lived in a seaside town and grown up with boats – rowing boats, fishing boats, sailing boats. He still remembered the thrill the first time he'd watched the sea bottom fall away below the clear water, as they pulled from shore in a row across the bay with his father – the feeling of inhabiting their own world, masters of their own fate, depending on no one, free agents.

So he knew about boats, which was as well, for the sea on that journey paid no heed to the importance of personages.

They drafted a few quick dispatches, to Commander Briggs, to Wardhope, and a personal one, which the Prime Minister penned with a lump in his throat.

Lynda, the thought and vision which had sustained him in captivity, must sustain him a little longer. He couldn't believe she had really decamped to Edwards' faction. He must keep faith in her, keep faith with her, and if she had kept faith too, then when they were together again, if she was willing, it would be for good.

Then they sealed them up, and handed them to the sailors standing by to return to the sub.

They did put ashore briefly, to raid Rory's sea chest and his wardrobe, and allow the surprised but excited Rory to collect himself.

The Inspector briefly argued the wisdom of the plan, but as quickly realised argument was futile, and started eating seasick pills from a little bottle produced by Rory.

He was wise in that, as he too was to find that the sea is no respecter of persons.

All down the west coast, running outside the islands to miss the inshore traffic, the wind blew harder and the seas grew lumpier. The only saving grace was that the wind was in the north-west, and so they were reaching, or running before it.

With a deep-reefed mainsail and storm jib they were surfing along at eight and nine knots.

In the Irish Sea, Rory reduced sail again, setting a trysail in place of the main.

Now the wind backed into the west, and as they passed out into the open Atlantic again, the ocean swell, on a fetch all the way from the Bahamas, began to hoist them to the sky, then take them down into troughs so deep only the top of their mainmast remained visible, while the yacht gyrated wildly in the seas built up by the winds of the past forty-eight hours.

For a time they considered running for port, and in other circumstances would have done so – but they could not take the risk.

So they toughed it out, though the Inspector's toughness owed more to the seasick pills than the development of sea legs. For twelve hours at the height of the gale they hove to, and for the next six ran under bare poles, with no sails set, and still made six knots.

And when Rory did spread his canvas again, albeit just a couple of scraps at first, they fairly raced up the Channel.

Earlier, as the yacht was slipping through the North Channel between Scotland and Ireland, in Wardhope's subterranean bunker the Acting Prime Minister was dumbfounded.

'They've done what?' he mouthed in an amazed whisper, as an officer read him a dispatch just arrived from Commander Briggs. 'Why, in God's name?'

'He doesn't say why, sir. Indeed, I gather he doesn't know why. He was simply told the Prime Minister wouldn't be coming back aboard, as he was going for a sail with the King, and that Commander Briggs should contact us for further orders.

'He did shadow them for a little, but all he can really tell us is that after going ashore briefly, they headed out into the Minch – oh, and they struck the red ensign and flew a Scottish Saltire in its place.'

'A Saltire? The blue and white St. Andrew's Cross?'

'Yes, sir.'

'But that's what Edwards' – or rather the Union's – Scottish stooges are using.'

'That's right, sir. Very strange. But as I said, another signal Cabinet-coded for you in person, followed this. Perhaps that will shed some more light,' and he handed the other dispatch to Wardhope, who immediately made for his office.

Five minutes later he emerged, still with a bemused look on his face.

'Any clearer, sir?' asked the signals officer.

'Not a jot!'

Then he turned to an aide.

'Get the Emergency Cabinet rounded up. We need to have a serious chat.'

A little after, ministers one by one made their way through the warren of tunnels to the stark, utilitarian, Emergency Cabinet room Wardhope had had set up in a storeroom – six desks pushed together with three army blankets for a tablecloth, and slatted wooden folding chairs to sit on.

'I've heard from the Prime Minister,' Wardhope began.

All were agog at this news, although they'd known that moves were afoot to locate him.

'Is he out, then?' queried Bryn Thomas, rippling a bushy eyebrow.

'Is he OK?'

'Where is he?'

'How did they get to him?'

The questions fairly flew from the others round the table.

Wardhope held up a hand. 'He was freed two nights ago, but for obvious reasons we've kept it on a strictly 'need to know' basis. But you need to know now, because I don't know what's going on, and we need to be ready for anything.'

He recapped Lynda Stalker's role, and the intelligence breakthrough that had led to the discovery of the Prime Minister's whereabouts, the special forces raid, the escape by submarine, and the rendezvous with the King.

'Thus far it's all gone according to plan – then this!' and he flung on to the coarse brown fibre of the army blanket a transcript of the Prime Minister's dispatch.

Bryn Thomas picked it up, scanned it briefly, and began to read it aloud.

' "Dear David, I am so glad to hear you have stayed out of their clutches – that's more than I managed, as you know.

"The way in which you have grabbed the reins and tried to keep the Government in the driving seat is no more than I would have expected of you – but amazing nonetheless. We could not have a better man for the job.

"My personal thanks, too, for engineering my rescue. I seem to have survived intact in mind and body.

"As you are aware, I have had a meeting with you-know-who. We have decided on a plan – which means I will not be coming in, as I had previously decided to do if it were possible.

"You will know immediately if it comes to fruition, and that within a few days. If it succeeds, it should have a major impact on the situation.

"If it does not, you must carry on the fight alone."

Bryn Thomas slowly folded the dispatch again. There was silence, which Bryn finally broke, saying, 'Dramatic – and a bit cryptic.'

'More than cryptic,' sighed Wardhope. 'We expected him to link up with the King, and either establish himself there, or make his way in here. Now we don't know where we stand. Ideas?'

'I don't see that we can do other than carry on the defence, and counter-attack where possible,' said the Home Office Minister.

'We have to continue as we have been,' said Keith Spencer. 'Then if the Prime Minister pulls his stroke successfully – whatever it is – we can review it again.'

'Indeed. I don't see that we can do more,' said Wardhope, 'but I wanted you all to be in the picture.'

'One thing's for sure, sir,' said the Chief of Staff, who now sat in on all Emergency Cabinet meetings, crucially concerned as he was in implementing most of their decisions, 'if they're still at sea they have more than Mr. Edwards and the Union forces to worry about. Conditions are atrocious. They'll run for shelter if they've any common sense.'

But aboard the Flying Fox, common sense told them the angry sea was more their friend than the enemy ashore, and so they persevered. They would be less easily spotted, and less likely to provoke interest in these conditions.

They needed this cover as the Dover Straits narrowed in front of them, and opened again behind on the evening of the fifth day - and that night as dusk fell, they raised the light at the mouth of the Schelde.

No one bothered with them, amazingly, as they buoy-hopped up the estuary, tracing channels between sandbanks where they could to escape notice by pilot and customs boats, and for safety's sake, just to stay clear of the relentless procession of huge vessels which made up the lifeblood of this great artery of commerce, flowing into the heart of Europe.

For the thirty miles of the Westerchelde to the Belgian border their luck held. They dared not trust it further.

Rory dropped anchor in a small inlet two or three miles downstream from the border on the Dutch side.

They made their way on foot over the border to the nearest village – not without difficulty adjusting to being on dry land, after so long upon a violent sea.

A taxi took them to Antwerp and a train to Brussels.

They could hardly believe how easy it was. The Prime Minister kept thinking of the comedian he'd found so funny as a boy, Tommy Cooper, and his famous catch-phrase - 'Jus' like that!'

And for now he was thankful for Europe's open borders, though he was so opposed to them for the UK.

Once, in Antwerp, they were almost recognised, but escaped by making a great joke of it, and laughing heartily with a still-suspicious ticket inspector, who joined in the merriment nonetheless.

From there was easy – just the train and another taxi ride. And not until they stepped from the taxi at the Summit, into a throng of the world's media, did their masquerade as ordinary travellers come to an end.

CHAPTER 42

As the President rose to reply to the widely divergent points from the floor of the Brussels Summit, to which he had listened for almost two hours with increasing frustration, there was a stir in the lobby leading to the Council chamber.

The President paused, and glanced aside. From the lobby a small crowd emerged – ushers and security guards trying to block access to the room, but obviously unwilling to use physical force, TV cameramen walking backwards at the edge of the throng, reporters thrusting tape recorders towards its centre.

And from the crowd emerged – the King, and a pace or two behind him, the Prime Minister.

Gasps ran round the room.

The President stepped back involuntarily in astonishment.

Delegates rose in their places and called out.

The President's glance flitted round the room. More were on their feet. He caught the tone of the shouts – greetings, encouragement, support.

Other delegates sat with heads hanging, sheepish almost - feeling, perhaps, that their part hadn't been an honourable one, or had been a mistaken one, at the least.

The King strode forward, free now of the press of media and security people, stopping a few feet in front of the President. The Prime Minister came up at his side.

'Good afternoon, Mr. President,' said the King with a wry smile.

The President mouthed a word of reply, but no sound came. He swallowed and tried again.

'Good afternoon, Your Majesty…Prime Minister.'

'Good afternoon,' said the Prime Minister. He was barely able to contain the deep rage he now felt when confronting this man, who had been the prime mover behind not only his country's torment, but his abduction and captivity, and the very private and personal torment he had suffered over Lynda – over her night of passion in the chateau, and then her defection. But at the same time, he felt an almost manic glee at so publicly and visibly confounding him at the heart of his empire.

'You have certainly achieved the element of surprise,' conceded Weurmann ruefully, gathering himself a little.

'We didn't know if we'd be welcome,' said the King simply, 'so we didn't ask for an invitation. We would like to say a few words.'

' "Who dares wins", eh?' murmured the President sarcastically.

But he stood aside, and gestured to the microphone, still bemused by the shock of this dramatic entrance.

The King stepped up.

The chaotic shouts and to-ing and fro-ing in the conference room quickly subsided.

'Ladies and gentlemen, you're surprised to see us here. We're somewhat surprised to be here.

'We don't wish to be melodramatic, but a great drama is, as you know, being played out the length and breadth of the United Kingdom.

'We thought we should speak to you direct. Much is at stake.

'Though I've been much involved personally because so much is at stake, a cornerstone of our democracy, by long tradition, is that the monarch should not enter the political arena.'

Delegates listened with rapt attention, heads cocked on one side, following the King with their eyes, and the simultaneous translation in their headsets with their ears.

'Though in extremis I've departed from that tradition, I wish to re-assert it, and will leave any further address to the Prime Minister.

'But let me say that for the sake of another long tradition – the long tradition of peace, and partnership, and prosperity, within our community of nations – for its sake, and for the sake of all the future generations, the dearest wish of my heart is for an end to this conflict, and for reconciliation amongst us all.'

As he stepped back, the Prime Minister moved to the microphone. As he did so, his eye caught and held Weurmann's, and in both their gazes, despite all, there lingered something still of that mutual admiration and liking which they had conceived for each other on first meeting, a seeming age ago.

Now, however, it was tempered on one side with rage, and glee, and a sense of moral victory – and on the other, with the surprise of the moment, moral confusion, and self-doubt. And on another level, tempered with the jealous rivalry of two men who had known the same woman.

The Prime Minister then shifted his gaze to the delegates. He stood back from the lectern, and assumed his full height.

He waited in dignified silence while a clerk scurried to adjust the microphone to suit him. Unhurried, he gazed round the room, seeming almost to eye each one there individually.

He produced no notes, yet did not hesitate for a single word – out of the full heart the mouth speaks....

No greeting, no salutation, no courteous form of words, preceded the overflow of that full heart.

'I do not believe,' he began in an implacable tone, 'that this Conference, or those it represents, or the Council, wish to destroy the United Kingdom.'

Murmurs of assent, nods, agreement, rippled round the chamber.

'And I know – and I re-state it here, now – that neither I , nor the Government, nor the people of the United Kingdom, want to destroy that community of nations which has become the United States of Europe.

'Yet the United Kingdom is effectively at war with the Union, and is on the verge of civil war within.

'We are killing, and being killed by, our erstwhile partners in the Union, as are you.

'And the Union itself is disintegrating, because some honourable nations will not agree to be party to the indefensible attempt to subjugate the United Kingdom by force of arms.

'Yet those who were willing parties to it, prime movers in it,' – and here he shot a glance at Weurmann, now seated near to the podium, 'acted honourably, according to their lights, in pursuit of an ideal – a European nation, at least a Union, "one and indivisible".'

Some shuffling in the room, glances between delegates, eyebrows here and there raised, indicated a general surprise at the Prime Minister's conciliatory and statesmanlike tone.

Having thrust his way in, catching all of them off their guard, most had expected a tirade of self-righteous invective – and many would have considered it justified.

But the Prime Minister continued on the same note. 'How then, has it come to this? To invasion, and counter-attack, and the descent into chaos of that which so many...' and here again he turned and looked directly at Weurmann, '...have striven for, so long and so hard?

'Ostensibly it is because the United Kingdom wished to withdraw from the Union.

'But did we seek to undermine it? No.

'Did we demand acceptance of our divergent views? No.

'Did we condemn the Union for the course it adopted? No – we disagreed with it, but no, we did not condemn it.

'If you disagree with your brother, do you knock him down? No. You agree to disagree. You agree to follow your own lights.

'And that is what we have done. That is all we have done.

'We have long supported the concept of a community of nations, acting together to advance their common interests – a "Common Market", a "European Community", even a "European Union".

'A community of nations. But I emphasise – "of nations".

'The people of the United Kingdom are clearly determined to maintain their status as a nation. It is this which has brought us into conflict with our friends and allies – but it should not have.

'We for our part have fully accepted – and respected – the decision of others to demit their national sovereignty and national identity, to become a state of the Union, rather than a nation state.

'But it is a first principle that a union can only be a union with the willing participation of its members.

'As soon as coercion comes in, breakdown of the ideal is inevitable.

'We ask you to recognise that principle, and reaffirm it anew.

'And we ask in the name of that ideal, in the name of the Union, and in the name of peace, that you desist from this attempted coercion.

'We ask that you acknowledge your brother's right to follow his own lights.

'And Mr. President, we demand safe passage to the UK.'

The President nodded wearily, conscious of the admiration, if not support, this daring stroke had generated amongst the delegates - but within him anger, indignation, and frustration were welling up to danger level.

That had been an incredible journey, the Prime Minister reflected. He pulled his coat collar up and his hat down, and pushed himself farther back into the corner of the official car. In the opposite corner the King, also with collar up and hat down, slept the sleep of the good, Brussels and the Summit now far behind them

As they sped through the Flanders countryside, flanked now by police outriders, back to the little inlet on the Westerschelde where the Flying Fox rode at anchor, the Prime Minister thought back to the first glimmerings of their plan.

It had all the romantic evocations, the suspense, the derring-do of an adventure story, this voyage of the Flying Fox from the sea lochs of the Scottish Highlands, to the Schelde estuary and the Low Countries.

Scotland evoked the landing and flight of Bonnie Prince Charlie, as they cast in their lot with a small boat on a big sea, in a spirit of great endeavour.

The Schelde was like Erskine Childers' "The Riddle of the Sands" – flirting with the sandbanks, dodging the enemy, the uncertainty, the suspicion, and the high purpose to which it tended.

Now the limousine rolled to a stop at the water's edge. The driver stepped out smartly and opened the door for his passengers. The outriders looked on impassively.

The yacht rocked at anchor two hundred metres offshore. Two figures were emerging from the companionway to investigate the commotion on the bank.

The Prime Minister left them in no doubt about what it portended, by opening his lungs and shouting at the top of his voice, 'Flying Fox, ahoy!' Then he and the King, and Rory and Johnson were all waving and laughing together.

As Rory came ashore in the dinghy to pick them up, a patrol boat appeared at the mouth of the inlet.

The car and the outriders sped off as they left the shore, and their new escort stood by, waiting till the Flying Fox was ready to sail.

They waited some time, for on board the Flying Fox there were toasts to be drunk and stories to be told, but a few hours later they escorted her down the Schelde, and waved her off into the open sea.

And an hour or two later, after some frantic radio traffic, an RAF helicopter hove into view, winched up the Prime Minister, the King, and Johnson, and winched down a three-man crew to help Rory sail the Flying Fox to a friendly port.

CHAPTER 43

Weurmann had peremptorily called a recess in the Conference as the King and the Prime Minister had made to leave.

Ostensibly this was to engage in some private dialogue with them, as well as to authorise their safe transit.

In reality, it was to give vent to his feelings, for something had snapped inside him when they had appeared at the dais.

Dialogue was an impossibility for him now.

He flung from the chamber with his train of advisers scurrying at his heels, then launched himself through the door of the security office and vented a tirade of abuse on the chief of security.

'You idiot! What kind of security is this? Our enemies are allowed to penetrate right to the heart of the State!'

'But...Monsieur le President... the British Prime Minister is entitled...'

'Fool! They are entitled to nothing! They are traitors. They have subverted the British Government and now they wish to subvert the Federal Government – and you stand by and watch!'

'Monsieur Le President, they arrived so suddenly and unexpectedly we could not...'

'Could not, or would not?' the President broke in. 'Are you in their pay, too, like the Spanish and the rest? Get out of here – you are dismissed.'

'But, sir,' said the security chief, reddening, ' I have security of tenure in my contract...'

'You have security of nothing! Your security of tenure is as good as your Summit security! Now, get out!'

'Lieutenant, get him out!' he shouted at a young officer who stood at the door. Transfixed by the President's psychotic demeanour, the lieutenant looked from one to the other and back, then stepped forward and tentatively touched his chief's elbow.

Defiantly the chief knocked his hand away, and marched from the office by himself, with the junior officer trotting after him.

'You!' Weurmann shouted at another officer. 'I want a report in the next half hour on how they got here! You can make arrangements to get them back to Britain, but I want that report immediately!'

Then Weurmann strode from the room and made for his own suite. His aides opened the doors ahead of him, but as he got to his private office he wrenched at the door handle, stalked in, and slammed it hard behind him, only avoiding injury to the aides by millimetres as they prepared to follow him in.

Alone now, he paced up and down the room and around his desk, ranting to himself as he did so.

Outside the door, a small group of staff had gathered. They could hear the shouted imprecations, and the bang and crash of furniture toppling over, as he barged from end to end of the room heedless of what stood in his way.

'My God!' they said. 'We have never seen him like this!'

Suddenly the door flew open. The President stood framed in it, glowering.

'What do you all stand there for?' he roared. 'No doubt gossiping and laughing! To your work, or you will have no work to go to!'

They hurriedly turned to leave, averting their gaze lest they draw down upon themselves a fresh outburst.

'Not you, Jacques and Carlo,' the President said a little less vehemently to his two principal aides, 'but get the rest of these oafs out of here!'

Then he began again to stalk about the ante-room.

'How dare they just arrive and take over the Summit? They are throwing down the gauntlet. They want to make me look a fool.

'I called the Summit to discuss how we could end this situation. Now they have stolen that from me. First they break up the Union – now they hi-jack the chance for me to reconcile friends who have become enemies.'

'But we can still reconcile them, sir,' ventured Jacques. 'The King and Prime Minister made very conciliatory speeches, and seemed disposed...'

'They do not "dispose",' shouted Weurmann. 'I "dispose". Who is the President, them or me?'

'You, sir.'

'That is correct! I am the President! It is not for them to conciliate. They are destroyers, wreckers!

'The Union is mine! I conceived it, fashioned it, guided it! It is one and indivisible, and will remain so!'

A timorous knock at the door of the ante-room heralded the entry of the security officer with the report of how the King and Prime Minister had got there.

'They what?' Weurmann asked, believing he had misheard the officer's first remarks.

'They sailed up to Antwerp in a yacht,' repeated the officer.

'In a yacht?' Weurmann questioned, incredulous.

'Yes, sir, then by train and taxi.'

'Train and taxi,' echoed Weurmann, again bemused. 'You mean they just sailed up the Schelde, took a train and a taxi from there, and hi-jacked the Summit?'

'Well, yes, sir,' said the officer.

'And this after they had attacked us with missiles here in Brussels?' he said to his aides in a deathly-quiet voice.

Then he continued in a sinister crescendo through clenched teeth, 'I want whoever is responsible for this dragged here in chains, made to beg forgiveness, and then thrown in the Schelde himself, chains and all!'

'I will investigate, sir,' said Carlo dutifully.

'Investigate? I want a head on a plate!' the President stormed. 'We have worked hard to maintain the solidarity of the Union in this crisis, and then they are allowed just to walk in, make fools of us, and undermine all that work! But I will show them who are the fools!'

With this he strode from the room and made for the Summit chamber, where the session was about to resume..

But before he reached the door of the chamber, he was intercepted by the Polish and Austrian premiers.

They delivered a simple and direct message. 'Mr. President,' they began,' we cannot have any more blood on our hands from this conflict.'

'Oh, and how do you propose to avoid it?' quizzed the President with heavy sarcasm.

'Simply by withdrawing our support from the operation. We no longer wish our forces to participate in this action.'

'Your troops are under the command of UHQ,' said Weurmann angrily.

'Nominally,' said the Austrian.

Weurmann stared. 'And actually!' he retorted vehemently.

'I would not put it to the test,' said the Polish premier. 'You will find that their national loyalties are stronger than their loyalty to the Union – as we have all found to our cost is the case with the British, too.'

The President opened his mouth to launch a tirade against the two statesmen, but was forestalled by an usher beckoning him into the chamber.

The mood was much more unsettled than it had been earlier - in that, it matched the President's own mood.

There had been a unity of purpose earlier - grim, reluctant, but determined to see the job done. The dissenters - Norway, Sweden, and Spain - were absent, and consensus possible.

But the dramatic intervention of the King and Prime Minister, and their appearance before the heads of government on the same podium as the President - personifications, as it were, of the victim and the oppressor - had a powerful effect.

Hopes of consensus were dashed by the position Poland and Austria were adopting.

There was unease as the President entered.

They eyes of the delegates were fixed on the Austrian and Polish leaders who entered a few paces behind him, trying to read their expressions.

Manifest undercurrents rippled the surface calm.

There was an almost tangible mood of division and dissent.

Weurmann, practised politician that he was, read all this as clearly as though it was written in front of him, and took it as a challenge and an affront.

When he again stepped up to the dais, it was in a very different spirit to that of two hours before.

Then he had risen as an arbitrator, committed to the policy of preventing secession, but wishing to reconcile differing viewpoints and present a united front to the world – and to Britain.

Now, as he began, he spoke like a dictator, determined on his course, heedless of the voices of protest raised against him, intent on crushing revolt or dissent from whatever quarter it came.

'Today we met to consider how we could stop the bloodshed caused by Britain's defiance of the Federal Government – so they came to defy us to our faces! So be it. We will set our faces against them!

'Their dissension has begotten dissension, and that has begotten more. If you doubt it, look around!

'The way forward is clear. We must protect the Union at all costs. To lose that is to lose all, and descend into a new dark age of war and strife between the peoples of Europe.'

The irony of this struck not a few delegates forcefully – the President seemed to be talking in a vacuum, from which the current reality was excluded.

The appeal of the King and the Prime Minister had struck them forcefully, too. Many delegates were already feeling, like Austria and Poland, that they could no longer support the President's policy. That is, if it still was a policy, and not a vendetta, which Weurmann's tone increasingly suggested.

But the mood of opposition which he sensed only inflamed his passion.

'Only a strong centre, controlling well-disciplined states in a tightly-bound Union will prevent that descent!' he all but shouted.

'We must not tolerate any further attempt to divide or weaken these United States of Europe. We must resolutely crush the attempt of Britain - and those who side with her - to do so.

'It is the duty of all states to support the Federal Government, and in this extremity I expect all states to do their duty.'

With that, he ended abruptly, turned on his heel without any valediction, and strode determinedly back to his suite.

Closing the door once more on the world, he visited again the dens of the dark furies which now beset him, and began again to rant unheard.

CHAPTER 44

For some reason no one seemed to have anticipated a full frontal assault on Chequers as a likely tactic to rescue the Cabinet.

When Wardhope got round to considering the problem of the captive ministers, he had been able to rely on Lynda Stalker's report that they were still being held there, together with some information on the daily routine and security measures.

The grounds were criss-crossed with trip-wires and infra-red detector beams. Additional floodlighting and look-out towers had been installed – all in expectation of a special forces operation, if any attempt was mounted.

Instead, a dozen tank rounds took out six key emplacements around the grounds – fired from tanks which had simply driven down the main road to take up their positions.

This had been Wardhope's own bright idea, as he planned the restoration of the Government with his chiefs of staff and the Emergency Cabinet.

'Do what I did when I walked out of Chequers that first day,' he had said.

'Send a tank squadron down the road looking as though it's meant to be there. If they're challenged, they say they're on the Union side. Confusion is still so bloody rife out there about which unit's gone with which side, that they might just get away with it.'

A day later a tank squadron backed by a company of infantry did just that, and they did get away with it.

They were stopped by a pimply Danish lieutenant with a nervous platoon at his back.

'Where are you going?' he called up to the turret of the leading tank, which had obligingly stopped in response to his upraised hand.

'Chequers, of course!' drawled the squadron commander leaning out of the turret with a disarming smile. 'Where else would we be going on this road?'

'I have thought you were with the King and the British resistance forces,' said the young lieutenant, eyeing the pennants and markings on the tanks dubiously.

'No, no. You must be thinking of the Blues and Royals – we're the Black and Blues. Easy mistake. Don't worry about it. Could happen to anyone.'

'Sorry, sir. Carry on,' and he stepped out of the roadway, saluting smartly.

The squadron commander gave him another smile and an airy wave, and signalled the column to move on.

When the last tank was round the bend in the road, all the heads disappeared from the turrets, and the hatches were clamped down.

Minutes later, panic gripped the detachments guarding Chequers.

With the gun emplacements out of action, the officer commanding played the only card he had left and paraded the Cabinet members in front of the building.

He hailed the tanks. 'Fire, and we will shoot them!'

A shiver ran down the line of ministers. One of the women began to sob.

'Withdraw immediately or we will shoot them,' shouted the officer.

The sobs became louder.

Then he made his mistake. He motioned to the soldiers who had escorted the ministers to take cover clear of the hostages.

They moved back several metres to shelter behind a low wall and stone balustrade.

'For God's sake withdraw!' screamed the woman minister at the tanks, her sobs becoming hysterical.

'Shirley! Hold on!' hissed the Home Secretary on one side of her.

'My children!' she sobbed. 'What will my children do? They're going to kill us!'

He moved to put his arm round her.

'They're not going to kill us,' he said, as he held her, and she turned her face into his shoulder.

'Stand apart! Leave her!' barked the officer behind him.

'For Heaven's sake! I'm just comforting her! Have you no compassion? What's the difference if you're going to shoot us anyway?' he shouted over his shoulder, meanwhile pulling her closer to him.

The hysterical sobs broke out anew. 'They mean it,' she groaned.

'They don't mean it! They don't dare kill us! Look how they've treated us – like guests, apart from the fact of holding us in the first place, and this business.'

'Withdraw your tanks!' shouted the officer again.

The Home Secretary looked to left and right.

'Here's what we're going to do,' he said steadily. 'I'm going to start walking towards the tanks, and keep on walking till I get there, and you're coming with me. We're all going to do it.'

'We can't! We can't! They'll kill us!'

'No they won't! They don't dare! They would bring down total international condemnation on themselves. At the moment the Union has the vestige of an argument – that they were entitled to prevent us seceding. Shooting us would be the action of barbarians, and they're not barbarians.

'Even Edwards, traitorous bastard though he is, wouldn't condone that.'

'Move out! Move out!' yelled the officer at the tanks, with increasing desperation.

The Cabinet members on either side who had heard the Home Secretary, had passed it down the line of their colleagues.

One or two demurred.

'They may not be bluffing, Charles,' one said.

'It's too risky,' said another.

'Look,' said Eager, 'there are fifteen of us. If we all start walking – slow, deliberate pace, all together – they'll do nothing. They can't shoot fifteen of us in the back!

'If one of us made a run, some trigger-happy squaddie might – not if we do it together. Come on now! With me!'

Slowly, as he glanced sidelong down the line, he got a nod or a muttered assent from each.

'All right. They're going to do a lot of screaming and shouting. They may fire over our heads. But they're not going to shoot us.

'Now, after my count of three – one…two…three. Walk!'

Shirley Alexander shuddered, and gave one last loud sob, but put her foot forward with the Home Secretary, who still held her tight.

'Don't look back,' he said. 'Look forward. We'll walk right up to and through the line of tanks. Keep going!'

The officer did do a lot of screaming and shouting in their rear – but the line of ministers, backs turned squarely to him, moved slowly on, one foot in front of the other.

'A funeral pace,' said the Attorney-General. 'Let's hope it's not our own we're walking to.'

'Shut up!' said another.

'It's Edwards' funeral we're walking to,' said a third.

The guards did fire over their heads, at which more than one of the line stumbled and almost fell.

All but Charles Eager started or shook involuntarily at the gunshots, and even on his head, beads of sweat stood out.

But step by step they came ever closer to the line of tanks.

They could see the machine guns projecting from the turrets being trained on targets behind them, and as they came even nearer, could hear them being cocked.

And now they were at the tanks, and as they moved through the line, the hatch of the squadron commander's tank opened, and he hauled himself out, dropping lightly down beside the Home Secretary.

In the same instant, the machine guns opened up a lethal crossfire which kept the Union troops' heads down.

'Well done, sir! Bravest thing I've ever seen!' and he took one of Shirley Alexander's arms, who now, with safety in her grasp, was on the point of collapse.

Then a single tank round was fired into a flower garden in front of the guards' position behind the wall.

The squadron commander hailed the Union officer in his turn.

'Lay down your weapons and surrender!'

There was a long pause. The squadron commander signalled to one of his troop commanders, and three tanks began to move slowly across the lawns.

They fired three more rounds into the flower garden.

As the smoke cleared, the watching ministers saw their captors stand up slowly and move out of their positions, their commanding officer in front, and their hands held high.

The battle of Chequers was won.

Later, in the room to room search of the building when the infantry moved in, hiding in the cellars they found Neville Edwards and three of the renegade ministers.

Unfortunately for them they'd chosen that day to hold a special meeting at Chequers, to discuss the problems posed by the further splits appearing in the Union.

After word had been flashed to the MOD, a special request came down for Edwards to be held until he received a visitor, and he was kept under close arrest in the butler's pantry.

The freed ministers moved back into Chequers as the safest and most comfortable place to recover from their ordeal, and avoid falling into enemy hands again until the country around was cleared.

The tanks ringed the stately pile, and turned their guns outwards in defensive formation.

And the two helicopters which came in the early hours to pick up the Cabinet, brought Neville Edwards his visitor.

'You are a bastard of the first water!' hissed the Prime Minister, with an up-welling of all the venom that had gathered in his spleen since he'd first heard of Edwards' treachery.

'There's no need for that, old chap,' smarmed Edwards with false bonhomie. 'I'm not a bad loser.'

'This is nothing to you, is it?' spat the Prime Minister. 'Just a game! The gratification of your own amoral, unprincipled lust for power!

'Do you feel nothing for the havoc and suffering you've wrought? All those young lives lost – on both sides? The country traumatised by virtual civil war?'

'That's politics!' snapped Edwards, stung now. 'Do you care nothing that the country is heading for economic extinction on the course you've set?'

'Empty rhetoric! You've never given a damn for anything or anyone but yourself, so don't presume to lecture me on the welfare of the country.'

'Why are you here, anyway?' Edwards asked, the sharp edge of anger now bare in his tone.

'I wanted to look you in the face once, before they lock you in the Tower and throw the key in the Thames! I've never seen a traitor face to face.

'I wanted to understand about treason. I wanted to see if there was a flicker of remorse or self-doubt.

'But you – you make a loathsome study! Arrogance, defiance, gamesmanship.'

'I see,' sneered Edwards. 'Did you expect me to grovel? Say I'm sorry?

"Lock me in the Tower and throw away the key!" Do you think you're judge and jury and executioner? Some justice!' he mouthed with bitter hatred.

'Justice!' fumed the Prime Minister, his eyes flashing. 'You set yourself up as judge, jury, and executioner for a nation!

'At least you will have your chance! You will have judge and jury very shortly – more than can be said for the thousands you condemned to death by your Machiavellian scheming.'

With that he turned from the room, leaving the two soldiers at the door standing guard over Edwards.

Now, for the first time, the Prime Minister had the opportunity to answer the question that burned at the core of him.

He'd asked it once before during this traumatic time, and even the uncertain answer he'd had then had been a disabling blow.

He hadn't dared to ask it again of anyone who could not know for sure, and had had no chance till now to ask it of anyone who could.

Having left the pantry in which Edwards was held, he made his way to the guest rooms, where his sometime colleagues were getting ready to leave in the helicopters.

There were gasps and astonished questions from those who caught a glimpse of him as he hurried along the corridor.

He smiled and waved and caught one or two hands, but hurried on saying, 'Later, later!'

A quick word with the sentry at the end of the corridor had pointed him to his destination - the Home Secretary's room.

He tapped on the door.

Eager opened it. 'Good God!' he exclaimed.

'Hello, Charles,' said the Prime Minister, and could hardly get through the flood of surprised questions, and his own concern over the Cabinet's ordeal, before coming to the question that haunted him, though he trembled to hear the answer.

'Charles – I've got to know – Lynda – I think you know how things stand – stood – between her and me. Has she really gone over?'

'No Prime Minister, she hasn't! She's been there as eyes and ears for David and the Emergency Government. We put her up for it when Edwards was trying to enlist some of us.'

'I knew it! I knew she couldn't really have sided with that toad! Thank God!'

Visible relief spread through him, he seemed to grow taller, and as he made his way back along the corridor, going from room to room, greeting and embracing the former captives, a huge beaming smile lit up his features.

CHAPTER 45

At the United Nations, Sir Richard Humphrey rocked back in his seat and fixed the Secretary-General with a baleful stare, across the floor of the chamber.

'Is this to be another Somalia, another Bosnia, another Sudan?' Sir Richard demanded after a long pause, throwing his considerable bulk forward again to reach the microphone.

'Are we to wait, and watch, and do nothing, while a member of the Security Council is crushed and dismembered before our eyes?

'We have come far from the need to prevent simple naked aggression which was the basis of my first address to this body. In the time since we have witnessed a headlong slide towards atrocity, and war crime, and what is in effect ethnic cleansing in Scotland.

'One wonders therefore, what has become of the "responsibility to protect". Surely it was for just such circumstances it was so lately agreed. Is that, too, fated to become just a pious form of words with no substance - like so much of what has gone before in this place?' '

Sir Richard's attack was born out of the frustration of the last few hours – indeed of the last few weeks.

But in particular, the present debate in the Security Council was winding down yet again to an inconclusive end, which would make it the third such meeting to end, in effect, in no action.

Today, as always, he had had to listen to the Union ambassador preach the sovereignty of the Union, lambast Britain, and refuse to countenance UN intervention.

'The United Kingdom, as I have said in this chamber twice before in discussing this issue, gave up her sovereign independence by the voluntary act of the Government of the day, in common with all the other states of the Union, in acceding to the Treaty of Berlin.

'From that day forward the United States of Europe has been a sovereign state, one and indivisible, every bit as much as the United States of America.

'It is for us to control our internal affairs. This is an internal matter, and so outwith the scope of the UN.'

At least in the General Assembly Sir Richard had had the comfort of other voices – many other voices – raised in support.

Britain's new allies – Spain, Norway, and Sweden – decried the Union and demanded action. They pointed to their own heavy involvement and the escalation of the conflict, and now Poland and Austria had joined their voices to these others, powerfully affected by the dramatic intervention of the King and Prime Minister at the Summit.

The Spanish ambassador had been particularly passionate.

'If we do nothing,' Senor Barras, had declared passionately, ' and this conflict escalates, it will not be just Britain and her three present allies versus the Union.'

Aware of the deep-seated discontent which had taken hold of the Brussels Summit, and the wave of sympathy for Britain which had surged up as a result of the Prime Minister's dignified and conciliatory appeal, he was increasingly haunted by the spectre of the limited conflict escalating into a pan-European war.

'There are those in the Union who, although now acquiescent, are uncomfortable with their role,' he warned. 'We have just heard the Polish and Austrian ambassadors join this protest.

'For some other members, any more will be too much, and they will at the least withdraw military support from the Union, and in all probability join with us.

'If the United Nations takes no action, and this conflict is allowed to continue, the Union will divide into two camps – and we have seen the beginning of that – like these United States of America a century and a half ago in the Civil War.

'And war between two great power blocs would then rage across the whole Continent of Europe. This would inevitably suck in other great powers as their support is canvassed, or their interests are threatened.'

He spoke well, and his words raised the demon of war before the eyes of the Assembly at large - and indeed changed the mood and tone of the debate.

Support came, too, from Commonwealth countries, and voices were raised against the atrocities which continued to be reported, and to demand relief for the refugees.

So Sir Richard had enjoyed brief respite in the Assembly from being in a minority of one. But here in the Security Council he was isolated and alone.

There were many who were sympathetic – old friends and old allies who could not with equanimity contemplate the fate now befalling Britain.

Their hearts felt for a friend and ally, but their heads told them that the Union 'internal affairs' argument was well-founded, and they felt unable to act.

The only really helpful voice had been New Zealand's.

Sir John Anderson, that redoubtable old Kiwi, could not stomach the complete inaction after the first meeting of the Security Council, though he had felt he had to accept the argument and vote with the Union.

For ten days before the next session, he canvassed support for sending UN observers in, successfully tapped the vein of sympathy, and at the second meeting got that through.

'Are we going to listen to this ghastly catalogue of death and atrocity, and do nothing at all?' he had thundered. 'Sounds to me like what're supposed to be some of the most civilised countries on the planet, can still get pretty uncivilised – and of course they've proved their credentials in the "uncivilised" stakes before.

'We have to let them know that even if we say it's their affair, the world is watching – watching and judging.'

Now in this third special session of the Security Council, with reports on the table from military and UNHCR observers, he entered the lists again to break a lance with Hallmeier, the German ambassador, who tried to play down the damaging content of some of the reports.

'They are only a few isolated incidents,' the German said. 'Soldiers suffer appalling stress in battle, and some go out of control – but it is only a few. the Union has condemned that indiscipline and taken steps to prevent it recurring.'

'Tell that to the parents of the schoolgirls who were raped,' growled Sir John. 'And what about the refugees?'

'An army advancing cannot keep stopping to let refugees get out of the way,' said Hallmeier. 'There is no policy of civilian terror. Fleeing refugees have been caught in shellfire or bombing because they are in the wrong place at the wrong time – not because they are being targeted.'

'That's not what the observers say,' retorted Sir John, ' and I would say that the UNHCR has just about enough experience of this sort of thing to be able to tell the difference.

'We have to demand strict observance of the Geneva Convention, and if we can't get it, we have to look again at the whole "internal affairs" argument and give serious consideration to our responsibility to protect, as Sir Richard has asked.'

''What of the Battle of the Tunnel?' Herr Hallmeier interjected. 'What of all those men buried alive, unable to defend themselves?'

'A desperate, tragic, grim act of war – appalling, and the mind shrinks from it,' Sir John replied. 'But it was an act of war. It was army against army, soldier against soldier.

'You can't draw a parallel with the shelling of refugees, and I say we can't stand back without guarantees of clear adherence to the Geneva Convention, internal affairs or no internal affairs. We only agreed the "responsibility to protect" in 2005 – and surely there is here a clear case for the application of that policy.

'Would you stand back and watch another six million Jews exterminated because it was someone else's internal affair?'

He still looked directly at Hallmeier, and the German visibly winced at this, but Sir John was not trying to score the easy, cheap point Hallmeier thought. The New Zealander had another parallel in mind.

'Will we stand back and watch what can only be called "ethnic cleansing" – of thousands of English people in Scotland, and now the murder of some?

'And how about that situation for some convoluted logic?

'The UK wants to secede from Europe. Many Scots want to secede from the UK. The Union goes to war over the principle of secession – then they encourage another country to secede from a 300-year-old Union because it suits them!

'I spy double standards!'

'Rubbish!' said Hallmeier, still smarting under the reference to the Holocaust, even if it was not directed at him. 'The Scots are being encouraged to take their own decision to stay in the Union.'

'And to murder any Englishman who thinks they should stay loyal to a Union three centuries old?' retorted Sir John.

'Of course not! We still adhere to the rule of law. Those committing war crimes or engaging in some sort of ethnic cleansing, if it is indeed happening as alleged, can be adequately dealt with – and will be – by the Union's normal justice machinery.

'You make much of the "responsibility to protect", but this is not a case of wilful disregard by a state of its duty to protect its citizens. Union action is predicated on precisely that duty – the Federal Government's duty to all the citizens of the Union, including those of the United Kingdom, to protect them from this illegal attempted secession, with all its economic and social consequences...'

So there is no case for UN intervention even in regard to those few extreme incidents which supposedly have occurred...'

'Supposedly!' spluttered Sir John. 'See no evil, hear no evil...! ''Order! Gentlemen, please!'

To all this, and much more, Sir Richard had listened with growing frustration.

And then he had launched that attack – '...Are we to wait, and watch, and do nothing, while a member of the Security Council is systematically crushed and dismembered before our eyes?

'You have heard New Zealand's condemnation of the Union's record on refugees and human rights. I am particularly grateful for Sir John's support in this, as it stems not simply from support for myself or the UK, for all his warm expressions, but from his well-known and often demonstrated refusal to tolerate injustice and oppression wherever he finds it.

'And he finds it here – right in front of us – and characteristically refuses to tolerate it. Is he alone in calling for, at the least, an expression of disapproval?

'Herr Hallmeier quibbles over when an atrocity is not an atrocity. As we know, a few days ago two UN observers were beaten to death by the so-called "Scottish Liberation Army" thugs in Glasgow. Is this an atrocity – or not an atrocity?

'And still we take no action. Is this not indicative of the supineness – no, craven-ness – of the UN today?'

'But these were, as you say, thugs, not Union soldiers,' interposed the Union ambassador.

'But they've been fellow travellers of the Union almost since the outset of the conflict,' rejoined Sir Richard. 'And they are now clearly the principal instruments of the Union in Scotland, along with their political front-men in the Scottish Liberation Party.'

Sir Richard now drew himself up in his place, and again fixed the Secretary-General with a direct stare.

'I have to ask if we are witnessing here the fallout of the United Nations' reverses over recent years ?

'Have the loss of credibility in Somalia, in Bosnia, in Georgia, in Iraq, and Sudan, so enervated us that we fear to try again, in case we are again found wanting?

'Surely we have learned the lessons of these conflicts – we can and we must play a positive role, and act now!

But in vain did Sir Richard prick the consciences of the members, and warn of the consequences of inaction. In vain did he exhort, and entreat, and goad, and cajole.

Yet again, 'internal affairs' carried the day.

CHAPTER 46

Wardhope began to feel that having got the Prime Minister out, and having got the Cabinet out, it was time he got himself and his staff out.

He'd been there...how many weeks now? He found it hard to keep track, not knowing night from day except by the hands of the clock.

They were all coping well, he told himself, but from time to time he'd noticed cracks appearing in some of the others, and occasionally he himself felt rather frayed at the edges.

So at daybreak four days later, the Parachute Regiment dropped out of the sky over Berkshire in battalion strength, and linking up with two armoured squadrons which had raced in from the Abingdon direction, fought a swift but sharp action with Union forces detailed to keep the lid on Wardhope's bunker.

After thirty minutes the parachute colonel in command was able to radio to those waiting several hundred feet below, 'Objectives one and two secured', confirming that both exits from the bunker could be used

One was the front door, and known to many.

The other was top secret, and few even knew of its existence.

Union patrols had by-passed it day and daily, criss-crossing the area in case a second entrance existed, but never uncovering its secret, though it lay under their very noses.

This was the route by which Bryn Thomas and the others had been brought in, to form the Emergency Government.

Now, for speed, both exits were used.

As they started to come out in groups, a squadron of helicopters swooped in low, to land on marks laid out by the paras beside each exit.

Rotors were kept turning, and none was on the ground for more than two or three minutes before whirling skywards again with its complement of grateful passengers.

As Wardhope reached the top of the shaft, with Bryn Thomas on one hand and the Chief of Staff on the other, he drank down the outside air in great gulps, like a man desperate with thirst in the desert, drinking at a water hole.

And now he gazed at the dawn, breaking then in all its rose-tinted glory. Broken cloud rose off the low rolling hills, and mist hung in the valleys, chastely concealing all the rare beauty of copse, and stream, and water-meadow, until the sun should come to claim them, and casting aside their morning raiment, bathe them in its warmth and light, possessing them, bestowing life upon them.

Wardhope was a plain man, but he could be a poet today, for his senses were sharpened to a pitch of poetic vision by being so long deprived of the stimuli of the upper world.

And then a helicopter crewman took his elbow, and they ran bent low under the whirling blades, and climbed in at the open doorway.

As they lifted off and wheeled into the wind, he felt he might have been a bird.

Bird poet, poet bird – free, alive, and breathing the upper air once more.

Ten minutes later they crossed what they now thought of as 'the front line', tree-hopping at two hundred feet to minimise the risk of detection.

Once, they had overflown a Union convoy, and a little farther on, an artillery battery, but were on them and gone before the troops on the ground had time to determine their status.

After forty minutes, skirting round the great industrial cities of the North, flying higher now that they were over friendly territory, they dropped down into the Yorkshire Dales.

They finally touched down at what even to the locals was an army engineering stores depot. When the door opened, they disembarked at a run into a drab warehouse building.

But half a minute later they were entrained in shuttle cars which sped them silently through brilliantly-lit tunnels, deep into the heather-clad hillsides, there to exchange one underground home for another.

As Wardhope stepped from the shuttle in a stark subterranean rock cavern, the Prime Minister, all smiles, strode forward out of the shadow of a massive steel pillar, and without a word – indeed, too moved to speak – grasped him by the hand.

Next moment – neither of them usually demonstrative men – they clutched each other in a long, back-slapping embrace, and each had a tear in his eye.

'It's so good to see you, and especially to see you looking so good, after all you've been through, Prime Minister!' said Wardhope at last.

'You too, David!' said the Prime Minister.

'But how did you get here?'

'We got the message that you were planning a moonlight flitting, and the RAF got us here about an hour ago.'

'Us?' queried Wardhope.

'I'm here, too, Mr. Wardhope, for my sins,' said the King, moving smilingly forward out of the shadows. 'Keep turning up like a bad penny and poking my nose into politics – got to stop it, I know, but I confess I've got rather a taste for it now.'

'Delighted to see you, sir!' exclaimed Wardhope in surprise. 'And far from thinking you're poking your nose in, I'm lost in admiration for yourself and the Prime Minister in pulling off such an amazing escapade. You won a lot of friends that day in Brussels!'

'In turn, Mr. Wardhope, I'm lost in admiration for what you've done these past few weeks. You've carried the country through some of the darkest days of the last thousand years – yes, a thousand years – checked the invasion, engineered the defence, and carried on the Government. The country owes you a great debt.'

'I was lucky, sir, but thank you.'

'Luck may have come into it, Mr. Wardhope, but you were also brave, selfless, and determined, and we could have had no better man as Acting Prime Minister.'

'Thank you, sir. I was greatly honoured, but will also be greatly relieved to hand back the reins to the Prime Minister.'

'Not so fast, David! You masterminded the whole of the response while I was out of commission, and I know you'll have your finger on the pulse of the overall situation. I need you there, and very much in control still.

'We don't need an Acting Prime Minister now, but I want to ask you to accept the post of Deputy Prime Minister – I don't think I'll be calling on Neville Edwards' services in that job again!' and all three men laughed heartily.

And then there was much shaking of hands, greetings, and mutual congratulations as the Prime Minister welcomed the Emergency Cabinet, Chief of Staff, and other senior officers, as they arrived in successive shuttle cars.

After a brief interlude while Wardhope and the others found their quarters, settled in, and freshened up, the Prime Minister presided over a working breakfast to take stock of the current situation.

'We've held them for now at a front, here,' said the Chief of Staff, running a light pointer along a line on the electronic map display, from the Bristol Channel to Cambridge, and north to The Wash. 'However, we have good intelligence on their movements, and they do seem to be engaged in a build-up. So they may be planning a further push soon.

'They could undoubtedly have moved forward in certain sectors on that front – so we consider it likely that there's a political check from Brussels on any further advance. But in the meantime, they're continuing to reinforce and stock-pile, presumably to be in a state of readiness for further action.

'They're continuing troop and equipment landings through the ferry ports they control, despite the heavy losses we've inflicted in the Channel, and have begun clearance work at the Tunnel landfall.'

'Thank you, General,' said the Prime Minister as the Chief of Staff resumed his seat.

Turning to the others he said, 'Certainly it seems they must have been checked by the Federal Government.

'The Union's in disarray politically, and as you know, we've now got considerable support among member states.

'His Majesty and I had a warm reception from some sections when we addressed the Summit, and obvious shamefacedness from others.

'As a result, we feel they may be hesitating.

'But I have to say, there was resolute opposition too. For all President Weurmann's pragmatic acceptance of our sudden appearance, and our safe conduct back here, he may yet be determined to continue.

'As you know, the Union was a long-dreamt of ideal for him, and he won't readily stand back and watch it unravel completely, as it now threatens to do.

'God knows, we didn't - and don't – wish to start that unravelling. It was the Council's outrageous response to secession which really started it fraying.

'President Weurmann's critical calculation now, is how best to reverse it.

'Is it better to let us go our own way, and then to restore relations with Spain, Norway, Sweden, and other sympathisers? But then he risks setting a precedent.

'Or is it better to finish the job, stamping the Federal Government's authority not only on us, but on the others who've taken our part?

'This is his calculation – his conclusion will determine whether it's war or peace.'

Round the breakfast table, his colleagues shifted uneasily in their seats at this stark analysis, and more than one pushed away his plate, all appetite gone.

CHAPTER 47

In Brussels, Weurmann's mind was already made up.

The pro-Unionists in Britain were a rudderless ship, with Edwards gone. It was now all up to him. He must dispense with the pretence of the puppet regime, and himself take power in the UK.

The irony was that his growing fanaticism for maintaining the integrity of the Union at all costs, was taking him down a road which could only end in internecine strife among the members.

Weurmann was not any longer the visionary coming upon the realisation of his dream. He was a man facing the ruination of his world, of his life's work. And worse, facing it with the knowledge – suppressed deep within himself for the sake of sanity – that he himself had precipitated the ruin.

But deep within him the knowledge festered and rankled, and the suppurations which rose from this canker within, distorted and clouded his judgment.

Now he lived the lie that the fault was Britain's alone because he, great architect of this United States of Europe, would not – could not – confront himself as author of its demise.

But he could still present a rational face to the world – and while taken aback at times by the changed manner and approach, neither his staff nor ministers in the Council, appreciated the full grip an evil alter ago had taken upon him.

They did protest a little, some of them.

'Mr. President, we have seen enough killing. It is not worth it. If Britain will go on her own, let her – we pay too great a price.'

'That is not what you said when we set out,' Weurmann reminded them tersely.

'No, but we say it now. When the King and the Prime Minister stood in front of us at the Summit, we were ashamed. Many of us realised the mistake we had made. These are friends, not enemies.

'We felt the British had been misled, whipped up to fever pitch by chauvinistic slogans for the election. Now we see they reject us and Edwards so completely that they give their lives.'

But Weurmann was so entrenched in power, had so firm a grip on the centre, that he would not vacillate in his course to quieten a few dissenting voices.

And from others he still enjoyed support – not perhaps so vehement in tone as the urgent voice within himself, but in principle they agreed.

'We cannot pull back now,' they argued along with him, ' and fiddle while Rome burns.

'We no longer have Edwards or his people, so we must finish the job ourselves. And we must do it now before Spain and the others mobilise properly.'

So the order went out from Brussels – 'Attack'.

No tear dimmed the President's eye as he signed the order, for his heart was hardened.

But through the ranks of ministers and officials, down through all the echelons of the Federal Government, through the general staff at UHQ, the commanders in the field, and the lowliest private soldier, a gloomy depression crept.

Before, they had come to the fight reluctant, and with misgivings, but imbued with the sense that they were recovering a wayward brother from the paths of unrighteousness, and that it was their duty to protect the Union.

But now they caught the stench of vengefulness from the President's order, and were no longer sure of their own motives, no longer certain that they fought with right on their side.

And they heard in that order, too, a deep bell-note of doom, and they knew it tolled for them, and for all of Europe.

And on the other side of that straggling line traced across the heartlands of England, the Prime Minister, Wardhope, and the King, in their subterranean HQ, and on the front line, the gangling major and the querulous private – they heard it too.

The Prime Minister and the King's secret descent on the Brussels Summit, and Wardhope's breakout from the bunker, had produced a brief euphoria, but that euphoria had evaporated some time since.

Now was unleashed upon them all the massed might pent up behind the Union lines, and it bore down upon them with a ferocity which could scarce be imagined.

No longer was there the caution, uncertainty, and reluctance which had characterised the first waves of the invasion, when the invaders were all too conscious of attacking erstwhile friends, though they felt they were fighting for the right.

Now there was the legacy of bitterness from the Battle of the Tunnel, and the Battle of the Channel, which was still continuing day on day – add to that the hardships of the campaign, and the rejection by the people, and it was easy to slip into the mindset that might was right, and theirs was the might.

No longer were the civilian population treated as citizens of the Union, half-expected to welcome the invading force. No longer were the atrocities isolated and untypical, the licentious madness of a few undisciplined troops.

Now the attack was indiscriminate, and the death and suffering of the populace written off as the fortunes of war.

Great tides of human misery began to flow northwards, as hundreds of thousands of proudly independent Englishmen – and Englishwomen, and children – donned the unaccustomed mantle of the refugee, and carrying with them such of their possessions as they could, abandoned their homes and villages to the implacable enemy.

No quarter was given, and no opposition brooked.

And the defenders - well-equipped, efficient, disciplined, determined as they were, fighting with all the commitment and passion which men display when they fight on their own soil, for their homes and families – were but a paltry opposition against the concentrated might of the score or so of other states which constituted the Union forces.

Inexorably the Union army began to roll forward the front line in the south, while the militant posture of the Scottish Liberation Army on the Scottish border, backed by some UHQ contingents and Union advisers, made the Prime Minister and Wardhope nervous of their rear.

There was no real invasion threat from this quarter. Both the rebel Scots and the Union preferred to secure the political detachment of the country without provoking intervention by the Emergency Government. But cross-border raids – by long historical example – could divert the Government's attention from the main task, and the Union wanted to keep this option open.

'If we can get our allies to put in ground forces – especially in the Union rear, say in Kent, the south coast or the West Country,' said the Chief of Staff, 'we'll give ourselves a chance – at the very least some respite to re-group and consolidate new positions.'

He eyed the silent, concerned group in the Prime Minister's office – the Prime Minister himself, Wardhope, Bryn Thomas, other ministers, and senior staff officers.

They were meeting within hours of the start of the Union offensive. Already it was becoming plain that the Union juggernaut was beginning to build up what would soon be an unstoppable momentum. Reports flooded in of reverses suffered by front line units, and of a terrible toll of lives, military and civilian, even in these first hours.

'Would the allies go for a ground offensive, do you think?' Bryn Thomas asked after a moment.

Everyone's eyes turned to the Prime Minister and Wardhope. There was a pause. They exchanged glances.

Then the Prime Minister said, almost as though delivering a prepared statement – 'We've considered this. The will is there, I believe, and we might be able to count on Norway and Sweden for help on the ground.

'Spain would have a problem with it. Don't forget she has common land borders with two other member states. Senor Perez has already provided substantial naval and air support, but has understandably had to make defending his land borders a priority for the army.

'But even if all three are willing, is it feasible militarily, even if it is logistically?

'We've had success in the Channel – but with raiding tactics. We can't pretend to control it – so could we even get the troops ashore?

'And even if that were possible, can we do it in any adequate timescale? I doubt it.

'Even if they were in place right now, how much good would it do us? Not enough, I think.'

'There is much for us all to consider together, and so I've called a meeting of the full Emergency cabinet for an hour from now. Some very hard decisions have to be taken.'

The Army Chief of Staff, willing enough to be optimistic, reflected the pessimism with a few nods of agreement during this analysis.

'I fear, gentlemen,' the Prime Minister continued after a portentous pause, 'that we're looking at an endgame scenario.'

Wardhope spent the hour with his Chief of Staff, poring over plans in the naval operations room. It was lunchtime, but he couldn't eat.

As the Emergency Cabinet session began, he tried a small sandwich with his coffee, but could only nibble at it.

The meeting continued for two hours – two very sombre hours.

Only one item was discussed. Only one decision was taken.

When the meeting ended, ministers, ashen-faced and silent, hung about the conference room in knots of two and three. Then gradually they dispersed, returning numbly to their offices, finding there was nothing they could say to each other.

The Prime Minister emerged last, and passing through the groups of ministers and advisers, made his way to the King's quarters.

As Bryn Thomas passed close by on the way to his own quarters, he heard the King's voice sound an anguished note – 'Prime Minister, I beg you to reconsider....'

Bryn passed on, taking his old pipe from his pocket and sucking on it for comfort, though he couldn't smoke it in the confines of the bunker, and had no tobacco anyway.

He barely saw the two giggling secretaries with the tray of red poppies, who hushed, and looked down guiltily as he went by.

But in his room, the image came to him again.

'Curious that,' he thought.

CHAPTER 48

Beneath the freezing Arctic seas, Captain McCormack had maintained the listen-only watch as ordered for what seemed an interminable age.

For captain and crew these had been weeks of tension, and also weeks of stultifying boredom.

The boredom ensued from the abandonment of normal patrol activity, and a stand-down from the day to day routine it demanded.

The tension was generated by the knowledge that far above, and far away, war was raging – raging around their homes and their families, raging across their country and across a continent. War raging before the hypnotised gaze of a world in suspense – a world which noted despondently, but perhaps with little surprise, that yet again, for the third time in just a century or so, Europe was tearing itself apart.

And the tension was generated too, by the knowledge that they were players in the drama now unfolding, though they knew not what their role would be - and prayed what it would not be.

McCormack passed and re-passed the gangways of his ship, with a friendly word here to a long-serving colleague, or a fatherly hand on the shoulder of a young rating on his first Trident trip, fear etched clearly on the youthful face, or drinking tea from an oily cup in the engine room, doing what he could to keep up morale.

In the wardroom gloomy silence prevailed, until the captain appeared. Somehow he managed always to elicit a laugh, prompt a discussion, provoke friendly argument. Anything to loosen the grip of boredom, break the intolerable tension.

But then in his cabin, no longer face to face with his responsibility as commanding officer, he lapsed into the self-same state as his men – yawing continually between one and the other state, pitching and rolling in the confused sea between boredom and tension.

Only his steward's gentle voice, firm hand, and strong tea, were specifics against the worst of these depressions. It sometimes seemed to McCormack that the steward was really in command, for it was he who roused the captain to his duties.

And day by day the chattering newsrooms of the world, which they constantly monitored, painted the picture they did not want to see, but could not take their eyes from. The Battle of the Tunnel, the strike on Brussels, the sea battle in the Channel – where a submarine many had served on had perished in a firestorm of depth charges, and many friends and colleagues with it – and in Scotland and Northern Ireland, virtual civil war.

And now the Union blitzkrieg, sweeping up through the Midland counties, pushing all before it – miserable throngs of refugees and Government troops alike. And in its wake death, and destruction, and the legacy of horror and atrocity which are the inevitable concomitants of war.

Tuesday the ninth of November began like any other day of those never-ending weeks of waiting and watching.

McCormack, fortified against the new day by the steward's strong brew and quiet but urgent encouragement, made his rounds as usual.

He stopped by a sailor whose wife was due to give birth that day, and exchanged a few words of support and a joke about being a dad.

In the sick bay he passed a few minutes with a gnarled chief petty officer with a broken arm.

He commiserated with the galley steward over the last of the supply of fresh vegetables, and eyed the huge catering cans of baked beans with distaste.

Now he stood in front of the missile firing console, in the little ritual he had daily observed since taking command. Mentally he rehearsed the procedures for authorisation and targeting, and the sequences for arming and firing the missiles.

Then he rehearsed the battle with the emotional and moral counter-attack from within himself, which he knew he would have to repulse before being able to carry out that ultimate order, if ever it came.

Now he focussed on the two red firing switches beneath their auto-locked clear protective cover, the invariable last act in this ritual. He visualised the cover flying back, and the first lieutenant's finger alongside his own, both pulling with awful finality on these two tiny components which could trigger such terrible forces.

He turned away – then turned back with a start as a sudden whirr arose behind him and the bank of computers kicked in. Digital displays began whirling through rapid sequences of numbers.

He hit the 'action stations' alarm. In an instant, tension and boredom were lost together. Men rushed to their stations, jumping from bunks, leaving half-finished meals on the mess table, each automatically going into his own prescribed routine.

Then the first lieutenant was at his side, and they exchanged doom-laden glances.

Each placed a palm on the electronic identity scanner.

The viewscope flipped up in front of them.

Together they scanned the coordinates beamed to them from the geo-stationary satellite 1500 miles up, which looked down upon the earth, seeing with all its vast array of sensors only a pleasant place of green temperate lands, orange-brown deserts, and cool blue seas – and which heard only the data-streams received and re-transmitted by its gleaming antennae, insensible of their import for all the suffering which had been, was now, and was to come.

The captain and the first lieutenant punched in their individual codes.

A limited strike.

The Emergency Government still had hope then – still hoped that this awful warning, this warning that they would play for maximum stakes, this game plan called 'unacceptable losses' – would yet bring the Union to reason, the war to an end, and everyone go home.

Unless, that is – they lived in Zone T1 or T2. There would be no going home for them.

Beyond that was the possibility of a full strike, warning duly given by the limited first strike.

The full strike would bring an annihilating response – no return to reason, but a journey into madness, and no going home for any of them.

The captain and first lieutenant looked at each other again.

Spontaneously they grasped each other's near hand and gripped tight, like kids in a surround-screen cinema when the action gets too scary, or at the top of the helter-skelter when the mat slips away beneath them and there's no going back, or the doors of the ghost train swing open in front of their carriage to reveal Pandemonium.

With their free hands they validated the steps of the procedure, punching in their codes again and again, at each pause in the sequence.

Then they hit the 'enter' key for the last time.

The auto-lock clicked and the clear cover flew open.

The two red switches lay unguarded beneath their hands, armed and ready.

CHAPTER 49

The peace marches had begun in Berlin of all places, and the irony was not lost on Weurmann - seething on the edge of fanaticism though he was - that it was from Berlin, not much more than a couple of decades before, that he had drawn his inspiration.

A group of students set up a vigil by the Brandenburg Gate and could hardly have known what they were setting in train.

It began with a few candles, a few placards, a few blankets on the ground.

But it caught the mood of this great city, from which war had been waged – waged and lost – twice in a century, and which had then fallen victim to the Cold War, dividing the city, dividing the nation, dividing Europe, dividing the world, East and West.

Berlin – the city and the infamous Wall for so long symbols of division – then raised its voice with the students against the divisive forces now at work within the Union.

There was paradox here as well as irony, thought Weurmann as he read or watched the reports.

The students marched for peace, against war – against a Europe divided, at odds with itself. But the war had been begun to forestall division, to prevent Britain – a part of the main – becoming an island again politically and economically, as well as geographically.

This was the Twitter and Facebook generation, and the student demonstrators found their ranks swelling night on night, until the glow of the candles lit up a thousand thronging faces and the great monument itself.

'We will have a march,' said the leaders, 'and invite the whole city to come.'

It seemed as though the whole city had come, that next Sunday – men, women, and children. Old men with haunting memories of the divided city, of families and friends driven apart; women, pregnant some of them, and pregnant with fear for the future of their unborn little ones; and the children, knowing nothing of war, or nations divided, but happy, laughing, enjoying the people, the bands, the goodwill between men – the children, symbol of hope for the future.

And as darkness fell and the candles were lit, a great moving ribbon of light began to wend its way through the city.

From across the Union other student groups came to join them. They knew from their books, if not from experience, of war and the horror of war, and they knew the sort of world they did not want to inherit, and argued endlessly about the sort they did.

Then, full of the inspiration of that Berlin Sunday, of the solidarity of young and old, rich and poor, they made their way back with the message of peace – to Paris, Rome, Helsinki, Ankara, and to Madrid and Stockholm and Oslo, to Vienna and Warsaw, and more – yes, and to Brussels and London, too.

And as the call went out, the word spreading in the ether as it had in the revolutions in North Africa and the Middle East, the social media revolutions, by the following Sunday all the capitals of Europe were lit by the flicker of a million candles, and the Sunday after that provincial capitals, towns, villages, and even the tiniest hamlets, had their vigils too, so that one would have thought the whole Continent would appear as a huge festival of light to satellites in their silent orbits, 1,000 miles above.

The popular mood would no longer countenance the war. There had been protests and demonstrations since the first landings of Union troops in Britain – but uncoordinated, isolated. This was a sea change, this great groundswell of popular opinion.

That third Sunday, Weurmann pondered all this in his heart, thinking, too, about his own experience at the Brandenburg Gate and at the Wall, a young man himself.

He still had on his desk the glass jar of pulverised brick from the wall.

And he reflected again on the paradox that this divisive war was being waged to prevent division, and on the fact that whether pro-Union or anti-Union, the peoples of Europe wanted peace above all – they had had too much of war, for too many centuries.

Both camps – pro and anti – strove after the same goal of peaceful co-existence and prosperity. The only argument was over how to achieve it.

No one had wanted war.

He had not – he wanted peace, and harmony, and the fulfilment of his Brandenburg vision.

The British had not – they wanted only to depart in peace.

The people had not – all those hopeful candles sending their smoky tracery aloft , as in prayer, testified to that.

Balancing the burgeoning peace movement, an ever more hawkish war party had risen up. As resistance had become counter-attack, and the Union side had begun to take heavy casualties, they had started crying for vengeance.

But even they had not wanted war, and their warlike posture was a reaction to the fierce resistance offered by the British, and the toll of Union lives.

And yet a terrible, relentless, force had been loosed – a dynamic of war and destruction which had coursed through the whole Continent, driven by its own momentum, and rather than spending itself, it seemed to have gathered greater momentum the longer it ran unchecked

And Weurmann and all the Council had been borne along by it.

In a moment of intense self-realisation he acknowledged that for some time now he had not only ridden this Juggernaut, but had held the reins and driven it on – and saw that he had lost sight of his true self, and perverted his once lofty ideals.

His gaze fell on the glass jar on his desk – the brick dust from the Wall – and one thought illuminated his mind.

'Did I help pull down that Wall, that hated symbol of division, only to go forward to divide another proud people against themselves?'

But even as he reflected, that Sunday, the President wondered if this madness could any longer be checked.

CHAPTER 50

Somehow, the madness did stop there – nobody really knew how.

Was it an Act of God, smiting insanity from men's minds and pouring reason in?

Was it the prayers of the millions who marched for peace, their flickering candles held earnestly aloft, sometimes seeming the only light that shone in Europe in the dark days of war?

Was it the hope, ever-present in the breasts of the young, all starry-eyed in this new century, this new millennium, proving more powerful than the forces of despair which had descended upon the souls of their elders?

Was it – two thousand years after Christ had taught 'love thy neighbour' – a triumph at last of civilisation over the anti-civilisation which had so often engulfed it?

Was it the jar of dust from the Wall, on the President's desk, or the poppy, laid casually on the Prime Minister's?

Certainly the poppy it was, and the images it stirred, which prompted the Prime Minister to pick up the Hotline that morning, and the little store of dust which softened the President into receptive mood.

As the Prime Minister had been briefing the King, as Bryn Thomas sucked on his pipe in the corridor, as the chiefs of staff relayed the dread decision to their staff, the two giggling girls had been doing the rounds of the subterranean offices - the two who had hushed, and pressed back against the wall, gaze cast shyly down, as Bryn passed by.

Traditions die hard in Britain, and this did not seem the time to let the tradition of Remembrance Day die. So they and a gaggle of other secretaries, isolated in the bunker with little to occupy such free time as they had, had begun to make poppies from some red paper they had found.

The Prime minister had returned to his desk with heavy steps, and with the words of the King still in his ears – 'I beg you to reconsider….'

In the secure confines of the naval operations room, he knew they would be inputting the final target data and code authorisations for relay to the Trident and Captain McCormack.

Then the Prime Minister's eye fell on the poppy, beautiful and terrible in its simplicity and its symbolism, beautiful in itself, terrible in the images it conjured up of blood, and wholesale slaughter, and death.

All man's inhumanity to man down the long march of history swam before him in his mind's eye.

Man, made in the image of God, gifted above the animals with intellect and reason to resolve the problems of survival, had yet returned to tooth and claw.

So the Prime Minister picked up the phone to the President.

It seemed so easy now. Why not before?

Anger? Pride? Face? All of these, he thought.

And then, the Hotline was there to ease the process of government from the distant centre of the Union – to bypass, when necessity dictated, all the cumbersome machinery of the federal state.

At war with the Union, and no longer under its governance, the Hotline had seemed redundant.

Now, the awful finality of the decision so lately taken set these selfish and self-indulgent emotions at nought, and the Hotline seemed a lifeline.

'I wish to speak to the President,' he said.

Alone in the dungeon-like office where no daylight ever entered, and from which he knew he might never again emerge, he felt the full ludicrousness of allies and friends bent on destroying each other, and felt, too, a sense of the equally ludicrous simplicity by which the situation could be resolved.

'Hello?' said the well-known voice of the President a moment or two later.

'Hello, Matthias,' said the Prime Minister. 'You don't mind if I call you Matthias?'

Silence.

'Please call me John.'

Silence.

'We are just men like the rest Matthias, are we not? But we inhabit these great offices of state.

'It seems to me that we are sometimes prisoners of the office – it lumbers forward on a set course, and we are carried along with it, unable to overcome the momentum.'

'I feel that, too, at times,' said Matthias.

'And sometimes people cannot reach us as men, because the office interposes.'

'Yes.'

'And sometimes we cannot even reach ourselves, because of it.'

'Yes – that too.'

'I have this thought, Matthias – that Presidents and Prime Ministers wage war – men don't. Men disagree, and quarrel, and fight – but they don't wage war.

'We must be men now, before President and Prime Minister destroy us all.'

Silence.

Then - 'Yes, John.'

'I am going to break the rules of war, Matthias, and tell you we are poised to launch a nuclear attack.'

Silence.

'And you must have contingency plans for a retaliatory strike.'

'Yes, John.'

'And that's crazy, isn't it? I don't want to kill you. I don't think you want to kill me. Yet if we die, we die at each other's hands as surely as if we had held a knife to each other's throat. Millions will die with us – and what for?

'All we want is an independent, sovereign United Kingdom, living in harmony with its neighbours – should I die because of that? Should you? All you want is a united, prosperous Europe.'

'That was my dream,' said Matthias.

'Matthias, you can build another dream. But this is the last moment – the very last moment – at which it is possible. If we do not agree now, Europe and Britain will be destroyed. There will be no dreams then, only nightmares!'

Silence.

'Then let us be men,' said the President. 'No more war.'
'And build a new dream,' said the Prime Minister.

EPILOGUE

In the Trident the clear plastic cover snapped back down over the two red switches, and the auto-lock clicked into place. The computers whirred again as the target data was unloaded and the system was stood down.

The first lieutenant was shaking from head to toe, and Captain McCormack had to support him en route for the wardroom, where he sat him down and poured each of them a double measure of pusser's rum, as cheering ran round the boat.

In the bunker, Wardhope and the Prime Minister embraced again, engaging in more mutual back-slapping.

The King wore a grin from ear to ear.

Bryn Thomas whooped with delight, and threw his pipe clear across the ops room in celebration.

In the Channel and the rolling Midlands countryside the guns fell silent. Troop-ships no longer followed complicated zig-zags to evade submarines. The flood-tide of refugees slowed, slowly turned, and began to ebb southwards again, as people returned to claim their homes.

A dishevelled but jubilant Lynda Stalker appeared at the entrance to the command centre.

The duty sergeant wanted to hold her there, uncertain of her status, knowing she had been part of Edwards' puppet regime.

But she was so effervescently happy and intent on gaining entry - and besides, dishevelled as she was, could still do as she would with men – that the duty officer rang through to the Prime Minister's office, from which, of course, she got immediate clearance, and a special escort to boot.

Soon she and the Prime Minister were in each other's arms for the first time in far too long, while Bryn Thomas grinned on, and finally roared out, 'Go on, boy-o, give 'er a big smacker!'

And the Prime Minister obliged, to the embarrassment of the duty sergeant, who had been part of the special escort.

In Brussels the President gathered his aides from the dark corners of the underground shelter, led them into the lift, pressed the button for the seventeenth floor, and opened the Presidential offices for the first time since the missile attack.

Sun streamed in through the blinds, and he took a great breath, sucking the air through his teeth with a hiss, expanding his chest to the full, and a twinkle appeared again in eyes which had grown dull with despair.

In Ireland the flames of civil war were not so readily quenched.

The Protestant backlash which had flared up in Northern Ireland over the massing of the Irish Army on the border continued unabated until all were withdrawn, and the Republic's soldiers had returned to their bases.

But the Province had returned to the deadlock of the early nineties. And if this represented progress from the violence of the last few weeks, it also pushed into a distant future any hope of a healing, and a renewal of that peace process which had held so much promise at the turn of the century.

In Scotland the SLA and the Leaguers continued their stand-off for some time. But as military support for the SLA was withdrawn, and funding from the Union slush funds dried up, its ranks dwindled in the face of universal unpopularity, and the end of wages and bounty payments for its men.

But though it dwindled to a rump, and had again been forced underground, it was a larger group than before, and the scars left by the deep divisions of the recent conflict – deeper than any Scotland had known since the Jacobite risings – would long be in evidence.

And as the First Minister and his team took up the reins of legitimate government again, and the Holyrood Parliament again took to their deliberations, it was a very different Scotland they watched over.

In Europe, too, there had been deep divisions, obvious as in the case of Spain, Sweden, and Norway, but as ominously, though less obviously, in Poland, in Austria, and not a few more.

These divisions arose not just out of member states' concerns or distaste for the hardening attitudes and ever-increasing military involvement in the war while it raged. They arose too after its cessation, out of fears for their own future within such a monolithic state, with so much power concentrated centrally.

A month after the telephone call, most Union forces were back on the mainland of Europe, and those which weren't were concentrated in transit camps around the ferry ports.

The Government was back in Whitehall, and the Prime Minister was back in No. 10.

The King was in the Palace, where he received a huge popular welcome from crowds teeming around the Victoria Monument and in The Mall. And to their great delight and his visible enjoyment, he kept re-appearing on the balcony throughout his first day back.

That same day Wardhope and the Chief of Staff paid a nostalgic visit to the bunker which had been the nerve-centre and driving engine of the resistance, although it had been ransacked by Union forces in the search for any useful intelligence, after the Emergency Government's break-out.

Neville Edwards and his supporters were given an amnesty, recognising that the context of their actions was a grey area legally, and remained so. But Edwards himself left the country, in fear of his life after a series of death threats from grieving families seeking revenge.

The London Conference was chaired jointly by the President and the Prime Minister, and the theme was reconciliation and the reconstruction of the shattered European ideal.

The war, the terrible toll of death and destruction, the secession of the United Kingdom, the alliance with Spain, Norway, and Sweden, and their reluctance to return to the Union fold in the same relationship as before, and the nervousness of other states – particularly the smaller ones – had rocked the Union to its core, and rendered the Federal Government impotent over whole regions.

Not for a very long time, if ever, would many of these states return themselves willingly to the central control of a federal union.

And never would they allow themselves to be returned unwillingly – ready to follow the example of Britain if need be.

That this was the political reality, was manifest well before the Conference.

The President, besides, with much honest heart-searching and earnest debate with recent enemies and old friends, had felt scales drop from his eyes, and seen with luminous clarity that Europe could be re-built only by cooperation and not by coercion, and would best endure as a community of independent states.

And so the first Act of the Conference reconstituted the United States of Europe as the European Community.

At the Conference, the newest member of the Community, the United Kingdom, took her seat, the Prime Minister heading her delegation

And as fervently as he had decried centralised control and the surrender of sovereignty, he reaffirmed his lifelong advocacy of consensus and cooperation between Community members.

In front of the Conference hall the national flags of all were once again arrayed.

And the flag which flew over it featured random gold stars on the blue background, one for each member country, signifying the free association of sovereign states.

ABOUT THE AUTHOR

Ken Jack currently works as a freelance photojournalist in Scotland - the latest incarnation in a career which has included newspaper and magazine journalism, teaching, and commerce. Other interests include video filmmaking, birdwatching and wildlife, the outdoors, and campervanning.

Author photo and cover layout by Pauline Johnson.

Made in the USA
Charleston, SC
03 December 2011